CLOCKWORK

FORTY STORIES

CLOCKWORK

FORTY STORIES

For Sarah—

BY JOHN M. FLOYD

Hope you like the stories!

Love, Johnny

(John M. Floyd)

DOGWOOD
PRESS

10-digit ISBN: 0972161198
13-digit ISBN: 9780972161190

Library of Congress Control Number
2010932655

Printed in the United States of America

Jacket design by Bill Wilson
Author photo of John M. Floyd by Carolyn Floyd
First Dogwood Press edition: October, 2010

DOGWOOD PRESS
P.O. Box 5958 • Brandon, MS 39047
www.dogwoodpress.com

For Lillian, Anna, Charlie, and Susannah

ACKNOWLEDGMENTS

Once again, many thanks to my friends and fellow writers for their continued support and inspiration. Although I'm certainly leaving out a great many names, I must mention the following: Ben Douglas, Bill Patrick, Janet Brown, Susan Weatherholt, Robert Angelo, Jim Ritchie, Donna Heubsch, Philip Levin, and Richelle Putnam. Thanks also to editors Johnene Granger, Andrew Gulli, and Linda Landrigan, and to my fellow weekly columnists and co-conspirators at the Criminal Brief web site.

A special nod of appreciation goes to my publisher, Joe Lee, for his willingness four years ago to take a chance on me and for his advice and encouragement at every turn. I only wish every writer could have a publisher as kind and knowledgeable and professional as Joe—I'm fortunate to have been issued an oat-bag in his stable of authors.

Last but not least, thank you to my wife Carolyn—my first reader, soulmate, best friend, and in-house psychiatrist, all rolled into one. I don't deserve you but I'm glad I caught you.

The stories included in *Clockwork* first appeared in the following publications:

"The Powder Room" and "Remembering Tally"—*Alfred Hitchcock's Mystery Magazine,* 2009; "The Judge's Wife," "An Hour at Finley's," "The Warden's Game," "Doctor's Orders," "Angel on Duty," "Thursday's Child," "The Willisburg Stage," "A Stranger in Town," "Appearances," and "Clockwork"—Amazon Shorts, 2005-2008; "Not One Word" and "Run Time"—*Futures,* 2001-2002; "True Colors," "Poetic Justice," "Early Retirement," "Backward Thinking," "A Day at the Office," "Sweet Caroline," "A Piece of Cake," "Cat Burglar," "Old Soldiers," "Hold the Phone," and "Smoke Test"—*Woman's World,* 1999-2000, 2003, and 2005-2009; "Christmas Gifts," "The Medicine Show," and "Vacationland"—*Reader's Break,* 1997-1998; "The Range"—*Mystery Time*, 2000; "High Anxiety" and "The Sixth Victim"—*Mouth Full of Bullets*, 2007; "Career Changes"—*Mysterical-E*, 2009; "Sightings"—T-Zero, 2003; "The Last Sunset"—*Dream International Quarterly,* 1994; "A Matter of Honor"—*Seven by Seven* anthology, Wolfmont Press, 2006; "The Home Front"—*Pebbles*, 1995; "Debbie and Bernie and Belle"—*The Strand Magazine,* 2008; "Last Chance"—Jupiter World Press, 2006; "Wheels of Fortune"—*Heist Magazine,* 2002; "Partners"—*The Oak,* 1996.

CONTENTS

The Powder Room

At exactly six-thirty Martin Field looked up from his desk to see a man standing in his office doorway. At first Field was surprised; his receptionist usually announced visitors. Then he remembered the time. He was probably the only one left on site.

The man at the door hesitated. "I don't have an appointment, Mr. Field. My name's Ed Loomis—and I realize it's late."

Field smiled. "No rest for the weary." He stood and extended a hand. "It seems you already know who I am."

"Everybody knows who Martin Field is." After shaking hands Ed Loomis settled into a chair facing the desk. He gave the room—and the view of the sunset through the office window—a long look. "Nice setup you have here."

Field nodded his thanks. He *was* proud of the place. When he'd decided years ago to start his own engineering firm, he'd also decided it would be no ordinary company. The layout of his corporate headquarters reflected that plan: the main office—this building—was a two-story farmhouse in the hills of west

Arkansas. The bedrooms had been converted into offices, the outbuildings into labs and equipment storage, the barn into an employee fitness center, the surrounding land into lawns and gardens. The front entrance was a simple gate in a split-rail fence.

Not surprisingly, his management style was as efficient and unassuming as his business site. The firm was widely praised for both its expertise and its results. But the main reason for his success, Field reminded himself now, was the company's regard and respect for its clients—whether they had appointments or not.

"What can I do for you, Mr. Loomis?" he asked.

Ed Loomis looked out the window again before answering, and Field studied him a moment. Nothing unusual: fortyish, sandy hair, sportcoat, jeans, loafers. But there was something odd about him too. Something about the face . . .

"I work for the government," Loomis said, without turning. "We're about to do some construction, down at the air base."

"You don't look like you work for the government."

Loomis grinned, and they locked eyes. "I said I *work.* Unlike most." When Field didn't reply, Loomis said, "Project manager. I'm outside more than in."

Field nodded again. "I miss those days. The base, you said. What kind of construction?"

"The highly confidential kind."

"Well, my firm's done classified government work before, Mr. Loomis—"

"Not like this." Loomis took a thick sheaf of folded papers from an inside pocket of his coat, but made no move to show them to Field. "You'll see what I mean, I think, once you read the report."

Field sat there a moment, waiting. "So are you going to show it to me?"

"There's a small problem," Loomis said. "On the one hand, I can't allow you to keep it. On the other, I must get back to my own office—I've not been granted the time to wait here tonight until you read through it all."

Field leaned back in his chair and clasped his hands. "Then why did you come?"

"Good question." Loomis tapped the report with a forefinger. "I've been authorized to leave it with you," he said, "*if* you can guarantee that it'll be properly secured, here on the premises."

"Are you telling me this is the only copy you have?"

"I'm telling you that the matter is—how did you put it?—classified."

Field stayed quiet a moment. "How classified?"

"Highly," Loomis said again. "Can you assure me, Mr. Field, that it'll be properly secured?"

"I have a vault, if that's what you're asking."

"What kind?"

"It's a Bingham wall safe. Model 3000, I believe. Burglarproof, fireproof."

Ed Loomis seemed to consider that.

"You want to see it?"

Instead of answering, Loomis said, "I understand you have explosives here."

Field frowned. "This is a civil engineering firm, Mr. Loomis, and this is the Ozarks. As you probably know, our work sometimes requires excavations, and excavations sometime require blasting. We have several hundred pounds here at the site." He paused a moment. "It presents no threat to the contents of my vault, if that's your concern."

"How so?"

Field pointed to the window. "You might've noticed the old storm cellar there in the yard. It's still a storm cellar in case a tornado comes through, but it's been converted into a bunker, of sorts. Steel door, steel roof underneath the sod, polycarbonate glass window, walls two feet thick. My employees call it the powder room."

"The powder room?"

"As in gunpowder," Field said. "The bunker contains all our explosives."

"So any accident, or mishap . . ."

Field nodded. "Any blast occurring inside would be confined largely to the bunker, and anything happening outside wouldn't affect the stored materials."

Loomis seemed to give that some thought. Then: "Back to the safe. That model has a time lock, doesn't it?"

"You've done your homework," Field said. "The timer's pre-set. This one ensures that the vault can be opened only once a day."

"And a day consists of . . ."

"In our case, from ten a.m. until ten a.m."

"Is that a problem?" Loomis asked.

"Not for you and me, it isn't. It hasn't been opened yet today."

Very slowly, Ed Loomis's eyes changed, and a cold smile spread across his face. At the same time, a cold dread spread through Field's stomach. Instantly he realized his mistake.

He had let his eagerness about a so-called government contract override caution. Loomis's questions—his whole act—had been no more than a means to obtain that one last answer.

Field felt his pulse thudding in his ears.

He shifted his gaze downward, to the sheaf of papers in his visitor's lap—and all doubt vanished.

In Loomis's left hand was a black revolver, peeking out from underneath the report. It was pointed at Martin Field's chest.

"I think now I *will* take a look at that safe, Mr. Field."

***

The engineer drew a long, shaky breath. He was alone and unarmed. Resistance, he knew, was futile. In those few seconds it occurred to him what had seemed strange about Ed Loomis's face, earlier. It looked too lined, and weathered. Too hard.

As if in a trance Field rose from his desk chair and crossed the room to a set of bookshelves. His legs, he noticed, didn't seem to want to work right.

On the top shelf, chest-high, were several notebooks, a set of surveyor's tools, a camera, and a vase of flowers. Beside them, hanging on the wall, was a framed painting of a misty mountain valley.

Without a word Field lifted the picture from its hook and set it aside, revealing a two-foot-square safe set into the wall.

"Open it," Loomis said. The folded papers had disappeared, presumably back into a coat pocket. In the midst of his other muddled thoughts Field found himself wondering what the "report" had really been. Blank sheets, probably.

He forced his mind back to the matter at hand.

"And if I don't?" he asked.

Ed Loomis cocked the pistol and tilted it a bit, so Field was staring down its barrel. "They told me you were smart," Loomis said. "Don't disappoint me."

Still Field hesitated. "You're sure you want to do this? It's not even full dark outside. Somebody could wander in here any minute—"

Loomis shook his head. "As you said, I do my homework, Mr. Field. I know you and your wife live in town, half an hour south, I know your nearest neighbor here is a mile away, I know you discourage your employees from staying after hours, and I know your car when I see it. Besides mine, it's the only one in the lot." He paused. "I suppose, under normal circumstances, someone could drive up and join us here . . . but these aren't normal circumstances. Matter of fact, there's a sawhorse in the middle of the road half a mile from your gate, with a ROAD CLOSED sign on it and a couple of those big orange witch's hats on each side, and they'll stay there until I drive back through and pick them up." He let that sink in, then nodded toward the vault. "Open it."

Two minutes later the door to the wall safe was standing open, and a stack of cash and securities was laid out on the glass-topped coffeetable. An expression somewhere between childish awe and adult greed had stamped itself on Ed Loomis's face.

Field felt, more than anything else, a deep sadness.

"You know, I think I'll need something to carry all this in," Loomis said, as if he'd just remembered being asked to stop by the market on his way home from work. Still holding the gun, he grabbed a leather monogrammed briefcase from Field's desk, emptied it onto the desktop, returned with it to the coffeetable, and began packing the case with bills.

Field studied him a moment. "So all you are," he said, "is a common thief."

"Not exactly." Loomis glanced up from his work and smiled. "It's just supposed to look that way."

"What?"

"I'm not here to rob you, Mr. Field. I'm here to kill you."

***

Martin Field just stared at him.

"It's true," Loomis said. "I was hired by one of your . . . how shall I put it? Your competitors. The robbery is just to throw the cops off the track." He resumed the task of loading the briefcase. "A nice bonus, though, I must say."

Field made no reply. He stood there beside the open vault, the bile rising in his throat, trying to process this new information. The idea that someone would want him dead for a price was almost as unsettling as the news that he was about to die. One by one, Martin Field's muscles began to sag. He felt tired and scared and sick, and thought he probably looked it too. What he *didn't* look, though, was threatening—he never had. And that was probably what made Ed Loomis take his eyes off him for a minute as Loomis continued to transfer the money from the tabletop to the briefcase.

A sudden noise brought Loomis's head up. A tight, solid THUMP, like the sound you hear when you close a refrigerator, or slam the door of an expensive car. The thump was followed by a series of tiny metallic clicks.

Loomis dropped the case, whirled around, raised the gun.

Martin Field stared back at him. Field was standing exactly as before, except that his right hand was raised and pressed flat against the vault door, which was now closed. He watched as understanding dawned on Loomis's face.

The little clicks had been the sounds of the lock's tumblers falling back into place.

"What the hell are you doing?" Loomis said.

"Just tidying up." To Field's surprise, despite his fear, he felt himself smile a little. "I wanted a little something to remember you by."

Loomis's eyes narrowed. "What do you mean?"

"I took your picture," Field said.

The room went dead quiet.

"What?"

"It'll be a good one, I think. You, leaning over my coffee-table with a gun in your hand and a grin on your face, stuffing money into a briefcase with my initials on the side. Self-explanatory, I think they call that."

Ed Loomis's gaze lasered into him. "What are you talking ab—"

"Remember the camera, Mr. Loomis? The camera sitting here on the bookshelf?" Together, they turned to look at the place where it had been. "It's my wife's, she left it here the other day. She photographs flowers, of all things."

"So?" Even as Field's voice had become more steady, Loomis's began to tremble. "Where is it?"

"It's in the safe. I told you, I took your picture. With these lamps I didn't even need a flash."

A long silence dragged by.

Realization, Field noticed, was beginning to set in.

"I don't believe you," Loomis whispered. He seemed suddenly to have lost all interest in packing the briefcase.

Field shrugged. "It's true."

"You couldn't have," Loomis said. "You didn't have time—"

"Oh, but I did. The time, the opportunity, and the motivation. Your likeness, my friend, is now preserved, on film inside a camera inside a safe that's locked until after ten o'clock tomorrow morning. And even then, I'm one of only three people who can open it." Field folded his arms across his chest. "I think this is what's called, in sports terms, a 'shift in momentum.'"

Loomis was the one sweating now. His face glistened in the lamplight.

But he didn't look ready to surrender.

"You're crazy if you think that'll stop me from killing you," he said. He raised the cocked pistol. "Even if you did what you said, nobody's gonna care anything about that camera."

"Is that so? Think a minute, Loomis. Imagine the sequence of events. A prominent businessman is robbed and murdered in his office—"

"Murdered," Loomis corrected. "Not robbed. Nobody'll know about the robbery." He drew his brows together, thinking.

"I won't leave anything lying around," he murmured, as if to himself. "I was going to, to throw 'em off, but I won't now. I'll pick everything up. Nobody'll know anything was taken."

"You're wrong," Field said. "The vault's the first thing they'll check. At least two people besides me know what's in it. They'll damn sure know what's *not*, when they see it gone." He paused for a beat, watching the other man's face. "Back to my scenario: Prominent businessman is robbed and murdered in his office. A small fortune is stolen from his wall safe. A camera is then found inside the otherwise empty safe. 'What the hell's *that* doing there, Lieutenant?' one detective asks the other . . ."

Field smiled, more easily this time, and did a palms-up.

"See the problem, Mr. Loomis? The first thing any sane cop would do is develop the film in the camera. They'll probably be expecting some kind of picture-message from the thief. Won't it be a pleasant surprise when they find—"

"No," Loomis said, shaking his head. "No. That can't happen." He focused on Field as if seeing him for the first time, then waved the gunbarrel toward one of the chairs. "Sit down. *Now*."

When Field was seated, Ed Loomis began to stomp back and forth across the room, his eyes glazed and dreamy. The money, forgotten now, lay scattered on the coffeetable, half in and half out of the briefcase. Loomis looked like a drugged wolf pacing a cage.

"I could take you with me," he said, his voice low. "I could take you now, and bring you back tomorrow night to open it. If you refused, I'd shoot off your kneecaps, and then your elbows, and then—"

"If you kidnap me now, Loomis, you can forget coming back. I'll be missed tonight at home, not to mention here at the office tomorrow. The place'll be swarming with cops, and it's my guess they'll have my people open the safe as soon as the timer allows it, at 10:01 tomorrow morning. After they find the camera they'll process the film, and when they see the film your face'll be on every police station's fax machine from here to Atlanta." Field shook his head. "Not a good plan."

Loomis swallowed, then wiped a palm across his forehead. "Then I'll . . . hell, I'll burn the place down." He continued pacing, nodding. "That's what I'll do. I'll burn it to the ground—"

"That won't work," Field said.

Loomis stopped in his tracks. "What?"

"Fireproof, remember? The safe's fireproof."

"Then I'll . . . I'll . . ." Loomis's eyes drifted to the west window. Twenty yards away, backlit by the last rays of the sun, was the grassy hump of the old storm cellar. A tiny square window in its side stared back, like the filmy eye of a subterranean monster. He looked at it for a long time, then turned to face Martin Field.

"I'll blow it up," he said.

***

Field felt a new flutter in his stomach. "What did you say?"

"The safe. I'll blow it to pieces." Loomis was nodding slowly.

"How would you do that?"

"How would I *do* it? How would you climb up a cliff if you saw a rope hanging there in front of you?" He seemed to be growing more excited with every word. "You said yourself there's plenty of explosives out there in that bunker of yours. Want me to draw you a picture?"

Martin Field leaned forward in his chair, pinning the other man with his gaze. "I don't doubt you could draw me a picture, Mr. Loomis. What I doubt is that you could wire an explosive charge."

His visitor smiled. "I won't have to."

The statement lingered there in the air between them.

"What do you mean by that?"

Loomis shrugged. "*You* can wire a charge. Right?"

"I can, sure. The question is, why should I?"

"I'll tell you why: I'll kill you if you don't."

"You'll kill me if I *do*! I'm no fool, Loomis. That camera inside my safe is all that's keeping me alive right now. If I blow it up, we're back where we started."

"No," Loomis said, shaking his head again.

"No what?"

"No I won't kill you. Not if you help me, I won't." His face hardened. "I need you, you can see that. No more threats of bullets in the knees or elbows, not now. I *need* you. And if you wire a blast that destroys that safe . . . or even if it just messes up the clock enough so you can open it, say, and get the camera out, or melts the film—"

"Yes?"

"Then I'll let you go. I'll vanish."

"You'll vanish," Field said.

"Into thin air. I swear it. Ed Loomis, as you've probably figured out, isn't my real name. I'll leave and you'll never see me again."

"If I help you, you mean."

"That's right."

Field studied him for a long moment. "And if I don't?"

"Then I *will* kill you." The man calling himself Loomis approached the engineer slowly, then reached forward and touched the cold muzzle of the gun to the center of his forehead. "I'll shoot you dead as Custer's last bugler, just like I started out to do."

Field shrank back in his seat. "You don't understand. If you let me live and the cops find the camera, you're guilty of burglary. If you kill me and the cops find the camera, you're guilty of burglary *and* murder. You're not making sense."

The reaction was swift and violent. Before he knew what was happening, Martin Field was grabbed by the shirtfront, snatched out of his chair, and thrown backward against the wall. Stunned, he stared into the wildest pair of eyes he'd ever seen. The two men's noses were two inches apart.

"Don't you tell me," Loomis said, his face fiery red, "what makes sense."

Field swallowed.

"What *doesn't* make sense is me letting you get the jump on me the way you did. Don't get me wrong, I'm not convinced you took that picture, Field. I'm not even convinced there's any film in the camera. But I can't take the chance, and both of us know it. And now that you've put me *in* this spot, you're gonna pull me out of it."

He fell silent then. It was so quiet Field thought he could hear the crickets in the woods behind the house.

"So you get yourself out there to that cellar," Loomis said, tipping his head toward the window, "and you fetch some dynamite or whatever you use, and you wire this safe to blow sky-high. It better split like a ripe watermelon. You understand me?"

"You're the one who doesn't understand." Field drew a breath, tried in vain to pull away from Loomis's iron grip. "A charge big enough to destroy the safe—it'd also destroy the building. The blast would be heard halfway to Little Rock."

"So? I'm not planning to linger, afterward." Loomis tightened his hold on Field's collar. "I'm telling you, once more: blow that safe to pieces, and do it fast. If you do that, you win your life. If you don't, or won't, or try to trick me . . . I'll kill you. I swear I'll kill you, Field, pure and simple. Logic doesn't have a thing to do with it." He paused, and the engineer could feel the other man's hot breath on his face. "You got that?"

Field made himself nod.

"Say it."

"I got it."

Loomis seemed to unwind a little, though his eyes still had a mad glint to them. "You have what you need to do it with? You have it here?"

"Yes. It's all locked in the powder room."

"Then do it."

With that, Field was shoved away from the wall and toward the center of the office, where he stood dazed and wobbling. Finally he asked, "How do you want it done?"

"What do you mean? You're the expert."

"There are a dozen ways," Field said, rubbing his bruised throat. "A remote, a fuse, a timer—"

"No timers. It has to be something I can control myself. No remotes either. I want wires, so I can see where they're going." Loomis frowned. "And a plunger, that's what I want. A box with an old-fashioned, T-shaped, bicycle-pump plunger, like in the movies."

Martin Field shook his head, then stopped when he found that it made him dizzy. "They don't make those anymore. I have a variation, though. It's wired, like you said, and has a handle you twist to set off the charge."

Loomis nodded. "I've seen 'em. That'll do fine." He glanced once more around the room, then took a minute to scoop the rest of the money into the briefcase and snap it shut. Case in one hand and pistol in the other, he motioned Field toward the outside door. "Walk slow," he said.

In the fading light they marched around the house to the driveway and climbed into Loomis's car. With Field held at gunpoint, Loomis drove a quarter mile down the road and parked. They trudged back to the house without a word.

At the door to the bunker Field flipped a switch that lit up the long stretch of yard between the office and where they now stood. Loomis nodded his approval. His pistol remained steady.

"Get to work," Loomis said.

***

It took forty minutes to rig the charges. The crickets were in full chorus by the time it was done, and a fat summer moon floated above the treeline to the south. Only twice had Martin Field been allowed to get more than a few feet away from his captor, and that had been the two times Field had entered through the steel door of the former storm-cellar he called the powder room, to prepare and retrieve the explosives and set up the wiring and the triggering device. During those times, about ten minutes each, Loomis had kept the door key and posted himself outside the inch-thick Lexan window in the east wall of the bunker. He remembered what Field had told him, he said, about everything *out*side the bunker being safe from accidents *in*side (and vice versa) and didn't want to be too close while Field was poking around in there, for fear a blunder might vaporize them both.

When all the preparations were finished, the two of them stood together just outside the open steel door of the shelter, the gun still pointed at Field's chest. Wires ran past them from the crank-style detonating device on the bunker's concrete floor and wound snakelike across the lawn to the side door of Field's private office, where eighty pounds of high explosives were sitting primed and waiting on the bookshelves beside the vault.

"You sure we'll be safe, in here?" Loomis asked.

"In the bunker? Yes."

"That little window, inside," Loomis said, pointing with the money-filled briefcase. "We can watch the explosion, from there?"

"Well, we can watch up until the moment I twist the handle

on the device. Then we'll have to duck. With that big a charge, that close to us, the window'll blow inward, blastproof glass or not."

"Okay."

"Anytime you're ready," Field said dully. Despite the constant tension—or maybe because of it—he was exhausted.

Loomis took in some air, held it, blew out a sigh. Then he squinted hard at the house, and the lighted window of Martin Field's office.

"My employer—your enemy—tells me you're a genius, Field. One of the brightest minds of our time." He kept his eyes on the house as he spoke. "Tell me, as a genius, what would you think the hardest thing is, about killing somebody?"

Field blinked. His mouth felt dry. "I don't know."

"Take a guess."

"Pulling the trigger, I suppose."

Loomis snorted. "That's the easiest thing. The hardest—well, two things are the hardest. The first is making it look like something other than foul play, and the second's the disposing of the body."

Field didn't reply. Somewhere in the woods south of the house, an owl hooted.

"And now and then," Loomis said, "not often, but now and then . . . you find you can do both at the same time."

Another silence.

"So," Field said. "You're going to kill me after all."

Slowly Loomis turned to look at him.

"You told me you'd let me go," Field said.

"Lying isn't my most serious character flaw," Loomis admitted, "but it's a flaw nonetheless." He tucked the briefcase under his arm, pulled the bunker's door open, and used the gun to point with. "Walk to the house, Mr. Field. I think I can handle things myself from here on out."

Field studied the killer's face in the moonlight. He could feel his heart hammering in his chest.

"But . . . if you blow me up along with the house—"

"And the safe," Loomis corrected.

"If you blow me up along with the house and the safe . . . how's that going to look like an accident? I don't normally keep bombs in my office."

"Not an accident," Loomis said. "Suicide."

"Suicide."

"I hear the rich guys like to go out with a bang."

Another silence, longer this time.

"Walk to the house, Mr. Field. Go inside and stand at your office window. I want to be able to see your face until the very last second."

"What if I run?" Field said.

"Then I'd catch you, and shoot you outside and drag you into the house. Unnecessary effort, for both of us. By the way, I made sure the inside door—the one from your office to the rest of the house—is blocked." Loomis took a step backward into the bunker and pointed again with the revolver. "Get moving."

Field said nothing more. There was nothing left to say.

He turned and crossed the twenty yards of floodlit lawn, following the trail of black wires on the ground, to his office door.

***

Field turned the knob, stepped through the door, and closed it behind him. He paused a minute and looked around. On the other side of the room, sitting on the bookshelves like stacks of wrapped gray hotdogs, was enough explosive power to blow this office and most of the headquarters of Field Engineering into pieces the size of a gnat's toothpick.

He moved to the west window and looked out at Ed

Loomis, who had entered the converted storm-cellar and was staring back at him through the foot-square Lexan window in its side. Grinning, Loomis held the triggering device up so Field could see it, and raised a hand in farewell.

At that moment, as the two men stared one last time into each other's eyes, Martin Field felt a rush of profound sorrow at what was about to happen. In his mind he pictured the scene afterward, and the army of policemen who would descend on the site tomorrow morning—or later tonight, maybe—when the neighbors reported hearing the explosion.

He had known, of course, that Loomis would lie to him, and doublecross him. That was a given. And the fact that Loomis had acted exactly as expected gave Field no sense of triumph or satisfaction.

It was all so needless, he thought. So unnecessary. But he'd had no choice.

As he watched, he saw Ed Loomis place his right hand on the handle of the device, and give it a sharp twist.

Then Loomis's face ducked out of sight. Field could picture him on the bunker floor with his head down and his eyes squeezed shut—

But nothing happened.

Seconds later Loomis's face reappeared in the window. It showed surprise, then puzzlement, then realization, then rage. His teeth were clenched, his eyes blazing.

Before he could act, Field took something from his pocket and held it up to the window so Loomis could see it. Almost casually Martin Field put his thumb on top of the little remote transmitter, paused a moment, and pressed the button. Then he closed his eyes and dropped to one knee below the window. He never really heard the blast, thanks to the steel bunker walls and the earplugs he had put in a moment ago when he came through the office door—but he felt it. For an instant his brain seemed to compress inside his skull, and the house quivered, and the earth itself heaved and shifted underneath him.

***

As it turned out, the losses were considerable: the entire contents of the bunker were of course obliterated, along with Ed Loomis and the money-filled briefcase he'd been holding at the time. By contrast, most everything *out*side the bunker was fine, including Martin Field and his office and the explosives piled on the bookshelves and the house itself, except for the west windows and the exterior on that side of the building.

The safe was of course untouched and intact, as was the camera inside it. The film in the camera might have been a surprise to Ed Loomis, though, if he had lived to hear about it.

It was a 12-exposure roll of Kodak 200, the only kind Mrs. Field liked to use. Every print, when the roll was developed, came out sharp and clear.

All twelve were photos of wildflowers, taken in the forests and meadows of western Arkansas.

The Judge's Wife

"Ms. Sanderford?"

"That's right."

The man on the porch took off his cap. "There's been an accident, ma'am." He turned and nodded in the direction of a second man, waiting at the foot of the steps. "The police sent us to fetch you."

Janice Sanderford put a hand to her throat. "Oh, no. My husband . . . ?"

"Yes ma'am. They're working on getting him out of the car. They don't think he's bad hurt, but he's asking for you."

"Oh my God." She looked around a moment, dazed, then came out and pulled the door shut behind her. "I'm ready," she said.

A moment later they were headed east on Highway 12, in an old blue Ford. The first man was at the wheel, Janice in the passenger seat, the other man in the back. She sat straight and stiff in her Polo shirt and jeans, hugging her elbows. Her face was chalk-white.

"What happened?" she asked. "Was it that bad intersection on the edge of town?"

The two men exchanged glances in the rear-view mirror. "What happened," the driver said, "was a kidnapping. And pretty well done, too." He looked thoughtful. "Imagine that: the wife of J.P. Sanderford, snatched in broad daylight."

Janice blinked. She studied his face, then turned to look at his partner. The man in the back seat held up a pistol so she could see it.

"I don't believe this," she said.

The driver was smiling now, his eyes glittering under the brim of the John Deere cap. "We been watching you. The plan was to wait till tomorrow morning, but when we saw your husband leave awhile ago, we decided—"

"Why not?" the partner said, from the back seat.

The driver gave Janice another grin. "We're the Mauronds, by the way."

"The morons?"

"Mauronds. I'm Eddie, that's my brother Nate in the back. We'll be spending some time together, the three of us, the next day or so."

Janice's face, so pale a moment ago, had turned the color of new brick. "You *are* morons," she said, "if you think this'll work."

Eddie narrowed his eyes. "What do you mean?"

"I mean you're idiots." She turned as if to make sure Nate knew he was included in her assessment. "You're going to hold me for ransom, is that the idea?"

"That's the idea." Eddie Maurond's grin had disappeared. "What's idiotic about that?"

"I'll tell you," she said. "Jason won't pay it."

"Your husband, you mean?"

"Yes, my husband. He won't pay it."

"How do you know? You don't know how much we'll ask for."

"Doesn't matter. Do you know anything about him? Anything about *us*?"

Eddie was quiet a moment. "We know he's rich. We ain't from here, but we heard of him. 'J.P. Sanderford, one of the most successful trial lawyers in the Southeast . . .' Anyhow, we got directions to your house, and—"

"We're getting a divorce. Did you know that? Jason won't pay to get me back because he doesn't *want* me back." She glared at him. "You beginning to get the picture?"

Eddie shot an uneasy glance at Nate, who looked even more worried. "I don't believe you," Eddie said to her.

"Fine. Wait till you call him, to ask for the money." She settled back in her seat, her color fading. Now she just looked tired.

Eddie braked, swerved onto a dirt road, and stopped the car fifty yards from the highway, in a thick stand of pines.

They sat there in dead silence. After a minute or so Eddie cranked down his window; birds sang and played in the trees beside the road. It was a warm, cloudless afternoon. The breeze through the open window smelled like freshly mown hay.

"This is crazy," he murmured.

"It's crazy all right," she said. "You made a mistake, Eddie or whatever your name really is. Why don't you just turn around and take me back to my house, and we'll forget this ever—"

"No. Not a chance." He removed his cap and ran a hand through his hair. "We've done this, we've come this far, we ain't turning back. He'll pay if we ask him."

"He won't. What he'll do is call the cops, and they'll

find you. Or, more likely, he'll just do nothing at all."

Eddie's face darkened. "Then we'll kill you."

"Kill me?" She did a palms-up. "What good would that do? Then you'd be murderers as well as kidnappers, and you still won't have your money."

"Well, we're not letting you go. Not now."

"Why not?"

Eddie squirmed in his seat. "Because we left him a message already."

"You what?"

"We left your husband a message on his office answering machine. I called there from a pay phone after we saw him leave your house, and said we have you and we want a quarter million in cash, or we'll kill you."

"You called his *office*?"

"That's right. A woman's voice on his machine said leave a message, and I did."

"I guess you probably spoke through a handkerchief, like in the movies," she said.

"Don't make fun of me. Yeah, I disguised my voice."

Suddenly her eyes widened. "You called the house last night, too. Didn't you."

Eddie made no reply.

"You did. I remember now. You called and talked to me, and said you were doing a survey, and asked if we had any children or other dependents living in the house. And I said no." She pinned him with her stare. "You asked me so you'd know no one else was there."

"Well, it worked, didn't it?"

She closed her eyes, shook her head. "Did you happen to notice, when Jason left—did either of you even *notice*—that he had a suitcase with him?"

Eddie frowned. "What?"

"He's not gone to the office. He's gone to our condo, on the Coast, for two days. He won't even check that message you left until Thursday morning."

A silence fell.

"Can we get in touch with him?"

"Why? I told you, he won't pay your ransom. He'll be thrilled to be rid of me."

"I said, can we get in touch with him?"

She sighed. "Not until tonight. He'll get to Pensacola around nine. But I'm serious, he won't even consider—"

She stopped and gazed off into space. "My God."

"What is it?"

Janice Sanderford looked stunned. After a moment her eyes came back into focus, and she turned to face him.

"I know how you can get your money," she said.

Eddie studied her carefully. "What do you mean?"

"I know how you can get Jason to pay your ransom. You're just using the wrong approach." She paused, as if deep in thought. "I could help you."

"Help us? Why would you help us?"

"So I could get half," she said.

"What?!"

"Why not? Without my help you'll get nothing, and God knows I could use the cash. I'm a software installer, in case you didn't know, and my debts—"

"But you're the wife of J.P. Sanderford."

"Grow up, Eddie. He's a lawyer. You really think I'll be getting much out of this divorce? If I help you, I guarantee you can pull this off, and for a lot more than a quarter million."

"How much?" he asked.

"How much more?"

"Total," he said.

"A million at least. Maybe two."

Nate leaned over the seat, watching them like a little kid. “I don’t follow this,” he said. “If he wouldn’t pay to get you back . . . what *would* he be paying for?”

“His reputation.” A slow smile had spread across her face.

“What?” Eddie asked.

“His good name,” she said. “I know his secret.”

“What kind of secret?”

Both men stared at her, waiting.

“The judge’s wife,” she said.

***

It was early evening now, and their meeting place had changed from a rusted 1992 Ford to a first-floor room at the Comfort Inn. Janice had put on Nate’s windbreaker and wrapped her hair in a bandanna from Eddie’s glove compartment to walk the ten paces from the car to the room. If anybody noticed her at all, they didn’t seem to care.

“So this affair he’s having,” Eddie said, “is with the wife of a judge.”

“A justice, actually. State Supreme Court.” Janice took a bite of the Double Whopper Nate had brought back from his trip through the BK drive-thru. The Maurond brothers had finished theirs and were sitting together on one of the beds, watching her. She was seated at a table the size of a bicycle wheel. “He’s one of the most powerful men around.”

“And he—this judge—don’t know what his wife and J.P. are up to?”

“Nobody knows but me,” she said, chewing. “They’ve been careful. If word did get out, the judge would destroy him. Jason’s career would be over.”

Eddie gave that some thought. “Wait a minute. If your husband’s playing around, why ain’t *you* divorcing *him*?”

“Because I have no proof. I told you, they’re careful.”

"But you're sure? About the affair, I mean."

"Yes, I'm sure." She took a swallow of Sprite. "This'll work, I tell you. We'll go to her house tonight, around midnight—"

"Whose house?"

"The judge's wife."

"Why would we go to her house?"

"Because that's where you'll call my husband from. The judge and his wife are out of town, we'll have the place to ourselves."

Nate still looked worried. "You mean we'll break in?"

"We could, but we won't. I have a key."

"On you?" Eddie said.

"No, not on me. It's at home, we'll just stop by there and pick it up."

"How is it you have a key to their house?"

She stared at him. "How do you think?"

"Oh. I guess she gave your husband one."

"And he doesn't know that I know he has it."

"But . . . you said you had no proof. Wouldn't the house key be proof?"

"Not in a courtroom. My husband and the judge used to be fishing buddies. Jason could say he had the key from back then."

Eddie shook his head. "I still don't get it. Why go to her *house*?"

"I told you, that's where you'll place the call to Jason. You'll tell him you broke into their house and you've found her diary—it tells the whole story."

"Does she have a diary?"

"Who knows? It doesn't matter, long as Jason believes she does."

"And why should he believe it?"

"Because you'll call him from her house," Janice said again. "Jason has caller ID on his phone at the condo. When he sees where you're calling from—believe me, he knows her number—he'll realize you're really there. He has to be paranoid anyway after walking a tightrope for so long, so this'll make perfect sense to him. He'll know the house is supposed to be empty while the judge and his wife are away."

Eddie nodded, thinking. "So I call your husband, tell him I'm onto him, ask for the money, then lay low until he delivers."

"Right. And believe me, he'll deliver."

"And you'll get a third—"

"I'll get half."

Eddie studied her a moment, but made no objection. "What about after?" he said. "Won't it look funny, you coming into a lot of money all of a sudden?"

"Why should it? I told you, we're in the process of a divorce. People will think I got a big settlement. Besides, I'm well thought of around here."

"How well?"

"Very well. I'm the police chief's sister."

"My, my. Your sneaky mind might be a surprise to your family."

"It's a surprise to me, sometimes. Now, is this a go, or not?"

The two men swapped a look and, almost at the same time, shrugged.

"I guess so," Eddie said.

"Good." She drained her Sprite and plunked the cup down on the table. "Now that that's settled, and we're partners, we need to get something else straight."

"What do you mean?"

"Is Maurond your real name?"

"Sure it is. Why?"

"Eddie and Nate?"

"That's us."

"And when you first kidnapped me—did you intend to let me go, eventually?"

"Yes. Why?"

She leaned forward in her chair. "Kidnapping Rule #1: Don't tell the kidnappee your real names."

Both men frowned, thinking that over.

"That was a mistake," she said. "Among others."

They looked embarrassed.

"And from now on, there'll be no mistakes. I don't plan to go to jail over this. Understood?"

Two nods. "Understood."

A silence passed. Finally she said, "Any questions?"

Nate slowly raised a hand.

"What?" she asked.

"You gonna eat the rest of them fries?"

***

They hung around the motel room for the next five hours, catnapping and gulping coffee and flipping channels on the remote. At a quarter past twelve they piled into the Ford, swung by the Sandersons' for the key, and drove the six miles to the house Janice identified as the judge's. A two-story colonial, on a wooded lot. No lights showed in the windows. Janice directed them to a deserted side street, where they left the car and doubled back through a patch of pineforest to the judge's back yard. Once, when she got a little too far ahead, Eddie caught up with her and gave her arm a hard squeeze.

"Partners or not, you're still kidnapped," he said. "I'd be disappointed, after all this, to have to kill you anyway."

"I would too," she assured him.

Her key worked fine. The three of them stood together

a minute in the moonlit kitchen, waiting and listening. Finally she led them along a shadowy back hallway. They'd agreed to be quiet and cautious, even though Janice seemed convinced the house was empty.

They paused outside what looked like a bedroom door. She had visited this house in happier times, she'd told them, and this was the room where Eddie should place his call: its only window faced the woods, so a light here wouldn't be seen from the road while he was on the phone.

"Wait here," she whispered. "I'll find a lamp and switch it on."

Eddie was still standing there in the hallway with Nate thirty seconds later, when the light came on. What it illuminated, however, was nothing a burglar would ever want to see.

"Hands up, boys," a voice said. "You're under arrest."

The voice's owner was a really large man with a really large gun, and the gun was pointing at Eddie's chest. Closer inspection revealed puffy eyes, mussed hair, and green pajamas, but the voice and the pistol were both rock-steady.

Eddie and Nate raised their hands.

"Don't tell me," Eddie said to Janice, who was standing beside the sleepy-looking gunman. "The police chief?"

"Afraid so," she said. Then, to her brother: "Glad you haven't had your locks changed lately. Or had an alarm installed."

"I'm just glad my heart didn't stop when you woke me up. Any guns in this group?"

"Just one," she said. "Nate?" He handed it over, then he and Eddie turned and held their wrists behind their backs while the chief handcuffed them. Over his shoulder, the chief called to his wife to phone the station to have a car sent over.

"You ready to explain all this, J.P.?" the chief asked his sister.

Eddie blinked, and twisted around to look at Janice. "J.P.?" he said. "*You're* J.P. Sanderford?"

"That's me."

"Good God." He gaped at her. "You're quite an actress, ain't you?"

"Just a lawyer."

"And your husband—"

"He's the software installer. That's where he is tonight, putting in a system."

Eddie couldn't stop staring at her. "So there ain't no judge, or judge's wife?"

"Sure there is," she said. "But this isn't their house. And they're happily married."

"Like you and your husband?"

She nodded. "Hell of a thing, all this marital bliss."

"And I suppose that was *your* recorded voice on the office answering machine?"

"Why not? It's my office." She regarded him a moment. "Let me ask you something, Eddie." She tipped her head toward the open bedroom door. "If this had been on the level, and you'd gotten the money . . . would you really have given me a share?"

Though he didn't quite smile, his eyes twinkled a little. "No," he said. "But I wouldn't have killed you, either."

She just nodded. "I believe you."

"I hate to break this up," the chief said, "but I'm sleepy, and it's late. I'm placing you boys under arrest for—" He glanced at Janice.

"Kidnapping," she said.

"Kidnapping. If you'll step outside with me, one of my associates will escort you two goobers to jail."

As they started away, she grabbed his sleeve and whispered, "Go easy on them, Bobby. They're more dumb than mean."

"Yeah, well, that makes three of us."

The chief's wife, a plain woman in a pink housecoat, came to stand beside her while the prisoners were marched outside.

"Who *are* they, J.P.?"

Janice thought a moment, watching them out the front window. "They're the Mauronds."

Her sister-in-law blinked. "Morons?"

"Yes," Janice said. "That too."

Not One Word

"Boys?"

Three ninth-graders in T-shirts and gym shorts turned to look as Father O'Neal hurried toward them down the empty hallway. Twenty feet away, through the open door of the teachers' lounge, a man in a sweatsuit was talking into a cell phone and rummaging through the drawers of a desk.

"You the boys who caught the snake?" O'Neal asked, puffing a bit.

Two of the youngsters pointed to the third. "There's your hero," one said. "Jungle Jimmy Todd."

O'Neal's eyes narrowed. "Ah yes," he said. "James and I are acquainted."

"Hello, Father," Jimmy murmured.

The priest—and head of the school—studied him a moment. "What happened, exactly?"

"We were helping Coach Steen bring some basketballs from the storeroom to the gym," Jimmy said, pointing to the half-dozen balls lined up against one wall, "when it crawled right up to us."

"Here in the hall?"

"Right over there," Jimmy said.

"What happened then?"

"It bit him," one of the other boys, Eddie Hendon, said.

Father O'Neal blinked. "Bit you?"

"Bit my sock," Jimmy said. He reached down to touch his ankle. "Then it wrapped itself around my leg."

"It was a python," Eddie said, looking pleased. "They're not poisonous."

"A python?!" O'Neal said.

"Or a boa constrictor. We're not sure which."

"A small one," Jimmy corrected. "A baby, probably."

"How small?"

"Four or five feet. I grabbed it behind the head, and Chuck and Eddie helped me uncoil it."

"What was it doing here, anyone know?"

All three boys shrugged. "Somebody's pet, maybe," Chuck Thomas said.

The priest looked around, frowning. Coach Steen was still on the phone in the teachers' lounge.

"Where's the snake now?" O'Neal asked.

"The broom closet," Jimmy said. "Just down the hall."

"How'd you get it in there?"

"Very quickly," Chuck said. Everybody grinned.

"Eddie opened the door and Chuck and I threw it in," Jimmy said.

Father O'Neal seemed to think that over, then asked, "What's Coach Steen doing in the lounge?"

"Looking for a key to the broom closet. To lock the door with."

O'Neal regarded the group a moment. "That was excellent work, boys. Excellent work." To Jimmy he added, "It appears you have redeemed yourself, James."

Jimmy looked uncomfortable. "You mean that thing last month?"

"You know what I mean."

"It was just butyric acid, Father. In a wastebasket. Nobody got hurt—"

"No, what everybody got," O'Neal said, "was a free day at home, because it stunk up the whole school."

"In my opinion," Chuck said helpfully, "the evacuation was very well organized."

The priest gave him a stern look, but didn't press the issue. "And I still haven't found out who switched the name-plates on the doors of the boys' and girls' restrooms last week."

"A terrible thing," Eddie agreed.

"Parents are still calling me about that," O'Neal said. "What a mess. Half the boys were in the girls' and half the girls in the boys'—"

"Sounded like an outside job to me," Chuck said, dead-pan. "St. Richard's, probably."

For a moment Father O'Neal actually looked amused.

"Regardless," he said, serious again, "you boys did a good thing today. If you hadn't been here, or if this had happened between classes ..." He shook his head. "Anyhow, I think this calls for an afternoon off. I'll speak to your teachers."

The boys all beamed. At that instant Coach Steen arrived, switching off the cell phone. "Couldn't find a key for the broom closet," he said. "It's still unlocked."

"Doesn't matter. That closet's hardly ever used, nobody'll go inside." O'Neal glanced at the phone. "I hope you were calling the fire department, or the zoo, or whoever can come take this thing off our hands."

"The carnival," Steen answered. The fairgrounds were on the far side of a wooded area that bordered the school property. "I heard on the news this morning some animals had got loose. Sure enough, they said it sounded like one of theirs. They're sending somebody over."

The priest nodded, then frowned. "Where were *you* during all this, by the way?"

Steen's face reddened. "I was, ah, on top of the lockers over there." He cleared his throat. "I hate snakes."

"I'd probably have been up there with you," O'Neal said. "Better get outside, Coach, and watch for the cavalry." As Steen hurried off O'Neal turned to the others. "I meant what I said, men. Outstanding work. Don't bother coming in after lunch."

"Aye aye, sir," Chuck said. Jimmy and Eddie grinned at each other.

"But not one word about this to Sister Agnes." O'Neal stared intensely into Jimmy's eyes. "Especially you," he said, pointing a finger. "Not *one word*."

Jimmy nodded. All of them had a healthy fear of the priest's Second in Command. Sister Agnes was a bitter, ruthless woman who disliked the schoolchildren only slightly less than she disliked Father O'Neal. This fact—though not very nun-like—was common knowledge. The only good thing about her was that she usually stayed in the batcave, which was the way most of the students referred to her office.

But this was, alas, no usual day. Ten seconds after Father O'Neal disappeared around the corner of the hallway, Sister Agnes appeared at the other end, striding along like an executioner on the way to the gallows.

When she saw the boys she stopped, her face darkening. She planted both hands on her hips and thrust her chin forward. "What are you hoodlums doing in the hall?"

All three stared at her, petrified. An enraged python was nothing compared to this woman.

"You heard me," she said. "Why aren't you in class?"

"We're on an errand with Coach Steen," Eddie croaked. He pointed to the row of basketballs, as if they explained everything.

"Coach Steen is in the gym," she said, giving him a laser stare. "You're supposed to be, too."

"He's outside," Eddie said. All three boys cast a hopeful look at the sunlit doors at the east exit, but there was no sign of Coach Steen's wide body.

"I thought you said you were helping him."

Jimmy started to answer, then hesitated.

Not one word, Father O'Neal had said . . .

"All of you stay right there," she snapped. She turned, marched through the still-open door of the teachers' lounge, and stood there a moment. Then she stormed out again.

"What were you doing in the teachers' lounge?" she asked.

"We weren't in the teachers' lounge," Chuck said.

"There's a basketball in there," she said.

"We didn't put it there."

"Then who did?"

"Coach Steen."

"Why would he do that?"

Eddie looked ill. No one answered.

"Why don't you just tell me," she said, glaring at them, "where it is."

Chuck blinked. "Where what is?"

"You know what. My cell phone."

"Your cell phone?!"

She nodded toward the teachers' lounge. "I left it there on that desk, twenty minutes ago. Now it's gone. And the door's open, everyone else is in class, you're in gym clothes, and there's a basketball where my phone was. Add it up."

Eddie Hendon swallowed. "We didn't steal your phone, Sister Ag—"

"You stole it," she said, through clenched teeth. "And I want to know what you did with it."

All of them stood and looked at her, wide-eyed.

Then she focused on Jimmy. "I know you, James Todd," she said, her eyes as black and still as a shark's. "You're the leader of this band of misfits. So tell me, where is it?"

Silence.

"WHERE," she roared, "*IS* IT?"

Jimmy took a deep breath.

"The broom closet," he said.

It was suddenly very quiet in the hall. She gave them another withering stare, then turned on her heel and stomped away toward the closet.

All three boys headed for the outside door. On the way there, Jimmy looked at Chuck and Eddie, who were gaping at him.

"That was *three* words," Jimmy explained.

Besides, her socks were at least as thick as his . . .

True Colors

"He's dead," Nicole Finney said. Teary-eyed, she led Officers Payne and Tyler down a dim hallway. Morris Dunn lay facedown in his office.

"This happened when?" Payne asked.

"Ten minutes ago."

"What'd you see?"

Nicole drew a shaky breath. "Nothing. I was up front at my desk, with the copier repairman, when we heard shots. We thought Mr. Dunn was the only other person in the building."

"Go on."

"Well, when I got back here, whoever did it was gone. But the copier guy . . . he said he saw the killer. Holding a gun."

"He saw him?"

"Her. He talks funny, but this was clear. He said, 'It was a woman. A woman with wet hair.'"

The officers exchanged glances. It had been raining all day. Whoever killed Dunn must've just come inside.

The frightened repairman had left, Nicole said. Tyler quickly phoned in orders to locate him. Meanwhile, employees Hilda Harper and Pam Brady stomped in with rain hats and umbrellas. Their hair—Harper's gray, Brady's blond—was as dry as Nicole's. They received the news in stunned silence.

When asked, Nicole revealed that there was also a back entrance, from a covered garage. "I can see only the front door from my desk," she said, "but anyone entering the back has to key in a door code."

Then, a break: they found Dunn's appointment book. According to the book, he was to meet his wife at noon today—around the time of the murder.

"Describe the wife," Officer Payne said.

Nicole wiped her eyes. "Nice enough lady. Fiftyish, red-headed, hot-tempered."

"Seen her today?"

"No. If she was here, she used the back door. She and the employees all know the code."

Suddenly a woman swept in, using that very door.

"I'm late, Nicole, is Morris—"

Mrs. Dunn stopped short. The policemen solemnly informed her of her husband's death, then stepped away.

"Her hair's dry too," Tyler whispered to Payne. "And check this out."

Another appointment-book entry said: HILDA'S EXIT INTERVIEW 4 P.M.

"Looks like Hilda Harper's getting the axe," Payne said. "The plot thickens."

Over the next hour they questioned everyone. Mrs. Dunn had been shopping all morning, the stonefaced Ms. Harper was resentful about being fired (enough to shoot her boss?), and the attractive young Pam Brady appeared more upset by Dunn's death than his wife was. This suspicion was verified by Nicole Finney:

"Yes," she said, "Pam and Mr. Dunn were having an affair. And yes, Mrs. Dunn knew. So did Pam's husband."

Not that that helped the case. Betrayed spouses are often vengeful, but Mrs. Dunn's hair didn't look rained-on, and even if Pam Brady's husband came here today soaking wet, the person the repairman saw in the hallway had been female. There was no solid evidence against anyone. Mrs. Dunn and the employees were allowed to leave.

"So how'd the killer get in?" Tyler said, as the lab team wrapped up. "The wet-hair description suggests the front door, but it was in plain view. And the back door requires a code."

The officers were pondering that when the copier repairman was brought in.

"I told Mith Finney what I thaw," he said. "The woman had wet hair. And a pithtol."

"Your name, sir?"

"John Wandolph."

Payne looked up from his notepad. "John Randolph?"

"That'th wight. Wandolph."

Payne blinked and turned to his partner. "It's Mrs. Dunn. She did it."

"What?"

"He talks funny, Nicole said. Remember?" Payne jumped to his feet. "The killer didn't have 'wet' hair—she had *red* hair."

Both cops rushed out into the rain. Randolph, left alone and confused in the office, stared after them.

"Who talkth funny?" he said.

John M. Floyd

An Hour at Finley's

I. Marco

Marco Tursi lit another cigarette and studied the room. The setup was a good one: corner table, window at his back, only a few customers in the bar. Rain spattered the windowpane behind him, gusting out of a gray afternoon sky.

Marco liked bar work. The people in bars almost never noticed you; they never noticed much of anything. As a rule, half of them were drunk and the other half didn't care.

Except for today.

Today the bartender was watching him.

At first he shrugged it off. After all, Marco was a big guy, dark, good-looking in a Tony Soprano kind of way. And who knew what kind of pervert the bartender might be.

But Marco had been on the streets a long time. Never in this bar before, but in enough others, and poolhalls and back rooms and dark alleys, to know when someone had him pegged.

His enemies were legion.

And he had a job to do. Too late to back out now.

Marco crushed out his smoke, picked up his empty beer glass, threaded his way through the tables to the bar. Despite his bulk his movements were smooth and precise. Marco liked that—he liked his look, his bearing. He liked it that most people thought he was Italian. His real name was Mark Turner.

"Another Bud," he said to the bartender. A small guy, with sandy hair and green eyes. The polar opposite of Marco.

"Comin' up," the guy said. He was polishing a shot glass with a worn dishtowel.

Marco took a slow look around. Hardwood countertop, brass footrail, mirror the length of the bar. The jukebox was blaring something about no mountain being high enough. Twenty feet away, a young man with red curly hair and a blue shirt had risen from a table and was walking to the restroom area in the back. Marco's narrowed eyes followed the man the way a snake's might follow a mouse, and stayed fixed on the closed bathroom door afterward.

He turned to find the bartender watching the same door.

Marco glanced at the name on the front window. S'YELNIF, in backward letters a foot high. The bartender was the only person behind the counter. "Are you Finley?" Marco asked him.

"One of them," he said. My brother owns the place. I'm Patrick."

Marco snorted. Once again he studied the dark alcove that ended at the door to the men's room. "You been watching me, Patrick Finley. Haven't you."

The bartender shrugged. He picked up Marco's beer glass, turned his back, took his time refilling it, set it down again. "Your face is familiar."

Marco took a swallow and licked his lips. "You're

mistaken," he said.

"It's not familiar?"

Again Marco's gaze drifted to the back alcove. In a low voice he said, "Not only don't you know me—you never saw me before. And you never saw me here today." He set the glass down carefully in the damp circle it had left on the countertop. "But I know you, now. I know your name, and I can find out where you live."

Marco faced the bartender then, and he knew it was the cold menace in his eyes that made the smaller man take a step back.

"Forget you saw me, Mr. Finley. Me, and anything that happens here today. You understand?"

Without another word Marco drained the beer, threw a five onto the bar, and strode to the restroom.

II. Eddie

Eddie Barton was sitting in the first of the three stalls. He had four hours to kill before his flight, and he was in no hurry. An out-of-the-way bar—better still, a restroom in an out-of-the-way bar—was a lot safer than an airport waiting area.

Not that anyplace was really safe. Not now. Not for him.

It had been a stupid fight, a disagreement over the payoff for a bet on a ballgame. Stupid, but fair. No guns or knives, just fists. And then the other guy had tripped and fallen wrong, hit his head on a table edge, out like a light. After that, pandemonium. Finger-pointing, phone calls, paramedics, an ambulance. Not Eddie's fault—not anyone's fault. But the other guy had been Jackie Castonza.

And now Eddie was on the run.

He checked his watch. He'd give it another hour, maybe one more drink, then a cab to the airport. Once there, he'd hide behind a newspaper in a coffeeshop, or in another bathroom—

Eddie heard the restroom door open and close. Footsteps, soft but clicking on the tiles. They approached his stall, passed it, stopped. Eddie's heart began to pound.

Then the door to the adjoining stall squeaked on its hinges. Eddie heard a zipper, and the rustle of clothing as someone settled onto the toilet seat. Below the partition to Eddie's left a right foot appeared, a big foot in an alligator loafer.

Eddie relaxed a bit, went back to his thoughts.

So far he should be okay. Plenty of traveling money, no paper trail, a new ID in his pocket bearing both his photo and a phony name he'd used to book the plane reservation. By midnight he'd be in L.A., and safe. At least until this blew over.

Again he looked down at his watch, and when he did he stiffened. The foot was gone. He frowned, leaned down, looked again.

No feet, left or right, in the next stall.

What was going on? He'd heard movement over there, but he was sure he hadn't heard the door open again—

At that moment a blur went past his eyes, and something snapped tight around his neck. He felt a jolt of pain, heard his own gagging as he was hauled upward off the toilet.

In a blind panic he clawed at his throat, waved his arms, thrashed from side to side like a hooked flounder. Slowly, he was pulled higher. Rolling his eyes upward, he caught an upside-down glimpse of his attacker—a large head, black hair, squinty eyes. The man he'd seen earlier, in the bar.

Eddie tried to scream, but nothing came out. He could hear, as if from a distance, the dull thumping of the heels of his sneakers against the metal partition. What a time for sneakers. He wished he were wearing hardsoled four-pound wingtips.

He wished a lot of things, in those few fleeting seconds. He wished he'd worn a cap to hide his red hair, he wished he'd checked more carefully for a tail on the way here, he wished he'd stayed outside where there were customers, he wished he'd remembered that when there are three stalls in a restroom and the first is occupied, no one ever takes the adjoining one—they go to the one farthest away. A basic fact of life.

The pain in his throat was unbearable. It made his chest ache, his insides boil. His head was roaring. Somewhere in the back of his mind he realized there was no wetness, no blood—whatever was around his neck wasn't piano wire, like in the gangster movies. This was something thicker, cord maybe. Not that it mattered. He was about to die, simple as that. He'd lived a hard and reckless life and now he was going to die. It made it worse that he was going to die with his pants bunched around his ankles, in the bathroom of a bar he'd never even been to before.

He knew exactly what had happened. He could see it in his mind, old Alligator Loafers climbing quietly onto the seat and then up onto the partition, lying there on his stomach over the top edge, crossing his arms and looping the garrote over Eddie's waiting head like a cowboy lassoing a calf, then uncrossing them and pulling it tight, and up—

Eddie's movements slowed, his vision blurred. His world was fading to black.

Eddie Barton was dying.

III. Patrick

Patrick Finley checked his watch again. They'd been in there almost twenty minutes.

He was about to go investigate when he saw the restroom door swing open, saw the redhaired young man in the blue shirt stumble out into the gloomy alcove. The shirt was wrinkled, the face pale. The man stood there a moment, blinking.

Then he looked across the room at Patrick, and staggered toward him.

Close up, the guy didn't look so young after all. His face was lined and world-weary.

The two men studied each other over the countertop. Patrick could see the ugly red marks at the man's throat, and along the sides of the neck.

Patrick swallowed. "Did you kill him?" he whispered.

The question didn't seem to surprise the young man. In a hoarse voice he said, "Kill who?"

"You know who."

The young/old face had regained some of its color. He gripped the edge of the bar as if to steady himself. "All I know," he said, "is that I saw you with him. On my way to the john, I saw you two standing here, talking."

"Listen, Mister—"

"The name's Eddie."

"Well, listen, Eddie, that man in there—in the restroom—he works for the Castonza family. I recognized him. I'd seen him watching you, and I knew something was about to happen—"

"I want to know what you said to him."

Patrick rubbed his face. He felt tired. "It's not what I said," he replied. "It's what I did."

"What you did?"

"While we were talking. While I was drawing his beer . . ."

Eddie watched him, waiting.

Still Patrick hesitated. Outside, the storm howled. The jukebox was playing something British, from the sixties.

Suddenly Eddie's eyes widened.

"You drugged him," he said. "Didn't you."

Patrick sighed. "I keep some powder here, behind the bar. Sedative. I gave him a pretty good dose. It was all I could think of to do."

Eddie's face had gone blank. He nodded slowly, as if a great mystery had been solved.

"It's supposed to work fast," Patrick added. "But he was so big, I guess—"

Eddie murmured something just as thunder boomed outside.

"What did you say?" Patrick asked.

"I said I think you saved my life." In hushed tones Eddie told Patrick about the restroom, told him about being choked from behind and then suddenly released at the last second, to fall gagging to the floor while his assailant fell also, on the other side of the partition.

"He had a cord wrapped around one hand but not the other," Eddie said. "When he passed out, it slipped free. So did I."

Patrick stayed quiet a minute, stunned. "Why was he after you?" he asked finally.

"Long story." Eddie touched his neck and winced. "Which reminds me, I have a plane to catch."

Patrick felt a chill. "You may need to save me a seat," he said.

"What?"

"When this guy wakes up"—he tilted his head toward the restroom door—"he might figure out what I did to him."

"He won't wake up."

Patrick stared. "So you did kill him?"

"He did it himself. Cracked his head on the john when he fell."

A silence passed. Patrick realized he'd been sweating, and drew a ragged breath. He felt a surge of both guilt and relief.

"That knockout stuff you gave him," Eddie said. "Does it leave traces?"

"Beats me."

"Then do us both a favor: block off your men's room, let everyone use the ladies' for a while. I need a head start."

"But it wasn't your fau—"

"I don't mean the cops. I wiped my prints off everything, and the cord he used is in my pocket. It's the Castonzas I'm worried about." Eddie cast a nervous look around. "And you didn't see me here, right?"

Patrick smiled without humor. "I been getting that a lot, lately."

Eddie drew himself up straighter, took a breath. He seemed about to leave, then paused.

"Why'd you do this for me?" he asked. "Why'd you help me?"

"That's a long story too." Patrick felt his jaw tighten. "My wife's sister had a run-in with the Castonzas, years ago. They sent Marco—our oversized friend in there—to deal with her. She didn't fare as well as you did."

Eddie just nodded, his eyes on the rain-streaked front window.

Watching his profile, Patrick said, "Tell me something. Would you have killed him just now? I mean, if he'd only been unconscious, and not dead already?"

Eddie swallowed without turning. It must have hurt his throat, because he grimaced again. "I honestly don't know."

Thunder rumbled. The house lights winked; the music wavered. A gust of wind and rain rattled the window.

"What about you?" Eddie asked.

"What about me?"

"Like you said, you had a stake in this, too. If he wasn't dead in there right now . . . would you finish him off?"

Patrick frowned. He thought about his sister-in-law, her case still unsolved, and about all the other murders attributed to

Marco Tursi. Had he deserved to die? Absolutely. Could Patrick have killed him? Probably. In fact he guessed he actually had, by indirect means. But in cold blood?

"I don't know either," he admitted.

And, at the same instant, they both smiled.

"Fine pair of thugs we are," Eddie said.

Solemn now, he reached across the bar, and they shook hands. For a long moment their gazes held.

Then, without a single look back, Eddie crossed the room and eased out into the blowing rain.

After a quick search Patrick found an OUT OF ORDER sign, locked the restroom door and hung the sign on it, returned to the bar, and picked up the phone. His wife's brother-in-law answered on the first ring. Patrick arranged for them to meet here at quitting time, and asked him to bring his van, but told him no more. He would be surprised, yes, but he'd be pleased as well.

Patrick hung up the phone, put up a stool behind the bar, and sat there listening to the storm and the jukebox and the faint conversation of the customers at one of the tables.

It would be a long night . . .

Christmas Gifts

Something was wrong with the lady in the elevator.

Dennis Bates knew it as soon as she walked in behind him on the nineteenth floor, then turned to stare blankly at the closing doors. For one thing, she hadn't noticed him (women always noticed Dennis Bates); for another, she stood too straight, too rigid. Her purse and her folded coat were held in a deathgrip. Once, as she stepped aside to let an old man get off on seventeen, Bates thought he saw the sparkle of tears on her cheek.

Alone with her now, between floors, he decided to make his move. In a friendly voice he asked, "Is everything all right, ma'am?"

She jumped as if he'd poked her in the ribs. "I'm fine," she said. She gave him a quick glance, then turned away again. Bates studied her a moment, noting the honey-blond hair and the pale profile and the inexpensive outfit, and remembering the glimpse of lovely but red-rimmed blue eyes.

He smiled to himself.

My kind of woman, he thought: good-looking and vulnerable.

They stopped again on fourteen, and two men in maintenance uniforms stomped inside, arguing about something called bolt-activating gear rings. The woman took a step backward as they entered, which put her within an inch of Bates's left elbow. He promptly removed a silk handkerchief from the pocket of his suit, leaned forward, and handed it to her. "Keep it," he whispered. "I have a spare."

She turned to stare at him. On cue, Bates raised his chin and smiled his best smile. At six-three and a trim 180, graying just a bit at the temples, J. Dennis Bates cut a dashing figure, and he knew it. This woman, however, seemed unimpressed. Her eyes, still damp with tears, held only sadness. "Thank you," she murmured.

"My pleasure. The name's Bates, by the way."

A silence passed as she dabbed at her eyes with the handkerchief. "Kathy Hastings," she said. She seemed about to turn away again, then asked distractedly, "Don't you work here?"

"I have an office here, on the nineteenth floor," he said. In fact, he owned the nineteenth floor, as well as most of the rest of the building. "What about you?"

He had spoken in a low voice, trying not to draw the attention of the others in the elevator. Not that it mattered: the two workmen were still deep in a conversation of their own.

"I'm with Rhodes & Ballinger, on twenty-two," she answered. She gave him another look, but it was clear that her mind was on other things. "I think I've seen you in the parking garage. White Toyota, right?"

"Gray Mercedes," Bates said. Amused, he watched her for a reaction, but she didn't even seem to have heard him. She was staring past him at the wall, lost in her own thoughts.

What kind of trouble are you *in*, Kathy Hastings? he wondered. He felt a tingling little thrill run up his spine.

Just as he was about to say something more, the elevator stopped again. Eleventh floor. The doors opened to reveal a hallway lined with holiday decorations. Not a soul was in sight. At ten a.m. on Christmas Eve, most of the building's occupants were either shopping or at home with their families. To Dennis Bates's relief, the two maintenance men got off. The doors closed behind them; the car continued downward.

Bates and the alluring Ms. Hastings were alone again.

Putting on a sympathetic face, he resumed his task. "I don't want to intrude," he said, "but can I do anything to help? Call someone, accompany you someplace . . . ?"

She blinked and focused on him. "No, no thank you," she said, and swallowed. "I'm just . . . I'm on my way to Kennington's, actually."

"Kennington's?" Bates glanced at the panel of lighted buttons. "But that's on the first floor. You pushed P2."

For a moment she continued to stare at him, saying nothing. Then, slowly, her face crumpled. New tears emerged, and after a second or two she lowered her face into her hands and wept like a baby.

"Here, here," Bates said, patting her shoulder. "What is it that's upset you so?"

Secretly, Dennis Bates was delighted. Whatever was troubling this exquisite young woman could be fixed, he was certain of that. Money could fix anything. And monetary favors—especially to people who really needed them—could bring a high return.

Just take it slow, Bates told himself. *One thing at a time*. "Tell me about it," he said gently.

She raised her head and replied, in sobbing little gasps,

"But . . . someone might—" Her eyes flicked to the elevator doors and back again.

Keeping a grave expression, Bates took a set of keys from his pocket, reached over to the lighted panel, opened it, and pressed a button. The car lurched to a stop between seven and eight.

"Tell me," he said again. "It might make you feel better."

She looked uncertainly at the open panel, then met his gaze.

After a long moment she said, still sniffling, "It's . . . it's Mr. Rhodes." She had calmed down a bit now, and took several deep breaths. "I work for him, three days a week."

She paused then, and seemed to notice him looking at her rather plain skirt and blouse.

"Not in his office," she explained. "Not yet anyway. I just make coffee, keep track of the equipment, water the plants, that kind of thing." She stopped long enough to blow her nose.

"But at least it's a job. A job I can't afford to lose."

Bates watched her, waiting.

She swallowed again, and heaved a sigh. "What happened was, Mr. Rhodes asked me yesterday to go pick up a Christmas present for his wife. A gold necklace he saw in Kennington's front window. He gave me the money to buy it with—two hundred dollars in fifties—but I worked late last night, and the store closed before I thought it did, before I could get there. I took the money home instead, planning to buy the necklace this morning, on my break."

She stopped once more, breathing hard. Bates saw that she was again close to tears. "Go on," he said.

"There's not much more to tell." She waved the handkerchief in a gesture so hopeless Bates was reminded of a white flag. "When I woke up this morning, the money was gone. I know where it went—my boyfriend's been making a habit lately of going through my purse while I'm asleep. Now he's gone, and so is the two hundred dollars." She lifted her shoulders tiredly and let them fall. "I tried to tell Mr. Rhodes a while ago, but I couldn't make myself do it. I'm afraid he'd fire me."

Bates just nodded. He knew Jason Rhodes well, and that's exactly what would have happened.

"But what now?" he asked her. "If you're not going to Kennington's, where *are* you going?"

"To my car," she said miserably. "My sister lives near here. Maybe she can help me raise the money. It's my only way out."

Bates let several seconds pass, savoring the moment. Finally he said, "You're wrong," and reached for his wallet. "There's another way."

She watched him, stunned, as he took two hundred-dollar bills from his wallet and held them out. "Take it," he told her.

She stepped back, her eyes searching his. Quietly she said, "I can't do that."

"Yes you can." He leaned forward and pressed the bills into her palm. "I insist. We'll call it a loan."

Her eyes were teary again, but now they showed a glimmer of real hope. "But . . . why?" she murmured. "You don't even know me . . ."

Oh, but I will, he thought. What he said was: "It's Christmas, Ms. Hastings. What better time for a good deed?"

He broke out a slow, winning smile, and as he watched she smiled too—just a little at first, then a wide, brilliant grin. It made her even more gorgeous.

Somewhere an alarm began beeping, and without looking away from her face Bates reached out, released the button, and closed the panel. The car began to descend again; the alarm stopped.

It took almost a full minute for the elevator to reach the first floor, and just before it arrived Kathy Hastings threw herself into Dennis Bates's arms. She held him tightly for a moment, then slowly broke away, pausing only to tuck the damp handkerchief back into his coat pocket. As the doors sighed open, she took a step back and looked him in the eye, her face flushed and radiant. "Thank you," she said, with deep feeling.

Their eyes held an instant longer, then she turned and left the elevator. Bates followed her for a few steps, keeping her in sight. And his thoughts, as he watched her hurry down the corridor toward the shops and disappear from view, had very little to do with the Christmas Spirit.

Pleased with himself, Bates strolled toward the lobby coffeeshop, where he always stopped around ten for orange juice and pastry. He was already considering his next move. Roses, maybe? A candlelit dinner? Several business associates greeted him as he passed, but he hardly noticed them. He couldn't get his mind off Kathy Hastings.

Which was unusual, he thought. He had had dozens of relationships over the years—both before and during his current marriage—but rarely had he felt this way about someone. She was, simply stated, the most attractive woman he'd ever seen. And it wasn't just her physical beauty. There was something about her that just . . . appealed to him.

Bates shook his head in wonder. How had Rhodes & Ballinger found someone like her? And why was she just a gofer? A lady like that shouldn't be spending her time tending office plants on the windowsills of the twenty-second—

Dennis Bates stopped in his tracks.

The twenty-second floor?

But she had boarded the elevator on nineteen. Right behind him.

Frowning, Bates took a cell phone from his pocket and

scrolled through his stored numbers. When he found the one he wanted, he pressed a button. Immediately a voice said, "Rhodes and Ballinger, may I help you?"

"Jason Rhodes, please."

A short pause. "I'm sorry, Mr. Rhodes is unavailable. May I take—"

"Margie, this is Dennis Bates. Where is he?"

"Oh. Mr. Bates. Well, actually, he's in Australia for the holidays, sir. He'll be back on the third."

"I see." Bates let out a sigh. "And I don't suppose you have a part-time employee named Kathy Hastings working there, do you."

"Hastings? No, I don't believe I know that name—"

Bates clicked the phone off and stared at his reflection in the mirrored wall of the lobby.

He had been conned. The ultimate con-man, the king of wheeler-dealers himself, had been tricked, right here in his own castle. And she'd been smooth, too, he had to give her that.

Disappointed but amused, he wandered on to the coffee-shop and sat at his usual table, replaying the past ten minutes in his mind. Her entire performance, he realized, had been flawless.

Moments later, munching on an apple danish, it occurred to him that that was probably what had been so enticing about her. She was just like *him*. He had sensed it, even then: The two of them were cast from the same mold.

Except for one thing.

That thought made him smile. They might both be as crooked as sidewinders, he and she, but their methods were vastly different in one respect: if Bates had been the one doing the conning, he wouldn't have asked for only two hundred dollars. Two hundred, to Dennis Bates, was chickenfeed. Pocket change. He had twenty times that in his wallet, and more in his money-clip. Bates chuckled to himself. A white Toyota, indeed. If her planning had been good enough, she would've known what he drove, and what he was worth.

She was a small-timer, and always would be. He grinned again, reassured. He might've been outsmarted this one time, but it was on a tiny scale. It had even been entertaining, in a sense.

Bates was still basking in the warmth of those thoughts when he finished his juice and sweet-roll and reached into his pocket to pay his check. And in that instant, as he groped for his wallet, another thought hit him.

He remembered her hugging him in the elevator. He remembered the long, clinging embrace, and, as the two of them parted, her slim fingers reaching into his jacket to replace his handkerchief.

Suddenly frantic, he searched all his pockets, and when he was done he knew the truth: Kathy Hastings, or whatever her real name was, hadn't been such a small-timer after all.

His wallet was indeed missing—along with his money-clip and his Cross pens and his gold watch.

And the keys to his new gray Mercedes.

The Range

At three a.m. Alice Howell jerked awake. Someone was outside her open bedroom window, pulling at the screen.

Her heart pounding, she grabbed her late husband's .38 revolver from the nightstand drawer, pointed it at the window, and shouted a warning.

For an instant the shadowy figure froze. Then, as she watched from her bed, its hand drew a long knife—it actually gleamed in the moonlight—and slit the screen from one side to the other, in one swipe.

That was when she shot him.

She fired twice, at what she hoped was the middle of his chest, and heard him cry out. A second later he was gone, the slashed screen moving gently in the breeze, the moonlit yard empty and silent. She kept the smoking gun aimed at the window while she called the police.

They found nothing. No blood, no weapon, no footprints. Because of the shots her neighbors were all up and awake now, but no one had seen a thing.

"It was the Phantom, wasn't it," she said to Officer McKee, who was sitting across from her in the living room. Two more cops were finishing up outside, and another was using the phone.

"We don't know," McKee said. But his eyes told a different story. There had been four victims in the past six months, all of them middle-aged and living alone in affluent, security-conscious neighborhoods. Just like Alice. And the attacker had always escaped without a trace—hence his nickname.

"Whoever he is," McKee added, "we'll get him."

"How? When he comes back to try again?"

"If it's the Phantom, he won't come back. He never did before."

"He never had a reason to, before," Alice said.

That was a valid point. All four women had been murdered, their throats cut in their beds in the middle of the night.

"We'll get him," McKee said again, as he rose to leave. Then he turned to look at her. "Meanwhile, just in case . . ."

"I'll keep my windows locked," she said.

***

The next morning Alice went to a gun shop, bought a dozen boxes of cartridges, and drove to the Federal Building downtown. The firing range was in the basement, and the agent in charge had been her husband's partner in the Bureau. They let her stay three hours, shooting at gangster-shaped targets, until her gun hand was too tired to hold the grip.

She went again the next day, and the next, and the next. She grew to like the roar of the pistols, the smell of smoke and gun oil, the stark white lights above the targets. After a week she could consistently put six rounds inside a six-inch circle at twenty-five feet. The younger agents on the range began calling her Grannie Oakley. She didn't mind.

That afternoon she stopped by an electrical-supply store, then went to the mall and bought five new outfits, each with baggy pockets. She had decided packing a gun might be a good idea.

If he did come back, she would be ready.

***

Three days later a tall, barrelchested police officer, one she hadn't seen before, showed up at her front door. He stood there holding his cap in both hands, as if he had come to ask her for a loan.

"Ms. Howell?" he said instead.

"Yes?"

"We found him."

Alice stared a moment, stunned, then invited him in. From his seat on the living-room sofa he said, "His name's Thomas Kraus. We matched his prints to those at three of the crime scenes, and found pictures of the victims in his bedroom closet. He confessed to everything, even the attempt on your life."

"Thank God." She had a sudden thought. "But you used the present tense—"

"Yes ma'am. He's alive."

"Then I didn't shoot him?"

"Oh, you shot him all right. He has a bruise this big"—he spread his fingers—"just under his right collarbone."

Alice blinked. "I don't understand."

"He was wearing body armor," the officer said. "A Kevlar vest."

She nodded grimly.

"It can leave a bruise?" she asked.

"It can if it's a big gun, at close range." Watching her eyes, he rubbed his upper chest. "It's still a little sore, actually."

At first that didn't register. Then he put his cap down on the sofa beside him, uncovering his nametag, and she understood.

It said T. KRAUS.

He smiled when he saw her reaction.

They stared at each other for a long moment.

Alice couldn't believe how calm she felt. Her heart was thudding, but her mind was clear. It all made sense now. That's why he was always able to get away, she realized. Nobody would look twice at a cop—especially in rich, heavily patrolled areas. Acceptability equals invisibility. He was probably among the first at each scene.

She sat very still, watching him carefully.

"By the way, I brought you something, Alice." His smile turned to a sneer as he pulled the long knife from his belt.

"Me too," she said, and took her hand from her pocket.

***

When the police arrived, it didn't take long to verify her story. Officer Thomas Kraus did indeed have a dark bruise underneath his armor, and a closetful of snapshots of the four victims—and of Alice Howell—at his suburban home. He also had a fresh, neat bullethole in the center of his forehead.

"I guess his vest didn't come quite high enough, this time," McKee said, staring down at the body on the sofa.

Alice just nodded. She felt tired.

"Are you okay?" he asked her.

"I am now."

It took another hour to finish up. Before leaving, McKee stood with her in the living room a moment, looking thoughtful.

"Have you changed the lighting in here?" he asked. "It looks a little . . . stark."

She smiled. "It's just right," she said.

When the police team finally left, Alice went to her bedroom and put the gun back in the nightstand drawer. The Phantom was dead; her pistol-packin' days were done.

"But I'll still keep the windows locked," she said aloud.

Just in case.

High Anxiety

Joe McClellan led a simple life. He had a wife, two kids, a mortgage, a respectable job, and very few complications. No excitement, no mystery, no oddities. At least until now.

Joe wondered, on his drive home from the airport, what could have happened in their quiet little neighborhood. His wife had left him a disturbing voicemail message before her commute to work this morning: last night in the wee hours she'd seen two police cars and an ambulance in the street in front of the Hickams's house, next door.

The only thing in front of it now was Bill Hickam, raking the leaves in his yard. Joe parked the car, plopped his luggage down on his driveway, and strolled over.

"Everything okay, Bill? Peggy said you had some excitement last night."

Bill Hickam stopped raking. He was a big man, blond and red-faced. Thanks to a recent downsizing he was unemployed, but his wife Mary—some kind of computer guru, Joe had heard—apparently kept their heads above water. "The police cars, you mean?"

"And she mentioned an ambulance," Joe said.

"Long story." Bill pointed his rake at the ground. "It's these dern leaves, caused it all."

Joe blinked. "The leaves?"

"Let me ask you something, McClellan. How do you keep leaves out of your rain gutters? You climb up there and clean 'em out yourself?"

"When they need it. Why?"

"Well, it's a little harder, for me." Bill nodded toward his roof. "The front's not that bad, but the back of the house—well, because of my basement, and the way our land slopes off, the edge of my back roof's a good three stories off the ground. I go up there and slip off, I'd kill myself."

Joe looked back and forth between Bill and the house, picturing his neighbor doing a nosedive onto the back patio. "Bill, what's this got to do with—"

"So what I decided was, I need to rig up a rope and harness of some kind, like mountain climbers use. All I'd have to do then is secure the rope to something solid here in front of the house, tie myself real good to the other end, and climb up onto the garage and over the peak of the roof. Then, if I slipped somewhere on the other side, the rope'd keep me from falling off. You with me so far?"

"No," Joe said.

"So that's what I did, yesterday. I backed Mary's car up close to the house, set the parking brake, tied one end of the rope to her back bumper, tied the other end real tight around my waist, and I was all set. I used the car to get up onto the garage roof, climbed over the top of the house to the back, and scooped the leaves out of my gutters there, safe and sound." Bill leaned on his rake and smiled. "How about that?"

Joe just stared at him. "What the hell are you talking about, Bill? I asked you about the ambulance."

"That's why I'm telling you this."

Suddenly Joe understood. His eyes widened. "You mean you fell off the house?"

"No, no, I didn't fall off. Just think for a second. Considering what I just told you, about the situation with the rope and the gutters, what's the worst thing that could happen?"

"While you're up on the roof, you mean?"

"Right."

"I don't know . . ." Joe pondered a moment. "The rope breaks?"

"Nope."

"It comes untied?"

"Nope."

"What, then?"

"You give up?"

"Yes, I give up."

"Mary drives off in her car," Bill said.

"*What?*"

Bill nodded, obviously delighted with his neighbor's reaction. "Let's say you're up there roped to her bumper, dumb and happy on the far side of the roof, and let's say Mary comes out and gets in her car, which is aimed out toward the road. She doesn't see the rope, starts the car, releases the brake, and drives off. What happens is"—he pointed to the house—"you get dragged up and over the peak, down this side of the roof, over the edge and SPLAT onto the driveway, and then she hauls you down the street a ways while you scream like a stuck hog."

"Good God, Bill," Joe said, in a hushed voice. "That actually *happened* to you?"

"Not to me. To the burglar."

Joe stood there a moment, his mouth hanging open. "The

burglar?"

"I figure he must've seen me yesterday, on the roof. Then last night we went to bed early, and since all the lights were off and my sister had come over after supper to borrow my truck, the guy must've thought nobody was home. There's a little balcony, you know, off that top-floor window in the back, and I guess he thought he could use my rope idea to get back there and break in. It was still hooked up and everything. What happened, though, is Mary had to go in to work at two a.m. to install some software—that's why we went to bed so early—and when she did, her car pulled his sorry butt right up off that balcony and up over the rooftop and down this side onto the driveway. I heard all the commotion, ran out the front door, tripped over my bicycle on the porch, and almost broke my neck."

Stunned, Joe asked, "What happened to the burglar?"

"He'll probably be okay, the ambulance crew said. Mary dragged him all the way to the corner, though, before she realized what happened."

"*Dragged* him?"

"To the corner."

"Unbelievable," Joe murmured. "How bad were the injuries, do you think?"

Bill looked thoughtful. "Not too bad, really." He stretched, held up one arm, winced a little. "Right shoulder, mostly. My own fault, leaving that bike in my way, on the porch."

As Joe watched his neighbor resume the raking, as he turned and walked back to his own house and his suitcase sitting in the driveway, he realized he had been wrong, on the way home a while ago. There *were* a few oddities in his life, after all.

One lived right next door.

The Warden's Game

Lars Hansen smelled trouble.

He also smelled woodsmoke and liquor and cigarettes and the occasional whiff of frosty air as the front door swung open to let someone in or out. None of those things were unusual—not in Whiterock, Alaska, in the dead of winter. But then again, neither was trouble. Not since the Grummonds came to town.

Hansen drained the rest of his beer and thumped the empty mug down on the polished surface of the bar. Behind him, the dozen or so other customers of the Side Pocket Tavern sat around in groups of two or three, telling tales and nursing their drinks and watching two old men in lumberjack shirts play nine-ball on what was said to be the only Brunswick pool table north of Anchorage.

Outside, the wind moaned in the trees—an ominous, lonely sound. Even the tethered sled dogs seemed uneasy. Hansen could hear them snapping and snarling at each other outside the back door. No one else seemed to notice.

Maybe it's just my nerves, he thought.

A sudden gust rattled the window at the end of the bar. Lars Hansen shifted his attention to the fogged and grimy pane of glass, and the view it offered of Front Street and the gray mountains beyond. Though it was barely past noon, the light was already fading. A sprinkling of snow had begun to fall; the wind howled in the icy street. It was a desolate scene, and except for the prices posted in the window of the general store, it probably hadn't changed one bit in the last thirty years.

Whiterock was little more than an outpost, one of dozens of small communities that dotted the great Alaskan interior. And Lars Hansen loved it—even at this time of year, when the roads were impassable and the nights were twenty hours long and the mighty Nanuk River was a solid sheet of ice that cut the town off from the rest of the world as surely as if it were on Jupiter.

The only place he loved more than Whiterock was his own cabin, just downriver. He and his wife had built it themselves eight years ago, with logs cut from their own land. It was home, and there was no spot in all the world where he'd rather live.

That's why the thought of losing it hurt so much . . .

But that was a long-range worry; the Grummonds had bigger fish to fry before they got to him. And the trouble he smelled today had nothing to do with that. It had to do with the man sitting on the barstool five feet away.

He'd been there for half an hour, and unless Hansen had missed something he hadn't moved a muscle except to sip from a glass of whiskey that old Sam Tidwell had refilled several times. Once more Lars Hansen tilted his head and studied the man from the corner of his eye.

He wasn't a local, that much was certain. Around here

everyone knew everyone within forty miles, and this man wouldn't be easy to forget. He was big, for one thing—six-four and 220 at least. And his clothes were different. Old and frayed, with a lot of buckles and fringe and fur. A battered cowboy hat was pushed back from his forehead, revealing a thatch of curly blond hair, and his face—what Hansen could see of it—looked as tough and weathered as his outfit. A wicked-looking scar added to the effect, running underneath his right eye and into the golden-brown beard that hid the rest of his features.

In short, he looked like one of *them*. And even if he wasn't, Hansen thought—even if he was only an innocent stranger—that meant trouble too, of a different kind. The Grummond brothers didn't like strangers.

Lars Hansen glanced at the clock on the back wall. 12:40. He had to get going. Martha usually liked him to be home before dark—

"Bartender," the stranger said.

Hansen turned to look at him.

Sam Tidwell wandered over, drying a shotglass with a ragged towel. Another towel hung over one shoulder; bags hung under his eyes.

The stranger held up his glass. Sam filled it. "And another beer," the man said.

It took Lars Hansen a couple of seconds to realize that that remark referred to him. Sam Tidwell drew the beer and plunked it down in front of Hansen, who stared at it a moment, watching the base of the cold mug breathe a ring of condensation onto the wood. Then he looked up at the stranger.

The big man was still gazing straight ahead. "You been giving me a lot of attention," he said. "Thought I'd return the favor."

Lars Hansen felt his face grow warm. The bartender was gone now, and no one was within earshot. "Sorry," Hansen said.

"I was . . . curious. Meant no offense."

"None taken." The stranger turned, and as the two men locked eyes for the first time Hansen's only thought was of something he'd heard years ago in another bar, the one in the Baranof Hotel in Juneau, with the rain pounding the windows and a plane ticket to Fairbanks burning a hole in his pocket.

Alaska, the old fisherman had told him, *has a way of bringing out the best or worst in people, kid. Kinda like the Old West. Folks up here are generally either good or evil, one or the other. There are very few in between*. In the time since, Hansen had found that to be true, and as he faced this stranger now he felt a vague sense of relief. The eyes were the giveaway. There was a look of kindness there, a simple, honest decency that would have been hard to fake. Whatever else this man was, he was not evil.

"I don't think I've seen you around here before," Hansen said.

"That's a good bet. I haven't been around here before."

Hansen smiled and held out his hand. "In that case, welcome to Whiterock. The name's Hansen."

The stranger nodded, and the thick beard moved in a way that suggested a grin somewhere underneath. "Abe Callendar. I run a mining camp upriver, near Fort Douglas."

They shook hands. The big man turned back to his drink, sipping it like a fine wine. Hansen was looking at the map he kept inside his head. Fort Douglas was two hundred miles away.

"What brings you *here*?" he asked.

The man named Callendar smiled. "To this bar, or to this town?"

"Both, I guess."

The stranger drained his glass and set it down. "I'm waiting for someone," he said.

Hansen didn't press further. He turned to the bar, took a long swallow from his new mug, and studied his reflection in the shiny countertop. This was his fourth beer, and he seldom drank more than one. He was feeling a little buzzed. It was the beer, he decided later, that made him say what he said next.

"I wouldn't wait too long if I was you," he murmured.

Abe Callendar looked at him. "Excuse me?"

Hansen hesitated. Behind him, pool balls clicked and tapped. "The Grummond boys stop by here sometimes," he said. "And that's a side of Whiterock I don't think you want to see."

"What do you mean?"

"I mean they run the town." Hansen gazed into his beer and added, "Before long they'll own it too."

Callendar said nothing.

"They're a 'protection agency,'" Hansen said, putting emphasis on the last two words. "They collect fees every month for their services. Problem is, they're the ones people need to be protected from."

"Who pays the fees?"

"The local businesses. Sam here, the general store, cafe, laundry, a couple others."

Callendar seemed to think about that awhile. "Why do they do it?"

Hansen chuckled bitterly. "Some didn't, at first. Eb Rasmussen—he ran the gas pumps down by the river—held out the longest." He drew a deep breath and let it out. "Then he disappeared. Vanished, along with his family. Some say we'll find them in the spring, when the snow melts."

Abe Callendar didn't reply. He had taken an old briar pipe from his pocket and was filling its bowl with tobacco. His manner was easy, his face calm. *He's not interested in this*, Hansen thought. *And why should he be? It isn't his problem.*

But at least he was listening. "Go on," he said.

Hansen hesitated, choosing his words. "There's three of them. Brothers. Ward, Billy, and Tyrell. Ward's the oldest, the ringleader. His brothers call him The Warden." Hansen felt his jaw tighten as he thought that over. "The name fits," he said. "The warden and his guards."

"And you're the inmates?" Callendar said, his face impassive.

"That's right. That's exactly what we are. Only difference is, we can leave if we want. In fact, they encourage it."

"How so?"

"The Grummond brothers have expanded their interests. They're into real estate now." Hansen stayed silent a moment, recalling the past few weeks. "So far, five families have sold out to them, at rockbottom prices. We figure they're planning to package a bunch of lots together and resell—probably to the oil companies."

"I don't suppose," Callendar said, still packing his pipe, "there was any pressure applied?"

Lars Hansen chuckled again, without humor. "Let's just say there's been a lot of freak accidents lately. Broken legs, burned-out cabins, dead livestock . . . and the victims don't seem to want to talk about it much."

Abe Callendar clamped the stem of his pipe between his teeth and searched his pockets for a match. "Last I heard, that kind of thing's against the law."

This time Hansen laughed aloud. Several customers glanced up at him, and he waited a minute before speaking.

"This ain't Seattle, Mr. Callendar, or San Francisco. The law's a long way off." His voice, already low, dropped lower. "We have only one transmitter, and it's in the sheriff's office. The Grummonds control it."

"What about your sheriff?"

"He's one of the missing. Or else they paid him to leave, we're not sure which."

Callendar produced a match and struck it with his thumbnail. "Nice town you got here, Hansen," he said, holding the flame to his tobacco.

Hansen sighed. "It actually used to be."

A screaming gust of wind shook the building, interrupting their thoughts. Hansen glanced out the window, at the low sky and the slate-gray clouds and the mountains that hung like a heavy brow over the west edge of town. As he watched, old Myra Kincaid emerged from the door of the general store fifty yards away and stomped down the wooden steps to the street. Head down, shoulders hunched, she struck out through the wind toward the Roadhouse Cafe. Despite his troubles, Hansen grinned to himself. The lady was well past seventy and here she was, marching down an icy street in workboots, carrying a box of supplies that probably weighed twenty pounds. It occurred to him that she was the very symbol of this kind of life.

Abe Callendar seemed to read his mind. "Don't give up hope," he said.

Hansen blinked. "What did you say?"

"I said I wouldn't give up hope, if I were you."

Hansen nodded wearily, turning back to the window. "Right," he murmured.

Both men watched the blowing snow for a while, saying nothing. Callendar puffed on his pipe.

"Ever heard of Nathan Cross?" he asked.

Lars Hansen turned to face him. "I been up here ten years. What do *you* think?"

"What have you heard?"

"Depends on who you talk to," Hansen said, remembering the stories. The most widely accepted version said Nathan Cross was a trapper who'd made a fortune in bear and wolf pelts and then disappeared somewhere in the Chugach Range years ago. That much, Hansen figured, was fact. The rest was another tale entirely. According to the legend, Cross had lost part of his left foot to a grizzly and had then killed the bear with his knife before freezing to death. The Eskimos believed he was some kind of god, an ageless, arctic Robin Hood whose ghost limped through the mountains feeding the poor and rescuing the unfortunate. It was the biggest pile of moose dung Hansen had ever heard. "Surely you don't buy any of that?"

Callendar scratched his beard. "The Natives do. They say he's alive."

"But you've never seen him?"

The big man looked amused. "I've never seen the wind either—but I've seen what it can do. I've felt it blow."

Lars Hansen stared at him a moment. "What the hell are you talking about?"

Callendar laughed. "I'm telling you what an old woman on the Susitna told me, when I asked her the same thing. They believe Cross only comes down out of the mountains when there's trouble—and even when he does come, you can't always see him. But you can feel his presence."

"Feel his presence?"

"That's what they say." Callendar waved his pipe and added, "Hell, stranger things than that have happened. Everything's weird up here anyway: colored lights in the sky at night, lakes a thousand feet deep, doors built to always open outward so the bears can't push them in—"

"—people who start their serious drinking at noon?" Hansen asked.

Callendar shrugged. "Why shouldn't we? Night starts at two in the afternoon. But I'm not drunk, if that's what you mean."

"You sure sound that way to me. All this talk of Nathan

Cross—"

"I'm just telling you what I've heard. To them"—Callendar nodded in the direction of the mountains—"he's the Guardian of all Alaskans, white or brown. If the trouble's bad enough he'll come, and that's that."

"And you think—you expect me to believe—he'll come *here*?"

Callendar turned and regarded him solemnly. The eyes were piercing, and blue as glacier ice. "I'm a prospector, Hansen—not a prophet. I don't care what you believe."

For a long moment they studied each other in silence, and it was as Hansen opened his mouth to reply that the front door swung open with a bang and Ward Grummond stepped into the room.

***

For a space of several seconds, everything stopped. Conversations, poker hands, the game of pool, everything. Even the wind seemed to die down and wait.

Grummond's two brothers followed him through the doorway, stomping wet snow from their boots. They fanned out along the front wall, their coats falling open in the manner of those who might need to reach underneath on short notice. Three pairs of eyes swept the room.

"Something's up," Hansen whispered. "Don't say a word."

Abe Callendar had swiveled his stool to face the front of the tavern. One hand rested on the bar, the other held his pipe. He was watching the man beside the doorway with open interest.

Ward Grummond looked like the villain in a Sergio Leone western. Lined face, hooked nose, black beard. A dead cigar poked through the underbrush. His coat was dark and heavy, and reached almost to the tops of his boots. Like

Callendar, he wore a hat; above its flat, straight brim it was a perfect hemisphere, like an upside-down mixing bowl. Loops of greasy hair hung over his ears. And his eyes—

His eyes made you want to crawl under the bar and hide.

They stopped on Abe Callendar. For what seemed an extremely long time, the two men stared at each other, then Grummond broke contact and looked at the bartender.

"Davenport," he said.

Sam Tidwell swallowed. Everyone in town knew Shorty Davenport—he owned the Whiterock Laundry and Bathhouse. Everyone also knew he was late with his payments.

"At his sister's, downriver," Sam said. Grummond's face hardened, and Sam added quickly, "Took a day off, is all. He'll be back by dark."

Ward Grummond considered that for a moment, then seemed to relax. "We'll wait," he said to the room in general, and nodded to his brothers, who slouched over to an empty table and pulled up chairs. The bartender followed them, sweating. Billy and Tyrell propped their feet on the tabletop and ordered beers. Sam nodded and hurried away, ignoring the other customers. Nobody seemed to mind.

The eldest Grummond shot another look at the stranger, then ambled to the bar and sat down alone at the far end. Tidwell stopped to pour him a whiskey on the way back to the table. Little by little, in slowly spreading waves, conversations and card games resumed.

During all this, Callendar sat motionless, watching and listening. Pipesmoke curled around him in a blue cloud. Lars Hansen, leaning toward him on the barstool, explained in a whisper who Davenport was and what was going on. Callendar's eyes never left Ward Grummond.

"Looks like a fine family," he said.

Hansen gave him an uneasy look, then turned to survey

the room. Uneasy looks, he noticed, seemed to be the order of the day. On the surface, things had returned more or less to normal—but only on the surface. Voices were strained, movements were measured and cautious. Tension had filled the room like a gas. Something was going to happen, and everyone there knew it.

It didn't take long.

"Colson," Grummond called from the end of the bar. "How about a game?"

It wasn't really a question, and no one understood that better than Ike Colson, who was sitting near the back of the tavern with a glass of beer halfway between the tabletop and his mouth. He stayed that way for a second or two, frozen in place like a snapshot. Slowly, the picture came to life; the beer glass descended to rest on the table. He turned to look at Ward Grummond.

Callendar glanced at Hansen. "What's all this?"

"I'll tell you what it is," Hansen said. He'd seen this same thing happen last week with Jed Bascom, and the week before with young Arthur Whittaker. Grummond had done his homework; he knew who the regular players were. "Ever been to the zoo, Mr. Callendar?" Hansen asked. "Ever seen the kids, the mean ones, poking the animals with sticks through the bars of the cages?"

"He mentioned a game," Callendar said, watching Ike Colson rise reluctantly from his chair. The look on Colson's face said he wished he hadn't gotten out of bed this morning.

Hansen nodded. "Straight pool. I once heard him tell Sam Tidwell it's one of the few real tests of skill left in the modern world."

Abe Callendar studied Colson's face as he approached the green-topped table. "Your man doesn't seem too thrilled."

Hansen shrugged. "What can we do? Like I said, he's in

a cage. We all are."

"I can think of worse things to be poked with than a pool cue."

"That depends on how bad he loses," Hansen said.

Callendar turned to face him. "Loses?"

"You think they're playing for fun?" Hansen asked. He suddenly felt tired.

"What are the stakes? Twenty a game? Fifty?"

"A dollar a ball. They play to 125, loser pays the difference."

"A new approach," Callendar said.

"They're Grummond's rules. More money in it that way."

Callendar seemed to ponder that for a while. "If you're good," he said.

Both of them watched as Ward Grummond rose from his stool and signaled to the bartender. Tidwell went into a back room, then reappeared with a long leather case, which he laid on the countertop. Grummond opened it with a flourish. The cuestick was a beauty—silver inlays gleamed in the overhead lights, and the shaft looked smooth as marble. With practiced ease he spun the two halves together and held it under one arm while he lit a new cigar.

"He's more than good," Hansen said. "He's the best I ever saw."

Ike Colson was waiting at the table, holding a cue he'd picked from the rack on the wall. He was a heavyset man with a red face and beard. He looked weary. The two oldtimers who had been playing earlier were gone, absorbed into the crowd. Just behind the pool table, a pine bench ran the length of the side wall; as Grummond approached, Colson walked to the bench, took out his wallet, and counted bills onto its wooden seat. The Warden did the same, placing his stack of money beside his opponent's.

"More rules," Hansen explained. "Last month Grummond won a game by almost a hundred balls, and the loser couldn't cover it all. Things got nasty. Now each player puts up the whole amount before the game."

Callendar nodded, watching.

Old Ben Gassaway from the bank retrieved the two stacks of bills, counted them again, and placed them on the bar in plain sight. Behind him, the players powdered their hands with talcum and rubbed chalk on the tips of their cues.

They lagged for the break. Colson lost. Sweating, he positioned the cue ball and aimed with great care.

Straight pool, Hansen knew, was harder than it looked. The balls, worth a point each, could be pocketed in any order, but each shot had to be called beforehand—even defensive strokes, or "safeties." It was a rule that essentially did away with the element of luck. The break, for example—usually a powerful stroke, and an advantage in other games—was a soft, delicate shot in straight pool. If badly done, the break could be disastrous.

It was disastrous for Ike Colson. The rulebook required that at least two balls from the rack, plus the cue ball, must touch a rail as a result of the break. When properly struck, the cue ball should then roll back to the head of the table and the two freed balls should tuck themselves neatly behind the rack, leaving no clear shot. Colson's didn't—they stayed out in the open, tempting Fate. Grummond hit them both, and used the second one to spread the rack. He ran twelve balls before missing.

"See what I mean?" Hansen whispered. Ben Gassaway was keeping score on a blackboard above the bench.

The game continued. The players were in the third rack, with a score of 29 to 5, when Colson was forced to shoot a safety. His cue ball rolled gently toward a tight cluster in the middle of the table, grazed the three-ball slightly, and coasted to the rail. A beautiful shot.

"Scratch," Grummond said, grinning. He took a ball at random from one of the pockets and looked up at Gassaway, nodding to him to subtract a ball from Colson's score. The old man was reaching for the blackboard when Abe Callendar spoke.

"The shot was good," he said. His voice was low but clear; it carried throughout the tavern. All eyes swung around to look at him.

The room went dead quiet.

"What are you *doing*?" Hansen whispered.

Ward Grummond stood there with a green six-ball in his hand, staring at the stranger in surprise. He'd been about to spot the ball on the table, to balance the altered score.

"What did you say?" Icicles hung from his voice.

"He brushed the three," Callendar said. "The shot was good."

Grummond walked to the bar, rolling the six-ball in his fingers. He stopped two feet from Abe Callendar.

"Who are you?" he asked.

Callendar studied him a moment, saying nothing. From the corner of his eye Lars Hansen saw the brothers rise from their table and saunter toward the other end of the bar. A clear field of fire, Hansen thought feverishly.

"I'm a tourist," Callendar answered.

Grummond took the cigar from between his teeth and spat out a shred of tobacco. It landed on Callendar's shirtfront. "You don't look like a tourist," he said.

"You don't look like a pool shark."

For the first time, Ward Grummond smiled. It was an unnerving sight, exposing rotten teeth and eyes that were as cold and dead as a lizard's. "Alaska's full of surprises, ain't it."

Callendar made no reply. Hansen sat and stared at them both. He wanted to look away, but he couldn't. He felt sure both men could hear his heart hammering.

"Do you play?" Grummond asked, nodding toward the table.

"I used to."

Without breaking eye contact Grummond raised his voice and spoke over his shoulder. "Colson," he called. "Give him your cue."

Ike Colson didn't look bright, but he was smart enough to realize a lifejacket was being thrown his way. He scooped up his stack of bills, hurried over, and leaned his cuestick against the bar. Seconds later a blast of wind and snow whistled through the door and then stopped again and he was gone into the swirling storm.

"Tournament rules," Grummond said. "Game of 125. We each put up twelve fifty at the start."

Callendar took out his pipe and examined its bowl. "Twelve fifty?"

"Ten dollars a ball."

Hansen sucked in his breath. He'd been afraid something like this would happen. He saw Callendar turn and look down the length of the bar. Tyrell and Billy Grummond stared back at him from the far end, silhouetted against the front window like dark vultures on a branch. Their coats and wool caps were off now, draped over the countertop, and the handles of what looked like Colt revolvers jutted from holsters at their sides.

Ward Grummond picked up Colson's cue and held it out. "You break," he said.

***

The room was as quiet as a crypt. Those in back had moved up close; poker hands and chips were left unattended;

half-finished drinks were forgotten. Not everyone in the crowd had heard the exchange at the bar a minute ago, but it would've taken a blind man not to notice the amount of money being counted into two stacks on the wooden bench.

Lars Hansen watched Callendar's face as the bundles of cash were recounted and taken aside. He didn't look worried and he didn't look happy, Hansen decided. His expression was neutral. Hansen interpreted it as simple acceptance, and admired him for it. *I tried to warn him*, Hansen thought.

As he watched, Abe Callendar walked to the head of the table, positioned the cue ball, planted his left hand, ran the cuestick smoothly through the crook of his forefinger, and took aim.

The storm was in full swing now. A sudden gust shook the windowpanes. Nobody cared.

All eyes were on the stranger.

It was a good break. The cue ball connected softly with the side of the rack; the two rear corner balls drifted to the rails and back again, leaving the rest of the rack intact, and the cue returned properly to the head of the table—but not quite far enough. The nine-ball was exposed, and it was all Ward Grummond needed.

Grummond fired the nine into the corner pocket, sending the cue ball expertly into the center of the rack. The balls spread, clicking, across the table. He ran ten straight, pausing between each only long enough to call his next shot. When he finally missed he didn't leave much, and Callendar missed also. Grummond finished out the table, leaving the cue ball positioned such that he could break the new rack easily off the one remaining ball.

He ran seven more. Callendar missed again. It went that way for a while, then Callendar managed to hit five in a row, making the crowd gain interest.

It didn't last. The game moved slowly, with short runs and unspectacular shots, but for every ball Callendar pocketed, Grummond hit four or five. By the fourth rack there was little doubt about the outcome, and half an hour later it was done.

The final score was 125 to 30. At ten bucks a ball, a difference of almost a thousand dollars.

Without a word Abe Callendar moved to the bench, counted nine hundreds and a fifty from his pile of bills, and dropped them onto Grummond's. He pocketed the rest and returned to his barstool. His pipe and empty glass lay where he'd left them; he tucked the pipe into his belt and waved for the bartender. Sam Tidwell gave him a refill, keeping one eye on the Grummonds, and moved away in a hurry.

It was as Callendar reached for his drink that he seemed to notice the blue chalk-dust on his hands. He gulped half his whiskey and rose to his feet.

Lars Hansen, who hadn't budged from his seat since all this started, looked up at him. "Where you going?" he whispered.

"To the john. Why?"

"I'll go with you."

"I think I can manage, Hansen." Callendar started to move past, but Hansen grabbed his arm and held on.

"We need to talk," Hansen said.

***

The tavern, like most bars in rural Alaska, had the best conveniences in town. The bathroom was a surprisingly clean sink and toilet tucked behind a curtain in the back corner of a huge adjoining storeroom—the same room Tidwell had entered earlier to retrieve Grummond's cuestick. Like the main room, it was poorly heated. Hansen's breath made little white clouds as he spoke.

"You must be crazy," he said to Callendar, who was

scrubbing his blue-stained hands in soapy water. His coat hung from a nail in the wall by the sink.

"Why? Because I lost a game of pool?"

"Because you played at all. I asked you to keep quiet."

"He was cheating," Callendar said, as if that explained everything. "Colson's shot was good."

Hansen sighed. "All right. Okay. But now you've got to get outa here. There's a door just to the left there, hidden behind them boxes—"

"No," Callendar said. "Not yet."

Hansen gaped at him. "You don't understand. You flashed a lot of money out there. And believe me, anytime money's involved—"

"—we're interested," a voice behind him said.

Hansen whirled around. Ward Grummond was leaning against a wall of packing crates twenty feet away, holding a match to a fresh cigar. He took his time getting it going. "That what you meant?" he asked, between puffs.

Lars Hansen didn't answer; there was no need to. Grummond's attention was focused on one man only, and that man was standing in front of the sink, drying his hands on a stringy towel.

"You never told me your name," Grummond said.

"No," Callendar said. "I never did."

Ward Grummond shook out his match and flipped it away. "You will," he said. Behind him, through the doorway that led to the bar, Tyrell Grummond stepped into the room. A second later Billy joined him.

Very slowly, Ward reached behind him and underneath his coat. The knife, when it emerged, was long and ugly. It glinted in the light from the naked bulb above their heads. He hefted it thoughtfully, then began cleaning his fingernails with the point of the blade.

"I want to know who you are," he said, "and I want to know now."

Callendar said nothing.

For an instant—just an instant—Grummond turned and looked hard at Lars Hansen. The message was clear: *Get out of here, little man. This doesn't concern you.*

But Hansen didn't leave. It was at that precise moment that he saw, deep in the cold soulless eyes of Ward Grummond, that what he'd suspected was true: (1) his missing neighbors weren't coming home, and (2) this was the man who had killed them. A feeling of utter despair swept through him like a wind.

"It's not worth dying for," Hansen said, as if to himself. All four men stared at him. To Ward Grummond he said, "His name is Abe Callendar."

The name had an effect. Grummond blinked, then squinted at the stranger as if from a great distance. "Callendar," he repeated. Without looking down, he dropped his cigar to the floor and ground it out with his bootheel.

"Who?" Billy Grummond asked.

Ward glanced absently at his brother. "Remember what we picked up on the radio awhile back?" Grummond paused, his eyes on the stranger. "A man from Fort Douglas had made a big strike—a goldminer named Abel Callendar. That was it all right—Abel Callendar. Sounded like he'd sold the mine for a fortune and would soon be headed for the Lower 48." Grummond added, "That true, Mister?"

Callendar didn't answer. He just stood there with that maddeningly calm look on his face. Outside the blocked door, the wind whooped and wailed.

After a moment Billy Grummond cleared his throat. "A gold strike?" he said.

Tyrell's voice cut in then: "Bet he's got a pack mule, Warden. Out back, probably." All three brothers exchanged glances.

"You guys are even dumber than I thought," Callendar said.

The three turned to look at him.

"There are twenty men in the other room right now. You think they're gonna sit still while you shoot the place up?"

"They'll do whatever I say," Ward said.

"So far they have. Up until now they haven't actually seen your dirty work. You gun me down—or Hansen, here—and they'll turn on you. I think you know that."

Grummond's face darkened. He fingered the handle of the knife, rolling it in his hand. The blade flashed silver as it caught the light. "We don't have to use guns."

Callendar didn't reply—but something like a smile flickered in his eyes.

Ward Grummond hesitated, licked his lips. Hansen knew what he was thinking. Callendar was a big man, and clearly unafraid. For all Grummond knew, the stranger might have a knife too, underneath that wool shirt. A minute dragged by.

"We could get you as you leave town," Ward said, his voice softer now.

Callendar looked even more amused. "What do you think brought me to Whiterock, Grummond? The travel brochures?"

"He's meeting someone here," Hansen said quickly. "He told me so."

Ward frowned, his eyes darting from one to the other. Uncertainty was apparently a new experience for him, and he didn't seem to like it much. Everyone in the storeroom was watching him except Abe Callendar, who had flipped down his sleeves, buttoned his cuffs, and was shrugging into his coat.

When he was done he said to Ward Grummond, "Excuse me," and walked straight past the three brothers to the door. Hansen stood rooted for a moment, then hurried after him.

"Wait!" Grummond called.

Callendar stopped in the doorway and turned. Hansen almost ran into him.

"One more game," Ward said, his breath smoking in the frigid air. The knife had disappeared.

Callendar shook his head. "I'm done with you, Grummond."

"One more. You're good, I could see that. We'll raise the stakes—"

Callendar walked out.

His barstool was unoccupied, his half-full drink still on the countertop. The men in the bar were quiet, watching him. Not a one of them had moved, it seemed, since he had left. Callendar sat down and picked up his glass, swirling the amber liquid inside.

The rest of the parade filed in. Hansen perched on the next stool, with Tyrell beside him. Billy strolled past and leaned against the bar to the stranger's right. Ward moved to a point just behind Calendar's seat and stood there, rubbing his coal-black beard and scowling.

"I'm waiting," he said.

The stranger sipped what was left of his whiskey. Without turning, he said, "You think I'm a fool, don't you, Grummond? You think you can walk over me the way you do Colson and Tidwell and everyone else in this town."

The Warden smiled crookedly. His confidence was back now, in force.

"Play me," he said again.

Callendar frowned into his glass. "Why should I?"

"Why did you before?"

Callendar swiveled on his stool. The two men studied each other.

"How much?" Callendar asked finally.

"How about a hundred a ball?"

A hush fell over the room. Ward Grummond glanced around, checking reactions, enjoying the moment. This was the kind of lesson they needed. His smile widened.

"Make it a thousand," Callendar said.

***

Grummond blinked. Behind him, the small crowd sat as still as a painting. No one even breathed.

"What?" he said.

"A thousand dollars a ball." Callendar reached into his coat pocket and took out a roll of cash as big around as a beer bottle. He thumped it down onto the countertop. "You," he called to Ben Gassaway. "Count it out."

The banker edged over, his eyes flicking from Grummond to the stranger and back again. He picked up the roll and counted silently, his beefy fingers trembling. When he was finished, not more than a dozen bills were left over. He folded them and handed them back to Abe Callendar. The rest he left on the bar, in a stack two inches high.

A hundred and twenty-five thousand dollars.

Ward Grummond stared at the pile of cash with slitted, sparkling eyes. He licked his lips and swallowed. "I . . . don't have that much," he murmured.

Callendar nodded as if in deep thought. "How much do you have?"

Grummond tore his gaze from the money, looked up into the clear blue eyes. After a moment he jerked his thumb toward the front door. "Get it," he said.

His brothers exchanged looks. Billy said, "I dunno, Warden—"

"Get it!" Ward roared.

Billy shrugged and left, slamming the door behind him.

Two minutes later he was back, a gray metal cashbox nestled under his arm. Ward Grummond opened the box and handed it to Ben Gassaway, who nervously counted out its contents onto the bar.

"One hundred thousand," he announced at last. "And some change."

Grummond grinned. "How's that, goldminer? You do think I can make 25 balls, don't you?" He seemed to be having trouble standing still.

"This time *you* break," Callendar said.

***

Grummond did just that, and it was perfect. Two balls to the cushions and back, the cue ball frozen obediently against the rail at the head of the table afterward. Abe Callendar shot a safety but left the edge of the eleven exposed. Grummond missed it; Callendar ran four and shot another safety. Again it fell short.

Ward Grummond called the two-ball, made it, and ran the table.

The score was ten to four as Ben Gassaway racked the balls, leaving the thirteen off to the side. Grummond drove it in hard, and the cue ball spread the rack.

The game continued, each man hitting only a few at a time. Shortly after the start of the third rack, Grummond shot a perfect safety that left the cue ball an inch from the corner pocket at the head of the table and ten balls clustered tightly around the spot at the other end. He was ahead of the stranger by a score of 23 to 11. In simpler terms, Callendar was behind by twelve thousand dollars. And he was left with no chance of making a ball on the next shot.

Callendar studied the layout awhile, then walked over to where Lars Hansen was sitting. He chalked the end of his cue and examined it as he spoke.

"You feel anything?" he asked.

Hansen stared at him. Callendar's face was impassive, almost indifferent. He went on chalking his cue tip.

"What do you mean?" Hansen said.

Abe Callendar raised his head and looked Lars in the eye. The storm whistled in the street.

"I think he's here," Callendar said. Then, very slowly, he grinned.

And Hansen felt it. He actually *felt* it. A warm, soothing rush, deep down. It said, *Everything's going to be fine, Lars Hansen. Just fine.*

Hansen's mind whirled. What was it Callendar had told him earlier? *You can feel his presence . . .*

Grummond's voice cut in, loud and harsh. "You gonna play, or what?"

Their eyes held for a moment more, then the stranger turned from Hansen and walked back to the table, to the impossible setup Grummond had left him. "Three-ball in the side," Callendar said, and fired. The cue ball went two rails and came in hard from the rear, driving into the partial rack with a sound like a pistol shot. The three-ball burst free, a red blur against the green, and smacked dead center into the left side pocket.

Abe Callendar never looked up. He moved around the table, sank the twelve in the corner, the seven in the side, the ten in the other side. The cue ball seemed to have a life all its own, drawing, spinning, sliding to a stop exactly where it should be for the next shot.

As Hansen watched, fascinated, Callendar finished the rack, broke on the ball he'd left, and kept going. The click-click-click of the balls was the only sound in the room, except for his soft voice, calling each shot as he aimed. And the cool confidence in that voice was the most fascinating thing of all.

He couldn't miss, and he knew it.

Callendar ran the next rack, and the next, and the next.

The crowd kept growing as the word spread. By two-thirty there were close to fifty people in the bar.

Lars found himself watching the crowd. *He's here*, Callendar had said. Had he really meant Nathan Cross?

Other words echoed in Hansen's mind. *If the trouble's bad enough, he'll come . . .*

If so, where was he? Lars Hansen's eyes swept the room, checking faces. All of them were local, all familiar. The only thing unfamiliar was their expressions, their sudden look of excitement. Of *hope*.

And then he understood.

It's his spirit, Hansen thought wildly. *That's what's here.*

And Abe Callendar kept shooting. Over and over and over, one ball after another. To Lars Hansen, time seemed to stand still. The ring of bearded faces, the clouds of cigarette smoke, the blowing snow in the gloom beyond the windows—all of that belonged to another world. For a fleeting moment, the very boundaries of the universe were the six rails of Sam Tidwell's pool table, where colored balls worth a thousand dollars each snapped and clicked and rolled one by one across the green felt into the padded leather pockets.

And then it was over. Old Ben Gassaway's stub of chalk scratched one last mark on the blackboard as the stranger rose from the table.

Abe Callendar had run 114 balls—almost eight full racks—without a miss. The final score was 125 to 23.

He strode to the bar. The bets lay in two stacks in front of Sam Tidwell, who hadn't drawn one beer or poured one drink for the past hour. Without a word Callendar took his own stack, pocketed it, and picked up the Warden's hundred thousand. He put it in his other pocket and then turned to

Grummond, who stood beside the table eight feet away.

"That's two grand you owe me," Callendar said.

Ward Grummond's face looked as if someone had cut off his air. A single vein pulsed in his pale forehead, and his lips had narrowed into a tight blue line. Hate and violence radiated from him in waves. The crowd sensed it, and was already pulling away when Grummond went for his gun.

Callendar was ready. In a move so fast Hansen scarcely saw it, Callendar stepped forward and swung the cue like a baseball bat, putting all his weight into it. The heavy butt of the stick caught Ward Grummond just below the nose. Blood and teeth flew everywhere; Grummond himself flew backward onto the pool table as if a team of horses had yanked a rope tied to his neck. He wound up spreadeagled on the felt, out cold, with each of his four limbs pointing toward a corner pocket.

Without turning, Callendar drove the point of the cue behind him into Billy Grummond's stomach. The .45 revolver in Billy's hand clattered to the floor as he was slammed back against the bar. Almost casually Callendar dropped the cuestick, plowed a fist into Billy's gut, and—when the younger man pitched forward—smashed a knee up into his face. The nose broke with a snap. Billy fell, unconscious, and even before he hit the floor Callendar knelt and snatched up the fallen gun. He thumbed back the hammer, spun to face the third Grummond—and relaxed. Slowly he lowered the pistol and rose to his feet.

Moments earlier, Brother Tyrell had reached for his holster. He had found that his gun wasn't there, and for good reason: Lars Hansen held it in his hand. Tyrell had a brief second for this to register—and to stare at Hansen with eyes as wide as the balls on the table—before Hansen brought the gun-barrel down as hard as he could on the top of Tyrell's shaggy head. The youngest of the Grummond brothers had collapsed like a ragdoll.

Abe Callendar returned to the bar, stepping over Tyrell's sprawled body on the way. Without being asked, the bartender poured a whiskey. Callendar knocked it back, placed the gun on the countertop, and looked him in the eye.

"If any of 'em are still alive—and I'm not sure about that one there," he said, waving his empty glass toward Ward's sprawled form, "lock 'em in that back room and get hold of the law in Anchorage. Can you handle that?"

Sam Tidwell nodded, his face blank and dreamy. Callendar set his glass down, seemed to consider for a moment, then turned to Lars Hansen, who was standing there awkwardly, Tyrell's pistol still in his hand.

"Payback time," Callendar said. He held out Ward Grummond's thick stack of bills. "See that this gets to the right folks."

Hansen's mouth fell open. He put down the gun and took the money, cupping it in both hands. The Hope Diamond couldn't have surprised him more.

Callendar buttoned his coat and pulled his hat low over his forehead. "Nice meeting you, Hansen," he said, and started for the door.

Hansen blinked. "I thought you were waiting for someone," he blurted.

Abe Callendar paused, and their eyes locked. For several seconds the two men stared at each other without a word.

Then Callendar smiled—a wide grin that lit up his rugged face. And once again Lars Hansen felt the warm, tingly feeling course through his veins, the way it had years ago when his mother had tucked him safe and snug into his bed.

"I was," Callendar said.

He turned again and approached the crowd. They parted silently so he could pass. Ike Colson, who had returned in time to see the fight, held the door open for him. Every eye in the room watched, some through the door and some through the front windows, while Callendar made his way across the porch and down the steps to the street.

Hansen was suddenly aware of Sam Tidwell standing beside him at the window. "Who is he?" Tidwell asked, never taking his eyes off the figure trudging alone through the snow.

"His name's Abe Callendar," Hansen said. "From upriver."

Tidwell turned and looked at Hansen. "I know where Abe Callendar's from. I've known him ten years." He added, "He's short, with black hair and a handlebar mustache."

Hansen stared at him. "What?"

"Besides, he's not even in Alaska anymore. My cousin—a charter pilot—set down near here last week to wait out a storm. He told me he'd flown Callendar to Anchorage awhile back, on his way south for good. Used his gold for a ranch in Arizona." Tidwell leaned closer to the window, squinting into the eerie gray twilight. "I don't know who that man is, my friend," he said, "but I know who he's not. And he's not Abe Callendar."

***

Lars Hansen sat there, on a chair he had pulled up close to the window, for the next hour or so, gazing out into the frozen, empty street. It was full dark now, and the storm had blown itself out. Snow fell softly from the black sky.

Hansen had watched the stranger all the way to the edge of town, fringed coat flapping behind him like a sail and head bowed into the screaming wind. Twice Hansen had risen from his seat, intending to run after him into the storm—perhaps to thank him, perhaps to confront him, he wasn't sure which. Both times he sat down again.

Hansen's mind kept returning to what he had seen just before the lone figure rounded the last building, the last turn in the path that led up to the high country. What Lars Hansen had noticed at that moment he would remember for the rest of his days; he had overlooked it earlier, in the close quarters of the bar.

Just as the stranger was about to vanish from sight, silhouetted against the snowy foothills, Hansen had seen that he was limping.

He was limping on his left foot . . .

Poetic Justice

Bertie Williams was almost asleep when she heard her roommate scream.

She jumped out of bed and sprinted down the apartment hallway to the den, where she fully expected to find JoAnne Sims either dead or dying. Instead Bertie found her sitting at her computer, grinning like an idiot.

"Look, Bert!" JoAnne said. "He's asked me out!"

Bertie stood there in the doorway, her heart still hammering in her chest. "What? Asked you out?"

JoAnne pointed at the computer screen, where the text of an email message lit up the darkened room. "Jim Jenson. I told you we've been swapping notes."

Bertie sighed. She should have known. Typical JoAnne Sims. If JoAnne spent half as much time studying as she did in Internet chat rooms, she'd probably have graduated by now. Instead, she was a fifth-year senior at a four-year university, and had a terminal case of men on the brain.

Bertie Williams wasted no time on email romances, or any other kind. She had a degree to pursue. Her name actually worked in her favor, there. Despite her friends' matchmaking efforts, and the fact that Bertie was cute and slim, a name like Bertha Mae—even shortened—apparently led potential suitors to expect a female wrestler in army boots. That was fine with Bertie. She hated blind dates anyway.

She also hated computers. And electronic mail.

"I thought you said he was at Ole Miss," Bertie said. Now that the crisis was over, she felt her eyelids drooping again.

"He is. He's driving up Saturday—we're going to dinner in Germantown."

Bertie had a sudden thought. "Isn't that a little risky? You've never actually met him."

"Doesn't matter." JoAnne pointed again. "Read this."

Squinting, Bertie read the entire email. The note from Jim Jenson wasn't just a request for a date; most of it was a long poem. And the poem—

Bertie blinked.

The poem was stunning. The language, the rhythm, the imagery . . . it was as heartfelt and beautiful a description of love as Bertie had ever seen. When she finished reading she felt a lump in her throat. Tears stung her eyes.

JoAnne was grinning from ear to ear. "It's really good, isn't it?"

That was an understatement. Bertie struggled to find her voice. "Who . . . who is this Jim—"

"Jim Jenson."

"Yes. Who is he? What does he do?"

"I told you, he's a student."

"Of what?"

"Law. But he also writes."

Obviously. What he'd written in his emailed poem was so powerful Bertie still had goosebumps. No wonder JoAnne wanted to meet him.

"So he just wrote that for you?" Bertie said. "Out of the blue?"

JoAnne hesitated. "I guess I kind of challenged him to."

"What?"

"He'd mentioned he was a writer, and I told him I was too."

"You're studying elementary ed, JoAnne."

"Well, I sort of wanted to impress him. So . . ."

Bertie waited.

"So I sent him a poem, last week," JoAnne said.

"About what?"

JoAnne shrugged. "Relationships. Feelings. Love. I told him if he liked mine, he could write one to send to me."

"I assume he liked yours?"

"He loved it. He said it was 'magnificent.'"

Bertie studied her a moment, eyes narrowed. "Since when do you write poetry, JoAnne?"

"Since never." Her face reddened. "It was yours."

Bertie's jaw dropped. "What?"

"It's the poem you published in the *Review* last year. The one that won the prizes. I didn't figure you'd mind."

Bertie sagged into a chair. This was too much to absorb. "You told him you wrote it? You *tricked* him?"

"I enticed him, that's all. I'll tell him the truth later."

"Unbelievable," Bertie said.

JoAnne leaned forward, her face solemn. "He'll like me, Bert, once he meets me. You know he will. I just wanted to get things moving." She smiled slyly. "And it worked."

Bertie shook her head. "This is crazy, JoAnne. You don't even know what he looks like."

"Yes I do." JoAnne clicked her mouse; a photo of a handsome young man appeared on the screen. He reminded Bertie of the actor in that remake of *Sabrina*. Greg something. "I also sent him one of me."

"But you don't really know him, JoAnne—"

"I know enough. You do too, from what he wrote."

That was true, Bertie thought. Anyone who could write those words *had* to be an impressive guy—lawyer or not. In fact, she wished she were the one meeting him.

"You'll meet him too," JoAnne added, as if mind-reading. "Saturday night at eight. Wear the green dress, okay?"

"What?!" Bertie sat up straight. "You think I'm going with you on your date?"

"I'll ask him to bring his cousin. Jim talks about him all the time." JoAnne squeezed Bertie's arm. "Please, Bert, I need you there. It'll be fun."

Bertie sighed, started to argue, and found she just didn't have the energy. "Fine. Whatever. I'll go along and meet your Prince Charming."

JoAnne clapped her hands underneath her chin like a trained seal. Then her face turned mischievous. "But he's not Prince Charming. I've already given him a fantasy name."

"Let me guess," Bertie said. "The bard lawyer?"

"Nope."

"Dis-barred lawyer?"

"Very funny."

"Poetic Justice?"

"Wrong again."

"Okay, I give up."

JoAnne grinned and nodded at the computer. "Electronic male."

Bertie snorted and turned to go back to bed. "In that case," she said, over her shoulder, "I might *not* like him."

***

They got to the restaurant at exactly eight o'clock. It was a nice place, remote and elegant. A kid in a tux parked JoAnne's car.

Inside, they were directed to a table in the back corner. Two young men rose to greet them. Bertie recognized Jim Jenson from his photo, and the other guy was just as handsome. Jim introduced him as Kevin Parker—"Second cousin on my mom's side."

JoAnne, Bertie noticed, was so nervous she could barely speak. It didn't matter; Jim talked enough for all of them. After half an hour tensions had eased, and Bertie found herself having a good time. Kevin was quiet but interesting, Jim was bubbling over, JoAnne was giggling as usual. In fact, Jim and JoAnne seemed alike in so many ways it was uncanny.

"Seems they're a good match," Bertie said to Kevin, when dinner was over and the other two were deep in a conversation of their own.

"Peas in a pod," Kevin agreed. He studied Bertie a moment in the dim lighting. "But I think I got the best of the deal."

Both of them smiled. Bertie couldn't remember ever feeling this comfortable with a date. "Me too," she said. "Things worked out well."

She saw an odd look on his face. "Is something wrong?"

He blushed. "No, no. You're right, everything's worked out great."

"But . . . ?"

He shrugged, shook his head. Bertie noticed he was staring a lot at Jim and JoAnne.

"What is it, Kevin?"

He turned to face her. "Nothing, really. It's just that the world's a funny place, Bertie. I mean, I'm beginning to think those two are truly meant for each other. Like it was Fate or something." He paused.

"Keep going."

Bertie watched his eyes. Friendly eyes. Honest. The kind she could learn to like, a lot—she knew that somehow.

"I read that poem JoAnne emailed to Jim," he said.

"And?"

"She didn't write it," Kevin said. "Did she."

Bertie felt her face grow warm. "What makes you think that?"

"I don't know. She's a great girl, I can see that. But she wouldn't have written that poem I read. That poem was . . ." He drew a slow breath and whooshed it out. "Bertie, that poem was amazing. It was *fantastic*. When Jim let me read it, it blew me away. I told him right then, 'This lady's special. One in a million. You've gotta meet her.'"

Bertie studied her wine glass, cleared her throat. "You were right. JoAnne is special."

"Of course. But . . ." He shrugged again, and smiled. A smile that made Bertie's heart tingle.

"But what?"

He appeared embarrassed. "Nothing. It's like you said, things have a way of working out."

Bertie took a sip from her glass, watching Kevin over the rim. So relaxed earlier, he now seemed preoccupied.

"Tell me, Kevin," she said. "Tell me what's worked out."

He fiddled with his napkin, looked up at the ceiling, then back at Bertie. With a glance at the others, he leaned closer to her ear.

"That poem Jim sent," he said. "It wasn't written for JoAnne. It was just a poem."

"What are you saying? He wrote it for someone else?"

"He didn't write it at all."

Bertie blinked. "Are you sure?"

"I'm positive."

She swallowed, looked Kevin in the eye. "How do you know?"

"Because I wrote it," he said.

In the silence that followed, while Bertie's eyes misted over and her heart sang and her smile broadened to light up her whole face, an odd thought locked itself into her mind:

Maybe computers aren't so bad after all.

Career Changes

By two a.m. Joe Burris had mopped all the floors, emptied the trash, and cleaned the windows. Finally he collapsed into a swivel chair and propped his feet on top of the fancy desk in the middle of the lobby. He deserved a break, he decided. After all, this was his birthday.

Joe had unwrapped a package of Hostess Twinkies and was taking a bite when the phone rang.

After five rings he gave in and picked up the receiver. “Front desk,” he said, since that was where his feet were propped.

“Front desk?” A female voice. It sounded uncertain.

“That’s right. Who were you trying to reach?”

A short pause. “You’ll do,” the voice said. “I need you to let me in.”

“The building, you mean?”

“Yes, the building.”

Joe studied the empty lobby. He couldn’t remember

ever seeing anyone arrive or leave after midnight. "Won't your ID badge open the door?" he asked, still chewing.

"I don't have a badge."

"Well, I'm sorry, ma'am, but I'm with the cleaning service. I'm not allowed to admit anyone, after hours."

"Damn," she said. "Is there someone else there I can talk to?"

"I'm the only one here."

"Well, I really do need to get in."

"Where are you now?" Joe asked.

"Down the street."

"Couldn't you just wait till morning, after seven?"

"No."

Joe heard her sigh, and something that sounded like fingernails tapping.

"I have an idea," she said. "How about you go get something for me? I could meet you outside and pick it up."

"Get what for you?"

"A package. It's in one of the rooms off the front hallway."

"One of the offices?"

"That's right."

"I can't," he said. "Not in one of the offices."

"Why not?"

"I'm not allowed anywhere except the lobby, the halls, and the restrooms. The other crew cleans the offices."

She stayed quiet a moment. "They're not locked, are they?"

"The offices? No, they're not locked. The building itself is a secure area. But there's confidential stuff about, and I'm not allowed—"

"What's your name?" the voice asked. "I didn't catch your name."

"Joe Burris."

"You're on the cleaning crew, you said?"

"I *am* the cleaning crew, tonight."

"Just one worker? That seems odd."

"I'm a hell of a worker," he said, with a chuckle that trailed off when he realized how stupid that sounded. He cleared his throat. "My partner's been out sick."

There was a long silence on the other end of the line. Then: "How much do you make in a year, Joe Burris?"

"Excuse me?"

"I said, what's your salary?"

Joe frowned. "I don't think that's any of your—"

"Let me confess something to you, Joe. I'm about to make a career change."

"What do you mean?"

"I was recently involved in a very profitable venture. A few days ago, I left a package—*hid* a package, actually—in the office of one of my business associates, in that building. No one knows it's there, not even him, and ever since I hid it, I've been trying to find a way to get back in there and get it. So far, well . . . circumstances have prevented that from happening."

"What circumstances?" Joe asked.

"I don't think you want to know."

Joe thought about that awhile, then said, "How about your . . ."

"Associate?"

"Yeah. How about him?"

"He's . . . unavailable, right now."

Joe swallowed. He decided he might not want to know about that, either.

"Let's just say I've had to be cautious," she added.

"What you're doing now doesn't seem too cautious."

"I'm running out of options," she said. "Besides, they think I've already left town. I have to act fast, while they're not watching me."

"Who's 'they'?"

When she made no reply, Joe figured he knew the answer to that one. 'They' probably wore guns and uniforms and badges made out of metal instead of plastic.

Joe's feet were off the desk now, his unfinished Twinkie forgotten in his hand. "Why are you telling me this?" he asked.

"I'm telling you this so you'll know I'm serious. I have to have that package, and I have to have it tonight. And . . ."

"And what?"

"I'm prepared to make you an offer."

Joe blinked. "What kind of offer?"

A long pause.

"The package contains eight hundred thousand dollars in wrapped twenties and fifties. Unmarked. If you get it for me, I'll let you keep"—he heard her breathing into the phone—"I'll let you keep a fourth of it."

Joe felt his mouth go dry. "A fourth?"

"You heard me. Twenty-five percent."

He leaned forward in his chair, gazing out through the dark windows. "Keep it how?"

"Take your share, and drop the rest off outside, at someplace we agree on."

Good God, he thought. *A fourth of eight hundred grand . . .*

"What's to keep me from turning you in?" he asked. He couldn't seem to control the squeak in his voice.

"I'm trusting you not to. I have no other choice."

He hesitated, then said, "What if I decide to keep more than a fourth? What if I decide to keep it all?"

The voice turned cold. "Don't even think about that."

"Why not?"

"Remember, I know your name," she said.

Joe felt a shiver ripple up his spine.

"What if I get caught?" he asked, as the thought occurred to him.

"Who's going to catch you?"

"Well . . ."

"Think about it, Joe. Is this line being recorded?"

"No."

"Is anyone else in the building?"

"No. I told you th—"

"You see anybody in the lot outside?"

"No."

"Any security cameras, where you are?"

"No . . ."

"Then why should you get caught?"

Joe mulled that over for a full thirty seconds. He also considered something else: two hundred thousand, tax free. What could he *do* with that much money?

But he knew the answer to that: He could make a career move of his own.

Joe found that he had sweated all the way through his uniform shirt. But he also found himself smiling. Smiling like a fool, at the deserted lobby.

He drew a long breath, let it out, and said, "Where do I find it?"

Her directions were quick but clear. Apparently the money was in a box underneath a stack of printouts somewhere in a closet in the third office on the left, counting from the front of the building. She would hold the line, she told him, while he went to fetch it.

"Okay," he said.

Eighteen minutes later Joe picked up the phone again, his hair mussed and his chest heaving. He could feel his pulse pounding in his ears. "I haven't found it yet. And I ran into a problem."

"What happened?"

"My boss stopped by with a new employee. They caught me in the office rummaging through the closet. He started shouting at me"—Joe stopped, and swallowed hard—"and I had to hit him over the head with a paperweight. The other guy took off up the hall."

"My God. Where is he now?"

"The second guy? He's unconscious too. He ran straight into the statue in the lobby and knocked himself out." Joe stopped again, to catch his breath. "I'm going back in now to keep looking for the package, okay?"

A pause. "The statue in the lobby?"

"Yeah. You know—the iron statue of the soldier, by the fountain."

"The fountain."

"Yeah."

A longer pause.

"Joe?" she said.

"What."

"Is this 354-8200 . . . ?"

He almost dropped the phone. Spots swam before his eyes.

"Just kidding," she said, chuckling. "Couldn't resist."

Joe Burris took a long, shaky breath. "Look, whoever you are, this isn't funny. I'm in a bad way, here, because of you. What should I do—go back and keep trying to find the money?"

"You could, I guess, but you know what? I have some sad news." She stopped for a beat, then said, her voice grave, "The money's not there."

"It's what?"

"There's no money. No package. I'm afraid I was kidding about that too."

Joe slumped into the chair he'd been sitting in when all

this started. "But . . ."

"I knew about your boss coming, Joe. He's there because I called him, on a throwaway cell phone, while you were looking through closets. I just didn't know he was bringing someone else along too."

Joe didn't respond. His head was spinning.

"This has actually gone quite well," she said, as if to herself. "Better even than I'd hoped."

"What . . . what are you saying?"

"I'm saying I'm not down the street, I'm *across* the street, in a phone booth, watching you through those big lobby windows." Her voice dropped lower then, and hardened. "Jeanette Bowers was my friend, Joe. She's the girl you got drunk at the Tiki Tavern awhile back, the one who got away from you and then wrecked her car on the way home that night."

"Who? Jeanette . . . ?"

"Don't worry, you'll have plenty of time to try to remember her. You're going to jail, Joe Burris. The cops should be there any minute."

"The cops?" He looked at the front door, and the black night beyond the glass. "How—"

"Because I called them, too," she said. And hung up.

Joe sat there a moment, listening to the dial tone and staring at the desktop and his half-eaten snack and the mop he'd propped against the wall and the inert body lying sprawled on the floor beside the statue.

This can't be real, he thought. It can't be happening.

It's my birthday.

He took out his key-card for the front door and looked at it. His employer's van was parked fifty feet from the lobby entrance; he wondered how fast it would go. *Should I try?*

Then he heard the siren, and the screech of tires in the

lot, and saw the blinking lights. After a deep sigh, Joe Burris hung up the phone, finished eating his Twinkie, and walked to the door to let them in.

Doctor's Orders

"You must be Monique."

The young lady at the table looked up at him. She had been watching the dance floor.

"And you're Tom," she said.

He hesitated, then sat in the chair across from her. He was about to say something else when the music stopped. Applause rippled through the crowd. They both turned to look at the band, and he studied her from the corner of his eye. She was even prettier than her photo.

She caught him staring at her and smiled.

"You'll have to excuse me," he said. "I'm new at this."

"Computer dating? Me too." She took her red billfold—their prearranged signal flag, in case he'd needed it—off the table and put it in her purse.

Tom Bartlett took a moment to look around. The restaurant was huge, with mahogany furnishings and a black-tie band and a vase of roses on every table. At least two hundred diners sat on tiers overlooking the dance floor, which gleamed like polished teak. Stone-faced waiters glided through the maze. Set in an area opposite the stage was a dessert table forty feet long, stocked with pastries and pies and a crystal punchbowl half as big as a bathtub.

"Is something wrong?" Monique asked.

Tom felt himself blush. He glanced at her gown and pearl necklace, then down at his sportcoat and Dockers. "It's just—I haven't been here before. I may be a tad underdressed."

She waved as if shooing a fly. "You look fine. If it makes you feel better, there's a girl over there in a sweatsuit and sneakers."

"The brunette?" He adjusted his glasses and squinted. "I think I recognize her from someplace."

"TV, probably. Or movies."

"No kidding. And the guy with her—"

"Him too."

Tom picked out half a dozen more familiar faces at other tables. It was a little like channel-surfing. "Is everyone here a celebrity?" he asked.

Her face darkened suddenly. Then the look passed, leaving him to wonder if it had been there at all. "Not everyone. But most are in show business, one way or another."

"Including you?"

A hint of a smile. "I'd forgotten," she said. "'Occupation' wasn't one of the items listed on the computer profile. I found that a little strange, didn't you?"

"I suppose they focused on the important things: astrological sign, favorite songs, hobbies, eye color—"

"One of my drawbacks," she admitted. "They should be blue."

"I beg your pardon?"

"Eye color. Mine are brown. Seventy percent are blue."

"Seventy percent of what?"

"My competition," she said. "I'm an actress."

He blinked. It made sense, he decided. The sleek black hair, the perfect figure, the sultry but sophisticated smile . . .

"An actress," he repeated. "Working or aspiring?"

Her face changed again, and he found himself wondering if he'd said something wrong.

"A little of both. A few bit parts, here and there."

"I'm impressed."

She shrugged. "Keeps me busy." She studied him a moment. "What about you?"

"Mine are green," he said.

Her smile returned, brilliant this time. "I can see that. What do you do?"

"I'm a sleep scientist."

She raised her eyebrows.

He grinned. "I love saying that."

"Is it true?"

"Well . . . halfway."

"Which half? Are you asleep, or are you a scientist?"

"Oh, I'm a scientist. I just do it half the time." He added, "I'm also a teacher."

"A schoolteacher?"

"College. I moved here from Nebraska two years ago. I teach psychology."

Her eyebrows went up again. "A professor?"

"That's me."

"A doctor, possibly?"

"Not medical. Ph.D."

"Now I'm the one who's impressed."

"Don't be," he said. "It'll be a long time before *I'm* on the silver screen."

She was quiet a moment. "It was a long time for me too."

A waitress arrived from the bar, and they ordered drinks. Both of them watched her as she left. Finally Tom broke the silence.

"So you knew, then, when you were little, that you wanted to act?"

"I was a dreamer," she said.

"Sounds like your dream came true."

"Well, one of them did. I'm disgustingly wealthy."

"I can think of worse fates."

"I have a rich father." She looked uncomfortable. "I thought we were talking about *you*."

"We changed the subject."

She turned again, to look at the dance floor. Only a handful of couples were there, swaying to music that was thankfully soft enough to allow conversation.

"Monique LaBont," he murmured. "It is LaBont, right?"

"Right."

"It sounds familiar." He paused for a beat. "Is it your real name?"

"Excuse me?"

"I'm serious," he said. "As an actress, did you have to change your name?"

She smiled. "No, it's mine. With a handle like LaBont, there's no need to come up with a new one. It sounds changed already." She took a sip from her water glass. "Daddy's folks were French, Mama's were Italian."

"They in show business too?"

"God, no. My mother was a housewife—she died when I was nine. And my father . . ." She rolled her eyes. "I don't really know how to describe my father."

"What does he do?"

"In his words? He arranges low-collateral, high-interest,

short-term investment opportunities."

"He sounds like a loan shark."

"That's half right," she said.

"Well, is he alone, or is he a shark?"

She laughed. "Oh, he's a shark, all right—he just does it half the time. He's also a minister."

"What?"

"A TV evangelist. That's how he made his *second* million."

"Excuse me, but . . . the two don't seem to go together."

She smiled. "Welcome to the West Coast, Mr. Bartlett."

The waitress came with their drinks. Monique picked hers up and held it while she watched the band. Tom traced rings around the rim of his glass with his forefinger.

"Tell me about you," she said when the song ended.

"What about me?"

"What exactly is a sleep scientist?"

He shrugged. "Nothing grand. I work nights with a research team at the university. We do experiments."

"What kind of experiments?"

"The sleep labs, mostly. Controlled-environment tests."

"Dreams, you mean?"

"And hypnosis."

"You're kidding."

He held up two fingers. "Scout's honor."

"You . . . hypnotize people?"

"You think it sounds childish."

"I think it sounds fantastic," she said. "How do you do it?"

"I do it very well."

Their eyes held. "I'll bet you do."

He chuckled. "Forgive me. I have no modesty." He picked up his drink and glanced at the stage. The band was taking a break. When he looked back at Monique, she was still staring at him. Her pearls gleamed in the muted lamplight.

"Tell me about it," she said.

"My modesty?"

"Your work."

"You sure? It's a long story."

She leaned forward, her elbows on the tabletop. "What's time to a dreamer?"

At that point a waiter appeared, standing ramrod-straight beside their table. "Would you like to see a menu?" he asked.

"Later," Monique said, keeping her eyes on Tom's face. The waiter scurried off.

To Tom she said, again, "Tell me."

He leaned back in his chair and thought for a moment before speaking.

"I suppose I was born with it. Even as a kid, growing up in Omaha, I was different. It was a little spooky, actually." He frowned, remembering. "I had a certain knack, a certain . . . control over the other kids. Grownups too, now and then."

"What do you mean, control?"

"I mean I could tell people to do something and they'd do it. Not always, mind you, but most of the time."

Amusement flickered in her eyes. "My dad can do the same thing. What's spooky about that?"

"I could do it without saying anything."

She blinked. "What?"

"Sounds crazy, doesn't it? Sometimes I could look at a person—the guy beside me in history class, let's say—and I could close my eyes and think really hard, and when I opened them again he'd do whatever I had asked him, in my mind, to do."

She tilted her head. "You're joking, right?"

He took a swallow of his drink. "It's the truth. It worked maybe eight times out of ten."

"But how . . . what would they *do*?"

"Most anything I told them. Take off their shoes, hand me a pencil, stick out their tongues, say the Pledge of Allegiance backward." He had a sudden thought, and grinned. "It could have worked wonders when I started dating."

"Could have?"

"Never got the chance to try it. My strange influence over others faded away, in the seventh grade. My high school years were as normal as anyone else's." He paused. "I never really figured out what happened, but I have a pretty good idea. Everything I've ever read indicates children are more susceptible to—and capable of—that kind of extra-sensory activity. I think puberty put an end to my magic. When I became a man, as the saying goes, I put away childish things."

Monique stared at him as if transfixed. "What then?"

"Then came college, and a course in psychology. I took it as an elective, my sophomore year. It was there I learned about hypnotism—what it was, how it was done, what it could do. I was fascinated. The next few months I read everything I could find about hypnotic phenomena—age regression, delusions, time distortion, attitude change, everything. End of that semester I changed my major, and six years later I was teaching in the same classes I'd attended as a student." Tom looked up at her. "That's my background," he said. "Two years ago I heard about the research being done here, I applied for a position . . . and here I am."

Their eyes held for a long time before she spoke. "I have a feeling there's more to it than that."

He hesitated. On the other side of the room, the band started up again.

Tom picked up his soup spoon and fiddled with it, seesawing it back and forth on the tabletop.

She waited, saying nothing.

"It came back," he said at last. "The gift, or knack, or whatever you want to call it—the mental games I played during childhood—came back." He let himself think that over. "Not as strong as before, but it was there. And reinforced now by my training in psychological behavior, by my knowledge of how and why the mind works as it does." He gave her what he knew was a sheepish look, but he couldn't help it. "Sure you want to hear all this?"

"Go on."

"Well . . . one of the things I'd learned over the years was that, in theory, the most difficult thing about hypnosis is the inducing of the hypnotic state. Some people are reluctant to submit, some refuse outright, some don't think it can be done at all, and some just don't have the concentration it requires. For those who are both willing and capable, the success of the session is related to the depth of the trance, and it's generally believed the deepest states are caused by things like flickering candles, swinging pendants, soothing voices, and so on. You with me so far?"

She nodded.

"I've found no need for any of those methods," he said. "In most of our experiments, I can put the subject under with ten to fifteen seconds of silent concentration on my part—regardless of his or her attitude. Also, the resulting trance is so sound that post-hypnotic suggestions are usually followed to the letter, even those the subject wouldn't normally obey if awake."

"That's . . . fascinating," she whispered.

"You're right. And it's effective. In our tests so far, we've cured everything from stuttering to bedwetting, eliminated phobias, helped people stop drinking and smoking and overeating. The therapeutic possibilities alone are endless."

He paused then, choosing his next words carefully.

"It also carries a responsibility," he said. "It's a power that's scary at times, even to me."

Monique was shaking her head. "Incredible." All of a sudden her brow wrinkled. "Why haven't you gone public with this? You'd be famous."

Tom chuckled. "Believe me, I've thought of it. Better still, I could quietly join the business world. Can you imagine the money a salesman or stockbroker or trial lawyer could make if he could control the decisions of those around him every day?" He shook his head. "But I could never do that. I'm no saint, but that's going too far. I wouldn't be able to sleep nights. And as for going public, that could backfire. Suppose, worst-case, some psycho got hold of it—or of *me*. I could be forced—or he might think I could be forced—to hypnotize people to assassinate heads of state, for example. A little farfetched, sure, but you get my drift."

He spread his hands. "Anyhow, that's my story and I'm sticking to it." He felt a sad smile on his lips. "It's the love, and the curse, of my life. But you'll have to admit, it's different."

"I'll say." She was looking a little overwhelmed. "By the way, Doc, before you get any ideas about later tonight, I should tell you I have a Doberman in my apartment. You might find him hard to influence."

Tom grinned. "I'll remember that." He put his spoon back where it was supposed to be and clasped his hands in front of him. "Now," he said, "you can tell me *your* story."

Her face changed again. It was amazing, he thought, how quickly her mood could shift. She cleared her throat. "To be honest, I've had a few setbacks lately. I doubt you'd be interested."

"Maybe not. But if you can't talk to a psychologist, who can you talk to?"

She gave him what looked like a grudging smile. "Well,

not on an empty stomach, at least." She glanced about. "Have you seen our waiter?"

"You sent him packing."

"That's right, I did. Why'd you let me do that?"

"I had the feeling," he said, "you're used to getting your own way."

"My, my. Not only persuasive—you're perceptive, too."

There was a smattering of applause on the other side of the room, and they saw the musicians taking their final bows. When the stage was cleared and the half-dozen dancers had returned to their tables, Tom marveled again at the size of the crowd. Every table was full.

Well, almost every table. He saw one young lady sitting alone—a short, pretty blonde in a blue dress—but even she appeared to be waiting for someone. When he looked again at Monique, he found her staring at the same table.

"That girl," Monique said. "Did you see her come in?"

"Excuse me?"

"The woman in the blue dress, six tables over. How long's she been sitting there?"

"I'm not sure. Why? You know her?"

Monique didn't answer. She continued watching the blonde, then turned to stare down at her plate. Finally she looked at Tom, studying his face as though she were about to do his portrait in oils.

"How would you like to have some fun?" she asked. A sly smile appeared.

"What do you mean?"

Monique shot another glance at the mystery lady, then hunched forward over the table. Mischievous lights danced in her eyes. "When you hypnotize someone," she said, "there are no ill effects, right? No aftershocks or anything?"

Tom grinned. "I get a little headache sometimes."

"You know what I mean."

"No," he said. "No negative after-effects. Matter of fact, subjects usually feel rested when it's over, like after a long night's sleep."

"Good. And it wouldn't be hard to do? I mean, in a situation like this? Here, tonight?"

"Not especially, no."

"In that case"—she looked him in the eye—"I'd like to ask a favor."

"You want me to hypnotize you," he said.

"Not exactly. I want you to hypnotize that girl over there, in the blue dress."

Tom blinked. "What?"

"Just listen for a second." She held up both hands. "Don't say no, yet."

"Monique, I really don't—"

"Just listen. Please."

He kept quiet. Involuntarily, he looked again at the young lady's table. She was still there, alone, tilting her wrist now and then to check her watch.

"Her name's Peggy Adams," Monique said, watching her too. "We were sorority sisters. I haven't seen her in years." She turned to face Tom. "We were really close in school, always playing practical jokes on each other. On graduation day—the last time I saw her, as a matter of fact—she played one on me. What the joke was isn't important, except that it was embarrassing. I laughed about it later, but it hurt me, and I swore—I *swore*—I'd get her back someday." She leaned closer, her eyes shining. "This is my chance, Tom. The fact that you're here too, with this wild talent of yours, is too good to pass up. You've got to help me do this."

He shook his head. "I don't know, Monique. Remember what I told you, about responsibility? I meant that."

"Come on, Professor," she said, her smile teasing. "All academics are stuffy, I know that. Break out of the mold for once."

Before he could answer she looked over her shoulder again. The blonde seemed to be getting impatient, shifting in her seat and checking the entrance every few seconds. "Her date's obviously late," Monique said. "We've got to hurry before he gets here, or she decides to leave." She grinned at him like a little kid. "Please. It'll be a blast."

Against his better judgment he asked, "What do you have in mind?"

"I've got it all figured out. There's a guy in the crowd named Bert Pendergrast—" As she spoke both of them saw the young woman look at her watch and signal a waiter.

"She's about to leave," Monique hissed. "Look, at least do this much: I'll go ask her to join us. Is there any way you could put her under for a minute while we talk this over, without her hearing what we're saying?"

"Well, that's possible, of course, but—"

"That's what we'll do. Wait here. When I get back with her we'll chat awhile and then I'll give you the signal."

He sighed. "All right, I guess there'd be no harm in—"

But Monique was already gone. Brooding over his decision, Tom watched her weave through the crowd to Peggy Adams's table, where she hugged the blonde and then plopped down in the seat across from her. After a minute or so he saw Monique point in his direction. He felt himself smile like an idiot. Then both women rose and made their way across the room toward him.

As they approached, Tom had a chance to observe them both. Each of the two, he thought, looked exactly like her name. Monique LaBont was tall, trim, dark, tough, sophisticated. Peggy Adams was short and fair and shapely, with a sweet smile and a girl-next-door freshness that was visible a mile away. Both were dressed to the teeth.

Together, they were two of the most stunning women Tom had ever seen. Maybe this computer dating thing wasn't such a bad deal.

He stood to greet them. Monique made the introductions.

"Won't you join us?" Tom asked. Peggy Adams's eyes, he noticed, were a deep, clear blue.

Peggy gave him a polite smile. "Only for a moment, thank you." She glanced over at her empty table. "It . . . appears I've gotten my signals crossed."

It appears you've gotten stood up, Tom thought. He wondered who in his right mind would have done that to a lady like this one.

Tom fetched an extra chair, and they sat. Monique said something about the restaurant, Tom mentioned the weather, Peggy made a flattering comment about Monique's earrings. After a few minutes of this, Peggy turned to check the entrance, and when she did Monique caught Tom's eye. NOW, she mouthed silently.

Tom sighed. Monique saw him hesitate, and glared at him.

What the hell, he decided. It won't hurt anything, and I can snap her out of it whenever I want . . .

He looked at Monique and nodded agreement. When Peggy faced their table again, she found both of them staring at her. "Is something wrong?" she asked.

Tom closed his eyes and concentrated.

Twelve seconds later he opened them again. Peggy Adams looked back at him, her face blank and her gaze unfocused.

"Peggy," he said, "can you hear me?"

She nodded. Her expression didn't change.

Across the table, Monique was watching them both, her eyes darting back and forth as if following a tennis match.

"Peggy," Tom said, "Monique and I are going to discuss something, between ourselves. You'll pay it no attention. Later, when I say the word 'Enjebi,' you'll wake up and rejoin the conversation. The word is 'Enjebi.' Understand?"

"Yes," she said.

Tom turned to Monique. "Okay."

She gaped first at Peggy, then at him. "Okay what?"

"She's under." He couldn't help feeling a twinge of pride.

"And she can't hear us?"

"She can hear us. She just doesn't understand what we're saying. She'll answer, though, if she's spoken to."

Monique stared at her as if she were Scarlett O'Hara, personified and beamed in from Tara. "Can I say something to her?"

"Sure."

Monique swallowed and said, "Peggy?"

The blond woman looked at her. "Yes?"

"How . . . do you feel?"

Peggy smiled vacantly. "I feel fine."

Monique turned to Tom. "This is weird," she murmured. She was silent a moment, as if in deep thought. "By the way, Tom," she said then, watching Peggy from the corner of her eye, "when I went to the restroom earlier, I noticed someone had cut off the governor's wife's head and stuffed it in the toilet bowl. I wonder if I should call the manager or just go try to fish it out myself." She turned to their guest. "What do you think, Peggy dear?"

Peggy's smile widened. "That sounds fine."

Monique stared at her a while longer, then pulled her eyes away. "Unbelievable," she whispered.

"I agree," Tom said, satisfied. "Now, what did you want to tell me? I don't think it's fair to keep her hanging like this."

"No, of course not." Monique still seemed shaken by the demonstration. "What I wanted to tell you is that there's a guy sitting over there"—she nodded toward the area near the long dessert table—"named Bert Pendergrast. He's a producer, a mutual friend of mine and Peggy's. What I want you to do is get her to go over and do something crazy in front of him, something embarrassing, like singing a dirty song or licking him on the nose or pulling her dress over her head."

Tom couldn't believe what he was hearing. "But . . . that wouldn't just be in front of *him*. It would be in front of everybody."

"So? What she did to me that day was in front of everybody, too."

He stared at her. "Surely you're not serious about this."

But she *was* serious. He could tell. A funny little grin, dangerously close to a sneer, had settled on her face, and her eyes were glowing like coals in a furnace. "Come on, Tom," she said. "It's all in fun. It's just a prank."

He shook his head. "I don't think so, Monique."

Her face darkened, but her strange little grin stayed put. "What is it, Doc? You don't think you can pull it off? Surely a man commended by the Surgeon General for his work could at least do something like this, as a favor to—"

She stopped in midsentence.

There was a moment of dead silence.

"What did you say?"

"I . . . read that in your profile," she mumbled.

He shook his head again. "It wasn't in my profile. Nobody knew about the commendation, at my own request. Nobody except my colleagues, and a handful of test subjects who were there when the call came in—" He stopped, watching her eyes, thinking.

LaBont.

Tom remembered him now. He'd said he was a preacher. A claustrophobia case, maybe a year ago. They'd cured him after half a dozen test visits—

"I knew your father," he said.

Her jaw dropped. That was, apparently, the last thing she'd expected to hear. "But—he said he never gave his name."

"He probably didn't, when he was awake." Tom was quiet a moment, studying her face. Beside them, Peggy Adams sat and stared blankly at the silverware.

Tom's voice turned cold. "He told you about me, and about what I could do, didn't he? You want to tell me the rest?"

For a while neither of them said a word. Monique had been thrown a curve, no question about that, but she didn't look overly upset by it.

"My cousin," she said, "runs the dating service."

Tom nodded. "So you had him arrange our meeting. But why?"

She avoided his eyes.

Then it came to him. "Peggy," he said. "Of course. You arranged that too." He frowned, thinking hard. "You made sure this girl"—he looked over at Peggy, who gave him a dopey smile—"you made sure she would be here too, at the same time we were. You had a friend call her for a date and then had him stand her up, didn't you? So you could step in and invite her to our table." He leaned forward. "Why, Monique? What's all this about?"

She glowered at him for a full ten seconds. "All right," she said. "I'll tell you."

Still she hesitated. At a table off to their left someone proposed a toast, and glasses tinkled above the hum of conversation.

"Almost two weeks ago, I went to Pendergrast's studio, for an audition. For the lead in a new film, one of the biggest jobs in town—and I had it locked. They practically told me so." Her face went rigid. "Then little Miss Adams came along."

Monique glared at Peggy. "I never went to school with her. I never even saw her before that day, a week ago Wednesday. We met when she strolled into Bert's office for *her* audition, just as I was leaving." Monique turned to Tom again, her eyes blazing. "She beat me. She won the part, hands down. I was out. Out of the role, out of work, out in the street. My big break went up in a puff of smoke, all because of her."

Tom was thunderstruck. It took him a moment to even formulate a reply. "That's what this is about? You want to get *back* at her?"

"No," she said, "not just get back at her. I want to disgrace her." She looked around at the crowd. "The people in this room right now are among the most powerful in the industry. An impropriety here, in front of them, would be career suicide." She pinned Tom with her gaze. "That's what I want. I want to humiliate her so badly she'll be told to give up the part. If that happens, I'll get it. Now do you understand?"

Tom felt his cheeks grow hot. "What I don't understand," he said, "is that you thought I would agree to do it."

Amusement lit up her face, surprising him. "Oh, let's not use past tense, Dr. Bartlett. You *will* do it."

Something in her voice made him pause.

"Does the name Amy Thornhill ring a bell?" she asked.

"Of course it does. She was one of my best students."

"Well, she likes you too. She also likes to go to Vegas every couple weeks. You didn't know that, did you?"

"What are you getting at?"

"Little Amy Thornhill enjoys gambling, I'm afraid. Trouble is, she's not good at it." Monique tipped her body forward over the table, her eyes drilling into his. "She owes my father a great deal of money, you see." Her voice dropped lower. "Do you remember, Dr. Bartlett, when she came to your office after hours a few times? Back in March, I think she said."

"Of course I do. She had questions for me, about class assignments. I helped her and she left."

Monique smiled then, and it was a smile that chilled Tom to the bone. "Understand this, Professor. One word from me, *one word*, and Amy Thornhill will swear you and she had an affair, against her will, so she could get the grades to pass your course."

Tom stiffened. "That's a lie and you know it. Nothing went on between—"

"Don't be stupid. It doesn't matter whether anything went on or not. What matters is that she will swear it *did*, and that you forced her into it. You'd be ruined at the university, and probably never allowed to work again in the field of psychology." Another smile. "A fine mess, don't you agree?"

"You're insane," he said wonderingly.

She threw back her head and laughed. "What I am, is a survivor." She nodded in Peggy's direction. "If I have to destroy this girl to get what I want, that's too bad. Just be careful I don't have to destroy you instead."

Tom shook his head. "So all this was an act. All the banter, the interest in my work, the talk of practical jokes, the stalling—" He studied her with a mixture of fascination and revulsion. "Tell me, Monique, was *any* of it true?"

"The part about Amy Thornhill is, I assure you. And I hope, for your sake, that you believe I will do what I've said I will."

"Oh, I believe you. I believe now that you're capable of anything."

"That I am," she said. "For the record, though, I'd hoped

I could talk you into it without force. I am not completely lacking in persuasive ability myself, you know." She sighed, and her face hardened. "Enough of that. Let's get on with the show."

He watched her look across the room. "Bert Pendergrast," she said, "is the white-haired guy at the table beside the big punchbowl. You see him?"

Still feeling shellshocked, Tom followed her gaze. "I see him."

"Good. You already know what I want: Have our friend here go over near his table and make a spectacle of herself. I don't care what she does, as long as it's outrageous. But whatever she does, make her keep doing it until she's dragged bodily from the room." She gave him a laser stare. "You get the message?"

He said nothing.

"And one more thing. I want you to have her forget she ever met you and me. Forget she was with us, forget our names, forget what we look like. Can you do that?"

He watched her for a long time before answering. "Yes," he murmured.

"Excellent." Monique wet her lips. It was almost time. "You remember everything I've said? She's to get up and walk over to him, and do her thing. No hesitation, no screwups. There's a coffeeshop just down the street—when it's done, and they've hauled her away, you and I will go there together, quietly. Do you understand?"

A silence passed.

"*Do you?*"

"Yes. I understand."

She drew a lungful of air, let it out, and scanned the crowd one last time.

"All right," she said. "Do it."

Tom Bartlett turned and looked at Peggy Adams, who gazed pleasantly back at him, a vacant smile on her lips.

Monique, watching them both, seemed to be holding her breath.

He closed his eyes and concentrated.

***

Half an hour later and half a block away, he sat with his head lowered, studying the bubbles in his coffee cup. Across the table from him, she stared out the dark window at the traffic. Though still beautiful, her aura seemed to have faded a bit. Her jewelry looked almost dull in the fluorescent lighting, her makeup pasty.

"That was unreal," she said. There was something like awe in her voice. "I saw it, I saw her with my own eyes . . . and I still don't believe it."

The coffeeshop smelled of plastic booths and pastry. The only sound was the clink of dishes from an unseen kitchen.

Tom took off his glasses and rubbed the corners of his eyes with a thumb and forefinger.

"You'll believe it when you watch the eleven o'clock news," he said. "There were probably a dozen anchors in the crowd."

And photographers. He'd never seen so many cameras.

But he'd been forced to do it. At least that's what he kept telling himself. He'd been forced to.

Hadn't he?

No. He had been forced into doing something, yes—but he could've stopped short of *that.* Part of it he'd done because . . .

Because I wanted to, he decided. Because, God help him, it had seemed *right*, somehow.

And now he'd have to live with that.

"What does 'Enjebi' mean?" she asked, still gazing into

the darkness.

Tom put his glasses back on. "It's an island in the Pacific. My granddad was there, in the Navy."

She didn't appear to have heard him. "As soon as you said that word—" She swallowed with a loud click. "It's like a dream. I saw her walking away, very slowly, from our table. And unzipping her dress . . ."

Tom took a sip of coffee.

"Why would she *do* that?" she said. "Why would someone like Monique LaBont take off all her clothes in front of two hundred people, climb onto the dessert table—and sit down in the *punchbowl*?"

Peggy Adams turned to look at him. "What could make someone *do* that?"

"Brown eyes," Tom said, as if talking to himself.

"What?"

"Nothing." He sighed and picked up the check. "Do you need a ride home?"

"I have my car." She studied him a moment. "Tell me, Mr. Bartlett—"

"Tom. The name's Tom."

"Tell me something, Tom: How well did you know her?"

"Monique? I didn't know her at all. It was a blind date—a computer date. I met her twenty minutes before I met you."

Peggy seemed to think that over. "But you did meet her. So did I, on two occasions now. And neither of us did a thing when the police took her away." She gave him a guilty look. "What do I do about that? What would I say to her if I ever saw her again?"

Tom rummaged in his pocket for a tip. "I don't think I'd worry about that, Ms. Adams."

"Why not?"

He put a dollar on the table and looked her in the eye. "Something tells me," he said, "she wouldn't remember either one of us."

She frowned at that, but nodded anyway.

"Ready?" he said. He rose to his feet.

She didn't move. Her face looked tired but her frown had smoothed out a bit now, and she stared up at him thoughtfully. "It's Peggy."

"Excuse me?"

"The name's Peggy," she said, and smiled.

And, for the first time since the restaurant, he felt like smiling too.

Sightings

Officer Jack Crowe was waiting with the engine running when his partner came out of the McDonald's restroom.

Get in," Crowe said. "We got a call."

"What kind of call?" Linda McBride asked, as their cruiser screeched out of the lot and into the late-night traffic.

"A UFO sighting."

"Are you kidding?"

"Nope. Lady says it flew over her house. Something big, fast, bright, and loud."

"Sounds like the Channel 5 News chopper."

"This one had green lights."

McBride chuckled. "To match the color of its passengers, probably." She turned to watch the dark city drift past outside her window. "This lady the one we're going to see?"

"No. She wouldn't give dispatch her name."

"Then where are we headed?"

"Her neighbor's address. Fred Hargroves. She said

whatever it was landed in his back yard."

"Why didn't Fred call us himself?" McBride asked.

"Who knows? Maybe he's asleep. Or not home."

"Or kidnapped. That's what aliens do."

Crowe grinned, hung a left, and headed west on Rosecrans. "Whatever you say—you're the *X-Files* guru."

"Am not. I didn't even like the show."

"Then why'd you watch it all the time?"

"I liked Agent Mulder," she said.

Fred Hargroves's house sat on a corner lot ten blocks from the beach. They parked, put on their hats, and waded through the weeds to the front porch. Crowe rang the doorbell. No answer.

"Let's check the back," he said.

The gate in the six-foot cedar fence was unlocked. They opened it and peeked inside, looking for anything from a dog to a spaceship. What they saw instead was a bald guy in a T-shirt and bermuda shorts, sitting with a can of Coors on a lighted patio.

"Mr. Hargroves?" Crowe said.

The man looked up at them. His face was blank, his eyes glassy and faraway. He showed no surprise at the sight of two of L.A.'s Finest standing at his back gate.

They crossed the yard to the patio, Crowe watching the man and McBride the house. You couldn't be too careful. "Are you Fred Hargroves?" Crowe asked again.

No reply.

"We were told you might have seen something unusual here tonight. Any truth to that?"

"Feenydoodle," Hargroves said.

"Excuse me?"

Hargroves just stared at them. His expression—lack of expression, actually—was spooky. "Zockyjabberdoo," he said.

"Googlepollywog."

"What do you think?" Crowe asked McBride.

"I think that's not the only beer Fred's had tonight. Isn't that right, Mr. Hargroves?"

"Crinkendiddlebaum," Hargroves said.

Crowe sighed. "Let's get out of here."

Ten minutes later they were parked on a street near the airport, sipping coffee from a Wendy's drive-thru. "Want to know my theory?" McBride said. "The whole country tilted a little once, a long time ago, and all the nuts rolled to the West Coast."

"That would explain it," Crowe agreed. "What do we do if we get another report of a sighting?"

"We let Jones and Kanosky check it out. Those two could use a little—"

A low hum filled the air, and then a roar like a hundred jet engines. The palms beside the road tossed and swayed as if in a hurricane; the police car rocked on its shocks. Thirty feet from its front bumper, an oblong ball the size of a double-wide trailer appeared, hovering just above the pavement. The entire scene was bathed in green light.

In the blink of an eye, it was gone again.

Officers Crowe and McBride sat staring at the windshield. Both their coffee cups were empty, the contents soaking into uniforms and seatcovers. The only sound was the metallic voice of their radio:

"One-tango-fourteen, come in. One-tango-fourteen?"

The cruiser sat dark and silent. The officers' faces remained expressionless, their eyes unfocused. Overhead, a fingernail moon rode a purple, cloudless sky.

"Calling one-tango-fourteen, do you read, please?"

Very slowly, never once moving his head or his eyes, Officer Crowe reached down and unclipped the radio mike. He raised it to his lips.

His face calm and dreamlike, Crowe thumbed the transmit button.

“Feenydoodle,” he said.

The Medicine Show

Colonel Puckett knew how to make an entrance.

When he rode into town—any town—he came in a tall, gaily-painted, horse-drawn wagon twice as big as a stagecoach, and was followed by a giant, a juggler, and an Indian maiden, all mounted on prancing horses with multicolored saddles and bridles. And it was always the same: some sharp-eyed youngster would spot the parade, word would spread, and by the time the procession reached Main Street everyone who was able had lined up to watch. As well they might. This was an odd occurrence, in the spring of 1806. Half a century later, Colonel Puckett's little entourage would be called a Wild West Show—after all, the Indian woman could do a little trick riding, and the juggler had a passable knife-throwing act. But this was the East, and long before the era of showmen like Bill Cody.

Colonel Puckett's odd-looking group was billed as a "medicine show." And Puckett himself was a forerunner of the fast-talking swindlers who would crisscross the country in years to come, rumbling into towns in wagons similar to his and leaving town again in the middle of the night, usually more quickly and quietly than they had arrived.

The medicine involved here, you see, was not the usual kind. It was, according to Colonel Puckett and his assistant Mr. Roy Biggs, a far superior product. And the show itself involved nothing so common as tickets or admission charges. It was all free. And its purpose was simple: draw and hold the crowd for what would come later, *after* the show—a presentation by the silver-tongued Amos Puckett himself, the discoverer and manufacturer of the Colonel's Magic Elixir.

It was, he proclaimed, the cure for every illness and misfortune known to man—colds, headaches, lumbago, snakebite, you name it. One swallow of the Magic Elixir (or one splash, if applied externally) would have you on your feet again and feeling perky in the wink of an eye. And all for only a dollar a bottle. Say hallelujah.

On this particular day, standing in the middle of a dusty street in northeastern New Jersey, Amos Puckett held a bottle of the miracle concoction high above his head as he shouted his message into the clear April morning and stared into the eyes of the spectators gathered around his wagon. For the past half hour, Thor the Giant had bent lengths of steel in his bare hands, Little Crow Feather had galloped through the streets while standing barefoot in her saddle, and the bored-looking juggler had spun flaming torches in the air. The crowd was excited and happy and ready to be fleeced, and Colonel Puckett felt equal to the task.

"No more pain and suffering, dear neighbors," he bellowed in his deep preacher's voice. "No more expensive trips to the doc or sickening doses of what he calls medicine. For this"—he made a long, slow turn so everyone could see the bottle and its precious contents—"this is the one and only absolute remedy for whatever ails you. The one incredible, secret formula that can transform you in minutes from sickness to health, pallor to radiance, fatigue to vitality. And there's even a bonus, my fine friends." He paused and studied them carefully. "It is not merely a cure," he said. "It is also a deterrent."

"A what?" someone asked, from way back in the crowd.

"A preventative," the Colonel said. "It can actually *protect* you from what has not yet happened."

A long silence. Then a different man, nearer to center stage, asked, "What do you mean, protect us?"

The Colonel grinned. "I mean, my good fellow, that the contents of this bottle, when used as directed, will actually shelter you from bodily harm." He paused again, watching their faces, and when he spoke next his voice was low and solemn. "We live in perilous times, ladies and gentlemen. We all know that. In our young country all sorts of dangers await us at every turn—thieves, murderers, diseases, natural disasters. In the midst of all this, how would you like to know, beyond a shadow of a doubt, that you and your family are safe from any physical harm?"

A hush fell over the gathering. Puckett, as he observed the looks of those near the front, saw a familiar sight: faces that had been curious and suspicious had turned downright scornful. Throughout the group, people frowned and shook their heads and murmured warnings to their neighbors.

The Colonel was undaunted. This always happened. A little skepticism was to be expected.

"Would it help," he called out, with a disarming smile, "if I were to offer proof that what I'm saying is true?"

Again the crowd fell silent. Several of them exchanged glances. No one had left.

"A demonstration, perhaps," he said, projecting his strong voice so that even those in the back ranks could hear.

Without waiting for a response, Amos Puckett looked down at his assistant, who was standing in the crowd to the left of the wagon. “Mr. Biggs. Do you have your weapon?”

Roy Biggs, a large man to begin with, drew himself up to his full height. “I have it, Colonel,” he said.

Immediately Puckett stripped off his coat and shirt and stood on the wagon seat. Even at the age of sixty-one the Colonel was in fine condition, with a barrel chest and broad shoulders. He cut an impressive figure, standing there above the crowd with his fists on his hips and his chin thrust forward like the prow of a warship.

The bottle of elixir was still in his left hand. Moving with great purpose, Amos Puckett popped the cork from the container, poured a dab of its contents into his right palm, and rubbed it briskly across his chest. Then he recorked the bottle and tossed it to Little Crow Feather, who caught it and tucked it into her waistband.

“Gather round, my friends,” the Colonel called, then turned and jumped lightly from the wagon to the ground. Murmuring, the crowd formed a circle around Puckett and his assistant. The two men faced each other from a distance of less than ten feet. Roy Biggs had drawn his heavy pistol and was holding it cocked and ready at his side.

Keeping his eyes on Biggs, the Colonel turned his head a bit. “You folks behind me might want to step aside,” he said. They did, and wasted no time doing it. Now the crowd formed a thick “U” with the Colonel standing alone in the open end.

“Observe, ladies and gentlemen,” Puckett said, then looked his assistant straight in the eye. “Whenever you’re ready, Mr. Biggs.”

For a long moment nobody moved. Somewhere far away a child called out, a dog barked, a hammer rang dully against an anvil, but these noises belonged to another world.

There in the shadow of the tall wagon in the middle of the street, in a crowd of nearly a hundred people, not a sound broke the silence.

Every eye was on the two strangers.

In one smooth motion, Roy Biggs raised his gun hand, pointed the musket at the Colonel's heart, and fired.

The crowd gasped; Colonel Puckett turned and fell face-down into the dirt. For an instant everyone, including Roy Biggs, stood frozen. Then, within seconds, Biggs was kneeling at his boss's side. Slowly Biggs rolled the Colonel over, and even more slowly helped him to his feet. As those gathered about him watched, Puckett blinked, opened his eyes wide, and looked dazedly around at the crowd. There was not a single mark on his chest.

A few spectators sighed with relief; several more laughed nervously. One or two clapped. But there were no cheers, no widespread applause.

Not yet.

After a moment one of the onlookers voiced the thought that had apparently occurred by now to almost everyone.

"How do we know that was on the level?" he shouted. "Anybody can load a blank charge."

Now other spectators joined in. *What's going on here*? they demanded.

And then, from the back of the group, someone else spoke up: "Let *me* have a try."

Everyone turned to look, though some had already recognized the shaky, raspy voice. It belonged to the town drunk, a small red-haired man who was making one of his rare appearances outside the walls of the jail. He looked sober for a change, but his voice always sounded the same. "Give *me* a shot at him, why don't you?"

As if on cue, all eyes swung back to the Colonel. He

seemed to have recovered completely now, and stood in the open space between Roy Biggs and the wagon. His eyes flicked to Biggs, and in that fraction of a second Puckett got his unspoken answer. Biggs's nod was almost imperceptible.

"Why not?" the Colonel said cheerfully, turning again to face the challenger. "Step to the front, my friend."

The small, poorly dressed man seemed taken aback. Then, apparently seeing the encouragement on the faces of his companions, he moved toward the front of the crowd. The throng parted to let him through.

He approached to within a few yards of Colonel Puckett and stopped. "Your name, sir?" the Colonel asked.

The small man opened his mouth, but the crowd beat him to it. "That's Zeb Hamilton," someone called. Others, too far back to see the action, repeated the name to their neighbors.

"Zeb?" most of them said. "What the hell's he doing up there?"

The murmur of the crowd became a buzz, then a rumble as everyone began to discuss this new turn of events.

But no one laughed, as they normally would have done at the mention of Zeb's name. This was serious business. Someone was trying to trick them, right here in their own town, and Zeb was attempting, at least, to do something about it.

The Colonel swiveled his head slowly, surveying the crowd. His fists were again on his hips, his chin held high. "You all know this man?" he said, in his booming voice.

Emphatic nods and replies, from all around. Zeblediah Woodthorpe Hamilton, while not well respected around these parts, was certainly well known.

"Good," Puckett said. After another glance at Biggs, the Colonel turned again to the small man. "I welcome your challenge, my friend. One should be allowed to prove for himself whether another's words are true." He stole one last look at the crowd, and was pleased this time with what he saw in their faces. He was winning them over.

"This'll only take a minute, ladies and gentlemen," he continued. "Get your money ready to make your purchases."

Colonel Puckett turned once more to the shabbily dressed man and smiled, showing him his wide white chest. They were standing less than eight feet apart.

"Draw your weapon, sir," the Colonel announced, "and fire when ready."

Zeb Hamilton, clearly uncomfortable as the center of attention, pulled his pistol from his belt, cocked it, aimed with both hands, and pulled the trigger.

***

It took almost an hour to pack up the wagon, disperse the crowd, and carry the Colonel's body down the street to the undertaker's. Now that that was done, there were only four people left at the scene. The little Indian woman sat on top of one of the wagon wheels, crying softly into her hands; Roy Biggs counted out wages to the juggler, who had a canvas pack thrown over one shoulder; and Zeb Hamilton stood in the middle of the street with his hands in his pockets, staring down at the fading, rust-colored patch of blood on the ground. The giant had already left, walking glumly toward the other end of town, where he had heard the blacksmith might need a hired hand.

Biggs finished paying the juggler, and the two men shook hands before parting. As the juggler left he stopped to talk to the woman, and after a moment she climbed down off the wheel, still sniffling, and walked away with him. Roy Biggs, alone now, stuffed the cashbox beneath the seat and wandered over to Zeb Hamilton. Biggs didn't look at him right away; for a while he just stared at the wagon, which looked even odder with three more horses tied onto the back end. Finally Biggs expelled a sigh and turned to Zeb.

The anger Biggs had felt at first had passed; now he was just tired.

"I can't figure you out, Mister," he said. "I really can't."

Zeb Hamilton nodded. "Guess this means I won't get my twenty dollars now, don't it?"

Biggs was struck with a sudden thought. Narrowing his eyes, he said, "You actually don't have any idea what's happened here today, do you?"

Zeb shrugged. "I suppose the guy wanted to commit suicide. Guess he talked you into helping him do it, and then you talked me into it too. That's what I suppose."

Roy Biggs shook his head. "What I suppose," he said, gazing sadly at the dark spot in the middle of the street, "is that Amos Puckett's probably the most surprised man in hell right now." He was quiet a moment, then looked again at Zeb. Out of long habit, he glanced around to make sure no one else was close by. Then he asked the question he had waited almost an hour to ask.

"Why on earth," Biggs said, "did you reload the gun? I told you it was ready to fire when I gave it to you, before the show."

Zeb looked surprised. "I didn't reload nothing," he said. "Neither did my cousin. Man gives you a weapon and says it's ready, another man don't check the load. That'd be an insult."

Biggs stared at him hard, thinking. "Show me the pistol."

Zeb Hamilton pulled the short musket from his belt and held it out. As soon as Biggs saw it he knew what had happened.

"That's not the gun I told you to use! Where's the one I gave you?"

Zeb looked uneasy. "I . . . loaned it to my cousin," he admitted.

"You what?!"

Zeb shrugged. "He's a rich man, my cousin. He needed a good gun, and quick, he told me—so I gave him yours and took his." Zeb quickly added, "He'll be back with it soon. Fact is, it should be over with by now."

Biggs could only stare at him. "*What* should be over with?"

"The fight. My cousin Alexander let himself get talked into a fight." Zeb shook his head. "Foolish thing, if you ask me."

Biggs swallowed. "A fight . . . ?"

"A duel," Zeb said. "With a guy named Aaron Burr."

Early Retirement

Arthur Speed was being downsized.

He was sixty-two years old, and had been a security guard at the bank's operations center for thirty of those years. This was to be his last. The announcement of the upcoming merger with a larger bank, in New York, had resulted in hundreds of similar job cuts throughout the organization. None of this was personal, the employees were told; this was business in the Modern Era. They would just have to make adjustments.

Today, on a Friday morning three weeks from the merger date and a week before his final day of employment, Arthur Speed leaned back in his chair at his post inside the north door of the op center and watched Estelle Feeney walk toward him along the main hallway. Estelle was the manager of the center's cafeteria, a small operation that was getting smaller every day, as more and more of the bank's workers left. In fact, next Friday would be Estelle's last day too. She sagged into a chair beside Arthur and heaved a sigh.

"Getting a little sparse around here, isn't it?" she said, with a glance down the deserted hallway.

"It's a shame, is what it is," Arthur said. He regarded Estelle's profile a moment, remembering happier times. He and she had dated several years ago, before their separate marriages. They were both alone again now, but he doubted Estelle would stay that way. Though she was no spring chicken, she was still an attractive lady. "We should both have quit, years ago."

She nodded. "At least you've got some retirement coming."

"Early retirement," he corrected. "You know how much this merger will cost me?"

She turned and studied him, waiting.

"Two hundred and fifty thousand," he said. "That's how much I'll lose, over the long haul, for having to leave here three years before I qualify for a full pension."

Estelle seemed to ponder that. "How much will I lose, do you think?"

Arthur Speed took a pen and notepad from his pocket. Despite his last name, his movements were slow and deliberate. "You're not fifty-five yet, are you?"

"Fifty-four," she said.

He crunched some numbers.

"About four hundred thousand," he said. "That's assuming you live to eighty-five."

She grunted and gazed through the glass door for a while. Outside, the almost-empty parking lot baked in the midday sun.

"Maybe you can get another guard job," she said. "If you change your ways a little, that is."

He nodded absently, then frowned. "What do you mean, change my ways?"

"The way you do things. Your routine."

"My what?"

She looked amused. "It's worked okay here, I'll admit. But there's not much of a problem here."

"What the hell are you talking about, Stella?"

"I'm talking about your routine, Artie. Your schedule. You come in at seven, you unlock the door at seven-fifteen, you go get a Coke at eight-thirty, you make your rounds at nine, you go to the bathroom at nine-fifteen."

"You know when I go to the bathroom?"

"Everybody knows. You do everything, all day long, at exactly the same time."

He fumed a little, then asked, "What's wrong with that?"

"Nothing, if you run the cafeteria. But if you're a security guard . . ."

"What."

She shrugged. "If I were a crook I could steal the place blind. This is a bank, Artie, money passes in and out of here all the time. It's not good for people to know where you are, and what you're doing, every minute of the day."

He gave that some thought. "So what are you suggesting?"

"I'm suggesting you change your pattern a little, this last week. Take your breaks at different times. Come in early, or stay later. Make a run over to Walmart now and then. It'll do you good."

Arthur scratched his chin. "What if the armored car came while I was gone?" He glanced at the north door. "Who'd let 'em in?"

She shrugged again. "You could leave me the key."

"Who'd open the vault?" The regional Federal Reserve depository was located here, in the basement.

"I could. I've done it before."

He thought that over. She was right: he'd been sick

once, in the john, and Estelle had let them in and out again.

"Maybe I will," he said. "Maybe it is time for a change."

And that was when the idea hit him.

After a long moment she seemed to sense his eyes on her, and turned to face him.

"What?" she said.

***

Five days later the investigation was in full swing. Half a dozen Feds had arrived last night, and the bank CEO himself had been there all day, wringing his hands and making phoned updates every ten minutes to the head of the acquiring bank. No one knew what had happened to the cash delivery that had arrived yesterday morning; they only knew that some of it had disappeared—and so had Estelle Feeney.

Arthur Speed answered all their questions calmly and professionally. He had been away from his post at the time, yes, but only to go to the break room. Everything had been locked, and he had the only key. If Ms. Feeney unlocked the vault, as some had implied, she must have been forced to, with a copied key, and was probably lying dead in a ditch somewhere by now. After much fingerprinting and cellphoning and gnashing of teeth, the authorities and executives left the scene, and even though Arthur Speed was investigated and cleared, he was advised not to leave town for the next week or so.

That, he figured, was no problem. After all, this Friday was his last day with the bank, and he wasn't due in Puerto Vallarta for another month. It would take that long for Estelle to find them a place there, and to make sure the cash—exactly $650,000—was safely laundered through the Caymans and deposited in the appropriate branches in Mexico.

Arthur and Estelle, you see, had decided they had nothing against banks—or even mergers.

They were just making adjustments.

The Last Sunset

All things considered, Jerry thought, it wasn't a bad day to die.

Not that he was happy about the idea. In fact, he was so scared his stomach was in knots. But if it had to happen . . .

He sighed. From the grassy hill where he was sitting he could see for miles, out past the golf course and the radio tower, to where the trees changed from green to blue to misty gray. Not a cloud was in sight. Off to his right, warming one side of his face with its dying glow, the sun balanced like a fat orange on the surface of the bay. It wouldn't be long now, he told himself.

He shivered as he remembered his dream.

It snapped on in his mind like a movie in a deserted theater, a private screening for him alone. Every detail was as clear and sharp and real as anything he'd ever experienced, asleep or awake.

Jerry had been told, in his dream last night, that this was to be his last day on earth. He had actually heard the words, four words, spoken in a deep and unfamiliar voice: "Tomorrow you will die." And he had seen, displayed on the wide screen of his subconscious, the image of a setting sun, and a grassy hillside.

Then, as the dream sun set into the waters of the dream sea, an eerie light appeared. Huge, boiling clouds materialized from nowhere. And as his sleeping eyes watched them, the clouds parted and the sky split open and . . .

Jerry had jerked awake in his bed, sweating and terrified, and had slept no more. At dawn, twelve hours ago, the dream had still been on his mind—how could it not have been?—but he discovered that his reaction to it had changed. In the light of the rising sun through his bedroom window, he felt a strange calmness. If he was truly destined to die this afternoon, said a voice inside his head, why waste time worrying about it? Why not make the best of the time he had left?

And that's exactly what he did. Since this was Saturday, he wheeled his bicycle out of the garage and pedalled to a park a few miles from his house. On the way he saw a group of homeless men and women sitting on the curb, and without a second thought—he wondered if he was in some kind of hypnotic trance—he stopped his bike and gave each of them a ten-dollar bill. Almost the entire contents of his billfold. When a raggedly dressed little girl appeared from behind one of the women, he gave her his bike.

Ten minutes later he passed an outdoor basketball court. Under one goal were several surly-looking black teenagers about his own age; under the other were white guys with preppie haircuts and expensive sneakers. Both groups were shooting baskets, but were also shooting angry looks at the other ends of the court. When Jerry strolled over to join the blacks, they stiffened and exchanged puzzled glances. Before a word could be spoken Jerry picked up a ball, took a few shots, and grinned at the players with such open confidence they didn't know how to respond. Then, looking pleased, he walked to the other end of the court. He told the preppie group the blacks wanted to play a game, but only if the teams were mixed, half and half. While the whites were pondering that surprising information, he went back to the other goal and told the black guys the same thing. Within minutes he had the groups combined and competing, though tentatively; and when he left half an hour later they were playing as if they'd known each other for years.

That was only the beginning. Over the next eight hours, he was a one-man goodwill mission. He treated a crippled war veteran to a hot dog, broke up two fistfights and a drug deal, waded into a duckpond to retrieve a toy sailboat for a weeping child, and spent two hours helping elementary-school kids wash cars for the Cancer Society.

Quite a day. And the strangest thing was, he had performed all these actions—these Good Samaritan deeds that until today he would never even have considered—without a moment's hesitation. He had done them because it had seemed the proper thing to do. And he found himself enjoying it. At one point in the afternoon, on an impulse, he had even sent an order of flowers to his mother, who lived alone a few blocks away.

He wondered now about the flowers as he sat in the cool grass of the hillside, watching the sun sink into the waves. He tried to imagine his mom's reaction when she saw the bouquet, when she read the card he'd enclosed. It had been two years since he and his father had last seen her. What would she feel? Surprise? Relief? Love? All three, probably.

He decided he was glad he'd sent them. They would almost certainly make her feel good.

The same way Jerry himself had been feeling good, all day long.

But now it was over, he thought. And not just the day—his life was over.

He heaved another sigh, and watched the blazing rim of the sun vanish below the horizon.

It was time.

He braced himself, waiting for the clouds and the strange light, waiting for the heavens to open, for the universe to split apart like a melon, for the rush of wind or the blast of heat or whatever would happen when the world came to an end . . .

But nothing happened.

He waited another minute, then five, then ten. The crickets were singing now, stars sparkled in an indigo sky, fireflies winked all around him. Somewhere over the hill to his left, a baseball game was underway. He could see the reflection of the field's lights on the trees, could hear the crack of a bat and the murmur of the crowd. A hawk circled overhead.

Still nothing happened.

Slowly, with a growing sense of relief, Jerry realized he was going to live. There would be no Armageddon, no fiery apocalypse—at least not tonight. The dream had only been a dream.

But he knew that wasn't quite true. Something had happened, something he didn't understand. Something was different, if only in his mind.

After a while, when it was full dark, Jerry rose to his feet. The ballgame on the far side of the hill was over; the night was still and quiet. The air smelled of honeysuckle. A full moon floated like a pearl in the cloudless sky.

A wonderful place, he thought, looking around him. A fine and wonderful night to be alive.

He glanced at his watch. Nine o'clock. It was early yet. He wondered, as he started down the hill, whether his mother was still up.

Her place, after all, was on his way home . . .

Angel on Duty

Since Sheriff Charles Jones had never been fond of work—even during normal business hours—he held overtime in especially low regard. And the very last thing he needed now, elbow deep in neglected paperwork at 9:50 p.m., was a complaint from retired schoolteacher and self-professed crime-fighter Angela Potts. But wouldn't you know it, here she was, looming over his desk with chin outthrust and fists planted on hips, bellowing loud enough to wake babies on the other side of town. The only things missing were blond braids and a spear and body armor.

"And a horned helmet," he murmured.

She stopped in midsentence. "What did you say?"

"Nothing. I was thinking you might need a new hat."

"What I *need*," she said, "is some cooperation, after I took the time to come over here."

Her presence here, of course, wasn't unusual at all—but her topic was. The current thorn under her saddle was neighborhood speed-demons, of all things. Angela had apparently heard from her buddy Bertha Woods that speedbumps had been installed in residential areas in the next county, and wanted to know why it hadn't been done here, where drunken hooligans roared up and down her street at all hours of the night. As an honest and law-abiding taxpayer, she informed him that she was sick and tired of living in a town with not only incompetent leaders but incompetent law enforcement, and so on and so on.

He listened to her rave awhile longer, then blew out a weary sigh.

"What can I say, Ms. Potts. Tell it to the mayor, tomorrow. I don't do speedbumps."

Angela snorted. "Trouble is, you don't do much of anything, Chunky Jones. If you ask me—"

He held up a finger to interrupt her. "Come to think of it, I *will* ask you something: Why are you out and roaming around at ten o'clock at night?" He pointed the same finger, unnecessarily, at the clock on his wall.

She didn't bother looking at it. What she did was stand up even straighter, fold her arms like Mr. Clean, and study him as if he were some kind of rare and interesting bug. It reminded him of thirty years ago, when she was his fifth-grade teacher. Her penetrating gaze, then and now, made him want to scurry under his desk and hide.

But she wasn't really mad at him—he knew that by now. Hell, she probably wasn't even that upset about the speed-bump issue. The simple truth was, Angela Potts just liked to complain. She also liked to aggravate him. For one thing, she always called him Chunky, an old nickname which she knew he hated. (Nicknames were abundant in small-town America, and he suspected it annoyed her that he never addressed her as "Angel" even though everyone else in town did, or even "Angela"—he insisted on calling her Ms. Potts, probably because his subconscious still considered her his school-teacher.) Another sore spot was that she tended to correct his grammar all the time, even in front of his deputies or the mayor or whoever else happened to be in the vicinity.

Angela Potts, bless her grouchy soul, was one of a kind. Thank God.

She informed him, in a patient voice, "I am 'out and roaming around at ten o'clock at night,' as you put it, so I can be back home before twelve."

"And why's that?"

Sudden amusement twinkled in her eyes. "Don't you know what happens to angels at midnight?"

Not only did he not know, he didn't care. But it turned out not to matter anyway, because at that moment a young man with red hair and a pimply face and a Dixie Chicks T-shirt burst into the office.

Timothy Weeks, the disc jockey at the local radio station, stood there in the doorway, wide-eyed and panting.

"Come quick, Sheriff," he said. "Funny Sonny Jackson's robbed the law office."

***

It took less than two minutes to follow Tim Weeks across the deserted street—no speeders were in sight—to the Grayson Building and up the stairs to a long hallway. The door on the right said J. BINGHAM COLLINS, ATTORNEY AT LAW; the one on the left said WXIF RADIO. At the end of the hall was what looked like a break room. Tim and Angela and the sheriff paraded through the first door, where Becky Drennan—Bing Collins's spaced-out twentysomething assistant—sat staring at them with her mouth hanging open.

The sheriff broke the silence. "Becky, you remember Ms. Potts, right? From school?"

She snapped her mouth shut, then opened it and said,

"Hi, Miss Angel."

Angela nodded but didn't reply. The sheriff knew her sharp eyes were already checking out the scene.

He took a moment too, to glance around the office. It was small and neat and functional. On one wall was the darkened doorway to the lawyer's inner sanctum; overhead, a sluggish ceiling fan shifted the warm air around. "Want to tell us what happened?"

Becky swallowed. "The cashbox," she said, tilting her bleached-blond head toward an empty shelf behind her. "It's missing. I was sitting right here at my desk when he took it."

"Sonny Jackson?"

"Yes sir."

"So you saw him?" Sheriff Jones was trying to keep his voice steady. He was still puffing a little from the climb to the second floor.

"Tim did."

All of them turned to look at Tim Weeks, whose goldfish eyes grew even wider. "I had just cued up Bon Jovi and was looking out my window," he said. "There's a streetlight outside—I saw Funny Sonny leave our building and go down the sidewalk."

"You sure it was Sonny Jackson?" the sheriff said.

"Yessir."

"But *you* didn't see him?" he asked Becky.

"I never saw anybody," she said. "I was turned the other way, like this"—she swiveled to face her computer—"typing a letter." She wiggled her fingers a little, apparently to make sure everyone understood the typing process. "Tim and I are the only ones here this time of night—him in his office, me in mine."

"Was Sonny carrying the cashbox when you saw him from the window, Tim?"

"Couldn't tell, Sheriff. But it was him all right. I came

in to ask Becky what he'd been doing here, and that's when she noticed the box was gone." Tim glanced at his watch and made a sound like a strangled chicken. "'Scuse me, I gotta go start my next song." He dashed out and across the hall to the radio station.

Sheriff Jones thought a moment. "Was your door—the one to the hallway—open or closed?" he asked Becky.

"Closed."

"And you didn't hear anybody come in?"

She held up her iPod. "I was listening to Garth," she said. At full blast, probably. Sheriff Jones, who had a teenaged niece, figured Tarzan could've driven a herd of elephants up the stairs with Cheetah screaming on his shoulder and Becky wouldn't have heard it.

Angela, quiet until now, said, "There's no A/C in here, Becky, and the fan doesn't help much—why keep your door closed, when it's this hot?"

Becky Drennan wrinkled her cute nose. "Folks smoke in the break room, during the day. I hate the smell, even after hours."

"But that room's all the way at the end of the hall, right?"

"I got a good sniffer." Becky looked at the sheriff. "Matter of fact I can smell smoke on you, right now, Sheriff."

"Wrong," he said. "I don't smoke."

"I didn't say you did. I can smell it on your clothes."

"His wife smokes," Angela explained.

"That's it, then." Becky made a face. "You might try baking soda, or vinegar."

A little irked at having two different women ordering him around when he wasn't even home, the sheriff said, "What're you doing with a cashbox anyway, in a law office?"

She frowned at him. "We're a small town, Sheriff. Some

of Bing's clients don't even have a checking account."

Which made sense, he realized. "But why would Sonny Jackson—or whoever it was—take the whole box?"

"Because it was locked." Becky dug two fingers into her skintight jeans pocket and finally produced a key. She seemed to have a sudden thought then, and her eyes bugged out as wide as Tim's had been. "Think he'll have to use explosives to get it open?"

***

Further questioning produced nothing useful, which was no great surprise. After fifteen sweltering minutes Angela and the sheriff left and trudged the three blocks to Bernardo's, the Mexican restaurant where Funny Sonny Jackson worked as a waiter. It was after closing time, but the sheriff's pained expression and a badge held up to the window got them inside. When they asked the manager if Sonny was still there, they were boredly directed to his section of tables in the back of the establishment.

Funny Sonny, a usually grinning fellow (hence his nickname), seemed especially happy at first to get a break from the challenging task of emptying ashtrays and stacking chairs. When the sheriff asked him the zillion-dollar question, though, Sonny's ready smile disappeared. In fact he appeared stunned by the news of the crime. He explained that he had worked the supper shift here and had then delivered a pre-ordered container of salsa to the empty break room on the second floor of the Grayson building around 9:45, just before the time Tim Weeks had said he'd spotted Sonny leaving. But the waiter swore he hadn't entered Bingham Collins's law office.

With a call on his cell phone the sheriff dispatched Deputy Fred Prewitt to the crime scene. Ten minutes later Prewitt reported that the delivery checked out—he'd found an unopened order of Bernardo's salsa in the break-room's refrigerator, along with a bill bearing today's date, taped to the fridge door. Which did not, of course, mean Sonny was innocent—it just gave him a reason to have been inside the building. But there was as yet no real proof that he was guilty, either.

If this job were easy, the sheriff thought glumly, anyone could do it.

At Angela's whispered suggestion and against his better judgment, he made no arrest. Instead he issued a firm warning to Sonny not to leave town—he loved telling people that—and then they headed back to the sheriff's office, where Angela assumed her usual station in the chair across from the desk. She seemed almost cheerful now that there was a mystery afoot, showing no hint of the formidable Viking soprano who'd stomped into the room half an hour ago.

It occurred to the sheriff that the reason Angela had been involved in so many of his cases over the years was that she'd usually been right here, hanging around his office, when he first received word about them. *I've got a nose for trouble, Chunky*, she'd once told him. *I can smell it a mile away*. He sometimes believed she could.

"The important thing," she said to him now, as she selected a Bite-Size Baby Ruth from a jar on his desk, "is that we verified that Sonny came straight to the building from his shift at the restaurant."

Sheriff Jones put his frustration aside and tried to concentrate. Angela Potts was smarter than he was, and he knew it. When he needed her help, he was actually pleased by that fact—her quick thinking had pulled his charred hindquarters out of the fire on many occasions. Other times it was just another of the things about her that irritated him. "Why's that important?" he asked.

Instead of answering, she said, "I think you should

search the WXIF office, Chunky. And Tim Weeks's car too, I saw it parked in the lot across the street. I doubt Becky Drennan's involved—she's not the brightest bulb in the chandelier, but she's not dumb enough to try something like this. Besides, if she had, she would've just taken the money, not the whole cashbox."

"So you think *Tim* stole it?"

The sheriff waited while she sampled another chocolate. "These things are great," she said, her mouth full. "I thought you were cutting back."

"I am. I only keep those for when you visit. So you think Tim Weeks—"

"Chocolate *and* peanuts. You don't know what you're missing."

He sighed and rubbed his eyes. "It's late, Ms. Potts. Bear with me. You think *Tim Weeks* stole the cashbox?"

"I don't know who stole it. I just know Funny Sonny didn't."

"How do you know that?"

"Trust me. Just check Tim's office and car."

He did a palms-up. "How? Judge Bailey won't okay a warrant without a reason."

"He will if you tell him it includes searching Sonny's car too. You'll be 'expediting justice'—you know, covering all the bases at once."

"Where'd you come up with that?"

"*CSI: Miami*." She paused. "Sure you don't want a Baby Ruth?"

"*CSI: Miami*?"

"Or *Law and Order*. Which one has Lieutenant Caine?"

Sheriff Jones thought he could actually feel his blood pressure spiking. "What if this doesn't work, Ms. Potts?"

"What do you mean?"

"What if we don't find anything? We'll look like a couple of fools, you and me."

"You and I," she said. Which irritated him even more.

***

An hour and a hasty search warrant later, Tim Weeks was in custody and cooling his heels in the jail next door. The cashbox had been found stashed in the trunk of his rusted Saturn, between a stack of *Entertainment Weekly* magazines and a pair of old high-topped Reeboks. When confronted with the evidence by the sheriff and both his deputies, Tim tearfully confessed to sneaking into the law office and stealing the box while Becky Drennan was merrily typing and grooving to her country music with her back turned, four feet away.

"How'd you know, Ms. Potts?" the sheriff asked again, when they were alone once more in his office. "Was it something Becky said?"

Angela smiled. "It was something she *didn't* say."

"What do you mean?"

She leaned back in her chair and lowered her head, an act which produced at least three chins. It crossed his mind that she was every bit as hefty as he was, despite his nickname.

"You of course know," she began, "that our good-for-nothing mayor continues to reject the smoke-free building ordinance."

"I of course know that," he said. Impatiently.

"And the smoking section at Bernardo's is located at the back of the restaurant, where we were awhile ago, right? I mean, that's where the tables with the ashtrays are."

"So?"

"So, we were told that that was Sonny Jackson's station tonight. He said he'd worked his shift there, before going over to the lawyer's building to deliver the order of salsa."

The sheriff sighed. "*So*?"

Angela took her time, along with another Baby Ruth mini from his jar. "Think about it. If Sonny worked the smoking section during supper, then came over and entered the office where Becky was and stood right behind her to grab the cash-box, she would've smelled the smoke on his clothing—especially since she has a sensitive nose—and would've been aware, *immediately* aware, of his presence." She unwrapped the chocolate and examined it as if it were a fine diamond. "In fact, she'd have smelled him even if it weren't for the smoke on him, with or without that creaky ceiling fan of hers. I love Bernardo's, but the odor of Mexican cooking has a way of seeping into your clothes. And since Becky *didn't* smell anything strange—"

"He wasn't there," the sheriff finished.

She popped the Baby Ruth into her mouth. "Right."

"So you suspected Tim—"

"Because there was no one else to suspect," she said, chewing. "I figure what happened was, Tim saw Sonny leaving the building, and since he now had someone to accuse, snuck into Becky's office right then and snatched the box. He probably stowed it in his car, ran back up to make sure Becky had discovered it was missing, then hotfooted over here to report the crime."

Sheriff Jones nodded slowly. He found himself staring out the window at the summer night, thinking. A soft breeze riffled the pear trees lining the sidewalk. Halfway down the block, in an island of yellow light from a streetlamp, old Claude Edgemore was being hauled along by a leash attached to a dog as big as he was. Thunder grumbled in the distance.

Her version made sense, the sheriff decided. He probably wouldn't have seen it if he had a hundred years to mull it over, but Angela Potts, a.k.a. Amateur Sleuth and Pain in the Patooty, had figured it out in no time.

"And now," she announced, "even though I know how much you enjoy my companionship and I certainly know how much I enjoy your snacks"—she licked her fingers, hoisted herself from the chair, and hitched her purse-strap higher on her shoulder—"I have to get home."

He looked up at the clock, and she followed his gaze. "You barely made it," he said. It was ten minutes to twelve.

She helped herself to another bite-sized chocolate for the road and turned to the door. As she opened it he said, "I have to ask."

"Ask what?"

"A while ago, you said something like, 'Don't you know what happens to angels at midnight?'"

"And?"

"Well, what's the answer?" he asked. "What does happen to angels at midnight?"

She grinned, and wiggled her eyebrows. "They become devils."

He stared at the closed door for a long time after she left, thinking about her and trying not to smile. Finally, just before leaving for home himself, he found a box of letterhead stationery and wrote up a formal request to the mayor and aldermen. He of course knew it was a waste of time. The board members would never install speedbumps in town—most of them were speeders themselves.

But what the hell.

He signed the letter, dropped it in his OUT basket, and regarded the stack of waiting paperwork for a full minute before deciding that it could wait another day. Then he picked up his hat and paused again, his eyes on the candy jar.

He ate three Baby Ruths on his way to the car.

Backward Thinking

"Hattie Phillips told you *what*?" Sheriff Jones asked.

Retired schoolteacher and professional nuisance Angela Potts was once again standing at the sheriff's desk, arms folded, staring down at him. She had stared at him the same way when he was a troublemaker in her fifth-grade class. It still gave him goosebumps.

"Are you deaf?" she said. "I said she told me somebody phoned her, and whoever phoned her said Delbert Smith was at home, dead."

"And she didn't recognize the caller's voice?"

"Only that it was a woman."

The sheriff didn't bother to ask if Hattie Phillips had Caller ID. At age ninety-four, she probably still had a rotary dial. "Fred and I'll go check on him," he said. He beckoned to Deputy Fred Prewitt, who followed him out to the sheriff's patrol car.

"I'll come with you," Angela said, hot on their heels.

"No, just go home, Ms. Potts. We can handle—"

"Take the back seat," she told Prewitt. "I'll ride shotgun."

***

They arrived to find Delbert Smith's house unlocked and his garage empty. Nobody was home. Two rubber-banded newspapers lay in the driveway.

"Looks like he left," the sheriff said, "two days ago."

"What a detective," Angela said. Deputy Prewitt grinned, but sobered quickly when his boss scowled at him.

"Okay, Ms. Potts, if you're so damn smart—why didn't he lock his doors?"

"Delbert? He never locks his doors. Some say he's so mean nobody'd dare steal from him." They were inside now, looking around.

"Mean enough for someone to want him dead?"

She snorted. "Get in line."

"What?"

"Some things in town you have to be old to know about. You're too young, Chunky, and Fred hasn't lived here long enough."

"What are you talking about?"

"Before you were born, Delbert Smith sold his daddy's paper mill, and put half this side of the county out of work. Not many folks liked him."

"Well, *some*body does," Prewitt said. He pointed to a note on the kitchen table:

> MR. SMITH—HOPE YOU HAD A NICE DAY AT CHARLES'S LAKE. BROUGHT YOU SOME FRESH-SQUEEZED ORANGE JUICE. GOOD VITAMINS!

It was signed L.M. Inside the refrigerator they found a

pitcher of OJ.

"What's that mean, 'a nice day'?" the sheriff asked. "He's been gone since Monday. And 'Charles's lake'?"

"Charles Baker's, I guess," Angela said. "Though that's more of a pond."

"And who's L.M.?"

"Probably Lisa Moon—she's a new home-health-care nurse. Fred, why don't you try to contact her? Chunky, you check with Delbert's relatives. I'll start questioning neighbors."

"Excuse me, Ms. Potts, but I'm the boss here. Not you."

"Right. By the way, you might try calling his son first," she said. "And Fred, you start with the hospital."

***

An hour later she found something. Mabel Judd, three doors down, had seen an '85 Chevy Impala with a 1990 license plate parked in Delbert Smith's driveway at 10:50 a.m. Monday.

"Nineteen ninety?" the sheriff said, when Angela reported in. "But that's sixteen years ago."

"My God—you finally learned how to subtract," she said.

"Wait a second. Old Lady Judd can't read her Bingo card. How could she read a license sticker?" In their county, car tags for even-numbered years took the form of a small two-digit sticker on the previous year's plate.

"Binoculars," Angela said. "Mabel spies on the neighbors."

"Well, did she happen to see who got back in the car?"

"She said she missed that. Her soap operas start at eleven."

The sheriff decided not to even respond to that. Instead he made some more calls. According to motor vehicle records, there were only two 1985 Impalas in the area—Joe Ames's and Emma Crump's—and both owners had recently bought 2006 stickers. Ames was away at college, and Emma Crump only came into town on Thursdays, for Ladies' Day at the church.

"Emma's a little unusual," Angela said. "She gets things turned around. She once hid Easter eggs at Halloween."

"Well, if he was murdered, I doubt it was the nurse," Prewitt said. "The hospital says she's in Memphis this week."

Angela frowned. "One thing's certain: Whoever called Hattie Phillips thought Delbert Smith was dead already."

They were mulling that over when the sheriff's cell phone rang. Moments later he said, "That was Delbert's son in Louisiana, returning my call. Delbert's down there visiting—he arrived Monday around noon."

"Where in Louisiana?" Angela asked.

"Lake Charles."

She blinked. "Excuse me a minute, boys."

When she'd left, Prewitt asked, "Where's she going?"

"Heaven only knows," the sheriff said. "Probably Dairy Queen."

***

An hour later Angela returned, wearing a wide grin.

"Chocolate sundae?" Sheriff Jones asked.

"Actually, I've been to the general store, Smartypants, and then to Emma Crump's."

"She tell you anything?"

"No," Angela said. "But I think she tried to kill Delbert."

"What?! How do you know?"

"Several things. Emma's father was one of those who lost his job, at Smith & Company. She was away then, living in California, and probably didn't know—but her dad died last month, and I bet she found something in his papers."

"But you said that was years ago—"

"I also said Emma's not the brightest light in the fixture."

Angela flopped into a chair. "I think that orange juice should be tested—and check the pitcher for prints."

"What for?"

"Jesse Tyler at the store says Emma bought rat poison last Saturday. I think she spiked the juice, stuck it in Delbert's fridge Monday morning, wrote the note, and signed Lisa Moon's initials to throw him—and us—off. Emma must've heard he'd be gone, but as usual she got things backward: He went three hundred miles to Lake Charles, not three miles to Charles's lake. She figured he'd be home soon and drink the poisoned OJ. Anyhow, she waited two days to be safe, then called the town gossip to report his death."

The sheriff frowned. "That's a long shot, Ms. Potts."

"There's one more thing."

"What?"

"Her car. It really was at Delbert's on Monday morning."

"How do you figure that?" he asked.

"Remember I said Emma sometimes gets things turned around?"

"Yes . . ."

"The new '06' sticker on her license plate looked like '90' in Mabel Judd's binoculars," Angela said. "Emma had put the sticker on upside down."

Both men stared at her. After a moment the sheriff shook his head and grinned. "Not bad, Ms. Potts. Not bad at all."

She seemed to be trying not to smile. "Did you say 'Ms. Potts'?" she asked.

"Isn't that your name?"

"I prefer 'Detective,'" she said.

A Day at the Office

Retired teacher Angela Potts was driving past the Dale mansion when she saw all three county patrol cars out front. She parked beside them, stomped up the steps to the porch, and asked, “What happened?”

Sheriff Chunky Jones, one of her former students in her former life, was—as usual—less than overjoyed to see her. He sighed and said, “Melvin Dale was shot dead in his office, two hours ago. His son Jimmy was with him. Jimmy says someone fired through the open window.”

“Show me,” she said.

She followed him to the “office,” a big one-room building in the muddy backyard. The body had already been removed. Hung on the wall above Melvin’s desk was a collection of old weapons: swords, spears, a bow strung and ready, a quiver of arrows, a cutlass. No guns.

“The maid at the main house says she heard the shot,” the sheriff said. “She came running, but found the door locked.

She called us on her cell phone."

"Locked?"

"A private meeting, Jimmy said."

"Did she see anyone else on the property?" Angela asked.

"Did who see anyone else?"

"Who do you think? The maid."

"No."

She thought that over. "I hear Jimmy has gambling debts. He's the only heir—maybe *he* shot Melvin."

"If he did, he's a magician. We were with the maid when Jimmy finally opened the door, and he didn't have a gun on him. We've searched the room top to bottom."

"The window's open—maybe he threw it out."

The sheriff shook his head. "Nope. We looked. And the window's too small for him to climb though, hide the gun, and climb back in."

Looking through it, Angela could see a lawn sloping down to a pond fifty feet away. "I assume you asked Jimmy to unlock the door. Why didn't he do it earlier?"

"Said he was in shock."

Angela studied the room. "Did the maid see anything out of place, in here?"

"Just this." The sheriff pointed to a Scotch Tape dispenser. "She says it's usually stored in a cabinet."

"How about this mud here, on the desktop?"

"Don't know."

She thought some more. "Where's Jimmy now?"

"With my deputy, at the main house. He's still pretty shaken."

Angela pointed to the sheriff's radio. "Let me talk to Prewitt."

Sheriff Jones hesitated, then buzzed Deputy Fred

Prewitt and handed his radio to Angela.

"Fred?" she said. "Angel Potts. Ask the maid if she cleans this office. She does? Good—ask her how many arrows are hanging on the wall." A pause. "Four, she says?"

Both Angela and the sheriff turned and looked. The quiver contained three arrows.

"Okay, Fred, listen. I want you to tell Jimmy that we know he killed Melvin—"

The sheriff gasped and reached for the handset, but Angela stepped away.

"—and that we can prove it. Understand?"

"Ms. Potts, give me that—"

"Tell him, Fred," Angela said, as the sheriff snatched the radio from her.

"Prewitt?" he shouted, into the handset. Then, to Angela: "He's gone. What do you think you're doing, telling him that?!"

"I know exactly what I'm doing. Just hold your water."

After a moment Prewitt's voice came back on the line. The sheriff listened, then said, "Okay. I'm coming." Stunned, he disconnected.

"What did he say?" Angela asked.

Sheriff Jones blinked and stared at her. "Prewitt says when he told Jimmy what you said—he snapped. He tried to run."

Angela smiled. "I figured he might."

"You going to tell me what happened?" the sheriff asked.

"What happened was well planned." She nodded toward the wall. "I think Jimmy Dale killed Melvin, climbed onto the desktop—hence the mud—got that bow down, taped his gun to an arrow, and shot it through the open window."

"What?"

"Then he hung the bow up again. The gun's probably tiny, and light. Derringer-sized."

"But—I told you, we searched the lawn."

"Not the lawn. He could've *thrown* it that far. He shot it into the pond."

"The pond? Is that even *possible?*"

"Sure. He didn't need accuracy, or style—it only had to go twenty yards." She pointed. "Get divers out here. I bet they'll find the gun and arrow on the bottom."

Slowly the sheriff nodded. "But . . . if that's what happened— how'd you figure it out?"

She grinned. "Jimmy didn't put everything back the way he found it."

"What do you mean?"

She pointed to the bow on the wall. "Bows are always stored with their strings loosened, to relieve the tension. But that one—"

"Is still strung," the sheriff finished.

"That's right. Because Jimmy used it."

Sheriff Jones pondered that a long time, then sighed.

"Guess my problem now is, where am I gonna find divers? This ain't exactly the Coast, you know."

Angela was grinning as she headed for the door. "You and Prewitt can do it yourselves—the city park'll let you borrow flippers and masks. But if you do"—she stopped and looked back at him—"call me and I'll bring my camcorder."

"For the ten o'clock news?"

"For *Funniest Home Videos.*"

Sweet Caroline

Sheriff Chunky Jones was hanging up the phone when Angela Potts barreled into his office. And—for once—he knew what she was going to say before she even opened her mouth.

"I heard already," he said to her. The news that Leonard Cobb's fancy boat had been stolen last night from his rural home was a big deal, in a town their size.

Angela dropped into a chair. "Effie Thompson's saying she saw the whole thing."

"Not the whole thing, she didn't."

"Explain."

The sheriff shrugged. "Effie had a good view, since she lives right across the street—but all she saw in the dark was a small pickup backing into Cobb's driveway and then towing Cobb's boat and trailer out again. And because she was staring into the headlights—and hiding—she couldn't see who jumped out to hook the trailer on. It left going east, though, toward town." He thought a moment. "How old is Effie now, do you know?"

"Ninety-two," Angela said, as she unwrapped a Tootsie Roll. "But don't worry, she can see like a hawk."

"If you say so."

"What color was the truck?" Angela asked.

"That, she didn't see."

"Even when it turned onto the main road?"

"She missed that part," he said. "Left her window too soon."

"What?"

"She said *Grey's Anatomy* was coming on."

"That's true—it moved to Thursday nights."

The sheriff rolled his eyes.

"But if Effie didn't see it leave," Angela said, chewing, "how do you know it went east?"

"Because there's another witness."

"Who?"

"Sam Shelton. He was out jogging—he lives west of Cobb, you know—and said he glimpsed a set of taillights going the other direction, down the long straightaway toward town."

"He only saw taillights?"

"Almost a mile away."

"How do we know it was the thief's taillights?" she asked.

"Well, that's an isolated road, and Shelton said he saw this around eight p.m.—the same time that Effie's TV show came on and she left her window. Gotta be the same vehicle."

Angela seemed to consider that, then nodded. "No one else saw anything?"

"Just Shelton and Effie Thompson."

"Who called you first?"

"Effie. Early this morning. She'd forgotten until then that the Cobbs are out of town for three days. She'd already phoned Shelton—he's her only other neighbor out there—and he called me later to give me his info."

A silence passed. "A small truck, you said?"

"According to Effie. And I know what you're thinking, Ms. Potts—Cobb's boat's a big one, a lot wider than a compact pickup. But it could still be towed."

Angela stayed quiet awhile, then asked, "What's the name of the boat?"

"It's an Aquasport, I think."

"No, I mean the *name.* Written on the side."

The sheriff checked his notes. "'Sweet Caroline.' Why?"

Instead of answering, she sat up straight and said, "This is someone local, Chunky."

"How so?"

"Two reasons. First, because it wasn't done in the wee hours. Someone knew the Cobbs were away, and probably that Effie was supposed to be away too—she had a cruise booked, and cancelled at the last minute."

"She's past ninety and she goes on cruises?"

"Effie's pretty spry. Point is, someone thought everyone would be gone, so it'd be safe to do this at eight o'clock at night." She seemed to think of something, and glanced at the candy jar on his desk. "You got any chocolates? Maybe a Baby Ruth?"

"Wouldn't he have seen Effie's lights on?"

"Ate 'em all already, huh?"

He sighed and repeated, "Wouldn't he have seen Effie's lights?"

"Probably—but a lot of folks put their lights on a timer when they're gone."

"What's the other reason?"

"I've seen Cobb's boat trailer," she said. "It's homemade

and low to the ground, with nothing but wheels and a hitch and a tall wooden frame. No wiring, no lights, no frills. It's for short trips and back roads. Whoever stole it wouldn't want to go far."

"But how could someone local keep, or even sell, that boat without being discovered?"

"Don't know." She frowned. "Maybe you should check out Sam Shelton."

"What?"

"Cobb married Shelton's ex-wife, remember? And her name's Caroline."

The sheriff thought that over. "And you figure Shelton still holds a grudge?"

"You have a better idea?"

"Matter of fact, I do." He rose from his chair. "It's called breakfast."

Angela stood also, studied his vast belly, and said, "Finally, something you're good at."

***

She phoned him before he'd finished half the donuts he'd brought back from Roscoe's Cafe.

"Guess where I am," she said.

"A meeting of Worrywarts Anonymous?"

"I'm at Sam Shelton's boathouse. And guess what I'm looking at."

"A boat?"

"A boat with SWEET CAROLINE painted on it. The trailer's hidden in the woods."

The sheriff almost choked on his donut. "You're kidding."

"There are also several concrete blocks inside the boat, and a cordless drill. I think he plans to sink it, Chunky." She added, "You better send Deputy Prewitt over here, quick."

"Where's Shelton?"

"Who knows. I tiptoed here through the trees by the

river."

The sheriff tried to picture Angela Potts tiptoeing anywhere, and failed.

Afterward, when Sam Shelton had been located and arrested, Sheriff Jones asked her, reluctantly, how she'd solved the case. "You didn't sneak down there just on a hunch," he said.

"No," she admitted. "Shelton lied to you."

"About what? Seeing the getaway vehicle?"

"Oh, he saw it all right—he was driving it. He lied about which way it went. And he knew to agree with Effie on the time, remember, because she called him before he called you."

"But how'd you know he lied?"

"Because," she said, "of something he *didn't* see."

"What do you mean?"

"The boat trailer was low-slung and tall and had no lights, right? Well, since the boat and trailer were so much bigger and wider than the truck towing them, the truck's taillights couldn't have been seen by someone a mile behind it on a straight road. Sam Shelton might well own a shirt with an S on it, but last I heard, he doesn't have X-ray vision."

"So he was lying," the sheriff said.

"Like a rug." Angela looked at her watch. "And I have to go—I promised Effie I'd drive her to Walmart."

"To buy new glasses, maybe?"

"To buy a big-screen TV."

A Piece of Cake

For at least the hundredth time, Sheriff Chunky Jones and his former schoolteacher Angela Potts were present at a crime scene. The differences were that (1) they were in the state capital, and (2) they were there by accident.

Sheriff Jones had come to the city for an old friend's retirement luncheon, and in a weak moment had agreed to take Angela along to visit her niece in the suburbs. That afternoon, before heading back to their hometown, they'd agreed on just about the only thing the two of them had in common: they both wanted to stop at a mall bakery shop for a snack.

They arrived the same time the local cops did—the shop had just been robbed.

The sheriff was reluctant to butt in on someone else's case, but Angela (who had perfected to a fine art the practice of butting in) dragged him close enough to overhear the story: a man dressed like John Wayne had held up the owner and escaped with the entire contents of the cash register.

"John Wayne?" one of the policemen asked.

"Spittin' image," said the aproned shopkeeper. "Big guy, hat, vest, red bandanna, six-shooter. He even squinted, and walked with the same swagger. 'Hand it over, Pilgrim,' he drawls to me. Sounded like the Duke himself."

"Sounds like a nut, to me," the cop said, then noticed the sheriff and Angela standing there. Sheriff Jones's reaction was to quietly back away; Angela's reaction, as usual, was to take charge. She blurted to the owner, "Which door did he use?"

Now both cops were staring at her. "Who are you?" one of them asked.

Angela lifted her chin. "This is Sheriff Charles Jones, and I'm his deputy," she lied.

"His what?"

She ignored that and asked again, "Where'd the robber enter from—mall or parking lot?"

"The mall," the owner said, pointing. "But he went out the other way."

Everyone looked at the mall door. Just beyond it were a long table and two girls in Scout uniforms. Without another word Angela turned and marched toward them. The sheriff followed. Before he left he heard one of the cops murmur something about country hicks.

When he caught up to Angela she was asking the Girl Scouts if they'd seen anyone come by dressed as a cowboy. One of them, wide-eyed, nodded.

"Mostly, I saw the top of his hat," the girl said.

"His hat?"

"He was bent over our table, writing."

"Writing what?"

"His raffle ticket." She pointed to a glass jar half-full of paper slips. "Our troop's giving away ten cakes from the bakery."

Angela and the sheriff swapped a glance. “You saw him write his name?” he asked.

“Name and phone number.”

“And the tickets go in that jar?”

“Yessir. Drawing’s next Saturday.”

Angela leaned over the jar. “Must be a hundred slips in there.” She looked up again. “You sure he filled one out?”

“Yes, ma’am.”

“Are the latest ones on top?”

“I doubt it. We shake ’em up now and then. Our leader said we should.”

Angela straightened up and tapped the sheriff’s badge. “This man’s a law officer, girls. We need to see those tickets.”

Without further explanation Angela dumped the jar’s contents onto the table. Carefully, touching only the corners, she began examining each slip.

“What’re you looking for?” the sheriff whispered.

“Don’t know yet.”

“Even if you find his ticket, which you can’t, you won’t know if it’s his real name.”

“It probably won’t be,” she agreed. “But I bet it’s his real phone number.”

“So you’re looking for a phone number?”

“I’m looking for a name.”

“What name?” he asked.

“I’m not sure yet.”

Sheriff Jones sighed. A typical exchange with Angela Potts. He wandered back past the stricken-looking Girl Scouts to the bakery shop, where more policemen were arriving.

Seven minutes later Angela called to him. On her little notepad she had written a number and the name MIKE MORRISON.

“Want to be a hero?” she asked. “Get the cops to find an

address for this phone number and send a car to that address. If that fails, they can lift fingerprints from the ticket."

"You think that's the robber?"

"Yep."

He studied the name. "Mike Morrison?"

"Just do it, okay?"

As it turned out, the man the police found at the address matching that phone number—Robert Nowell—was later positively ID'ed as the robber by the shopowner. Nowell proudly confessed that he used several false names, and that John Wayne was his lifelong hero.

Afterward, on the drive home, Sheriff Jones said, "That's a first—getting caught for trying to win a cake."

"Ten cakes," Angela corrected. "Like the cop said, the guy was crazy."

"Because he registered for the drawing?"

"No, that was just dumb. Writing the name was crazy. Either that, or he secretly wanted to be caught."

"About the name—how'd you know it was *him?*"

She grinned. "I used to read fan magazines."

"Explain," he said.

"John Wayne's real name wasn't John Wayne."

"What was it?"

"Marion Michael Morrison," she said.

The sheriff barked a laugh. "So that's why the police chief phoned you, before we left the scene? To congratulate the country bumpkin for solving their big-city crime?"

She gave him a smug look. "Not exactly."

"Well, then, what *did* he say?"

"He wanted to hire me away from you."

John M. Floyd

Cat Burglar

Sheriff Chunky Jones pushed through his office door just as Angela Potts was huffing up the outside steps. "There's a sale at the dollar store," she said. She held up a glass globe the size of a baseball; inside it, snowflakes swirled around a tiny log cabin. "I bought this for your desk."

The sheriff sighed. "Very nice, Ms. Potts. But I'm on my way out, right now—"

"Where to?" She stuffed the snow-globe into her purse and fell into step beside him.

"A lady in that new subdivision called in, said someone she didn't recognize was peeking into the window next door. She said the owner's name's Tim Brolin, some kind of writer who stays home while his wife works in town. I tried to phone him but there was no answer."

"So you're going to check it out, right? Come on, I'll give you a ride."

"I'm going alone. Besides, I thought your car was in the

shop."

"That's right, I forgot," she said, grinning. "I'll ride with you."

***

Five minutes later they arrived on Tim Brolin's front porch. The door opened just as the sheriff was about to ring the doorbell. "Mr. Brolin?" he said.

The man standing before them was tall and casually dressed. "Yes. Is something wrong?"

Sheriff Jones introduced himself and Angela, told Brolin about the reported prowler, and followed him inside. "Any problems, today?" the sheriff asked. "Seen any strangers around?"

"Not a soul. Maybe my neighbor was mistaken."

"Could be. Have you been out? I tried to call a few minutes ago."

"I was in the back yard. Can't hear the phone ring, from there."

A big calico glided into the room and curled into a chair. "Pretty cat," Angela said.

Brolin smiled. "We've had him for years—he's good company. A little grumpy sometimes, though."

"Lot of that going around," she said, with a glance at the sheriff. He scowled at her and was about to say something when he heard a siren wailing. He jumped, then realized it was coming from a TV. He could see the screen through a doorway into what looked like a den.

"Sorry," Brolin said. "I'll turn that off."

While he was gone Angela tugged the sheriff's shirt-sleeve. "Tell him you want to search the house," she hissed.

"What?"

"You heard me. Something's strange, here."

"But I don't have a warrant—"

"I didn't say *do* it. Just tell him you want to, and see what happens."

"But—"

"Tell him," she said.

When Tim Brolin returned and asked if there was anything else they needed, the sheriff cleared his throat and said, "Actually, I'd like to take a look around, if that's okay."

Brolin hesitated, then seemed to force a smile. "Of course. Help yourself."

The sheriff gave Angela a frustrated look, then nodded his thanks to Brolin and moved past him, toward the doorway to the den.

As soon as the sheriff's back was turned, Brolin shoved him with both hands and ran for the front door. The multicolored cat sprang from the chair and scooted under the couch.

Angela grabbed her new snow-globe from her purse, cocked her arm, and threw the globe—hard—at the fleeing man. It caught him square in the back of the head. He fell like a dropped ragdoll and lay still in the entranceway.

The sheriff had recovered in time to see what happened. Trembling and with gun drawn, he knelt beside the fallen man. "Out cold." To Angela he said, "Pretty good throw."

"I've won a few teddy bears at the state fair."

In the man's pockets they found cash and credit cards and tangled handfuls of jewelry. "We must've arrived just as he was leaving," the sheriff said.

After the suspect was handcuffed and revived, they checked the house. In a back bedroom they discovered an overturned jewelry box, along with another unconscious man. Inside the otherwise-empty wallet beside him was a driver's license that said TIMOTHY BROLIN. Angela fetched a damp cloth for the swelling bruise over his eyebrow, and within minutes the real homeowner was sitting up and moaning. The sheriff had already called for assistance.

While they waited the sheriff asked her, "How'd you know the first guy was a burglar?"

"I didn't," she said. She was examining her snow-globe, which appeared undamaged. "I just knew he didn't live here."

"How could you know that?"

She smiled. "Because my cousin's a veterinarian." She gave the globe a shake, then watched it snow.

"What?" he asked.

"Our burglar referred to the household cat as 'he.' Did you hear him say that?"

"I heard him. So?"

"So that made me ninety-nine percent certain he was lying."

The sheriff groaned. This was exactly the kind of thing that made Angela Potts such a pain. Wearily he said what he knew she wanted him to say:

"Why?"

"I'm glad you asked," she said. "More than ninety-nine percent of calico cats, because of the two X chromosomes needed for their unique coloring, are . . ."

"Are what?"

She grinned, like a cat. "Females."

Old Soldiers

Sheriff Charles Jones was sitting on the pedestal underneath the statue of Civil War hero Virgil Pinkard when he saw Angela Potts approaching. As she trudged up the hill, General Pinkard and his rearing stallion glared down at her. So did the sheriff.

"Why so glum?" Angela asked him. "The look on your face is scaring Pinky's horse."

"I'm not glum, I'm unmotivated."

"A five-syllable word? I'm proud of you." Angela had been the sheriff's fifth-grade teacher. He didn't know her age, but he was tempted to ask if she'd also taught Virgil Pinkard.

"Why are you here, Ms. Potts?"

"I'm here to motivate you." She pointed east. "A traveling peddler's drawn a crowd over on Jefferson. Calls himself Warren Kelbrick."

"And?"

She looked up at the bronze hooves hovering above the

sheriff's head. "He says he's the great-great-great-grandson of General Pinkard here. Says his great-grandmother Kelbrick, when she was a kid, was at Pinky's bedside in Alabama when he died, after the war. He says the general professed his love for our town to her on his deathbed, and that's why we got the statue." She frowned. "The crowd thinks this guy's wonderful."

"And . . . ?"

"He's a fraud and a liar."

"Is that so."

"I think you should send him packing."

"Should I tar and feather him first?"

"I'm serious, Chunky. He's cheating people."

The sheriff sighed. "Don't call me that, Ms. Potts. I've asked you a hundred times—"

"You head on over there. I need to stop by my house first."

Angela stormed off. With a grunt Sheriff Jones heaved himself to his feet.

Halfway down Jefferson Street he spotted the crowd, gathered around a tall fellow in a cowboy hat. The sheriff saw him hand someone a metal weathervane in exchange for bills.

Ten minutes later Angela appeared, scowling. "Why haven't you done something?"

"Because this don't exactly look like a crime scene."

"Doesn't," she corrected. "But it is. You know how Edna Larson loves antiques and such?"

"So?"

"Half an hour ago I saw this doofus sell her a hat that he swore had belonged to the Pilgrims. Said it was authentic because it's black and steepled and has a buckle on it."

"What's your point?"

"Buckles didn't appear until the late 1600s. I just looked it up on Google." She held up a printout. "The Pilgrims were 1620."

Without waiting for a response, she waved the sheet and bellowed the same information to the surprised and silent crowd. The most surprised were Warren Kelbrick and Edna Larson. Edna was gaping at her newly purchased "artifact."

The sheriff hesitated, then called: "Is that accusation true, Mr. Kelbrick?"

The salesman's face reddened. "No!"

"Edna's son's a lawyer," Angela shouted. "Should I phone him?"

Kelbrick fumed a moment, then both his face and his shoulders sagged. Scowling, he found Edna Larson's money and returned it to her.

"And you get on out of here," the sheriff told him.

"But I've committed no crime," Kelbrick whined.

"False advertising's illegal. You got twenty minutes to clear out."

When the crowd had dispersed and Kelbrick was gone, Angela gave the sheriff a smile. "Well done, Chunky."

They turned and headed back downtown. "You better tell me the rest," he said.

"What?"

"You said you checked to make sure he was swindling Edna. But that was *after* you told me to run him out of town. How'd you know he was a crook?"

She grinned. "Because he lied about his ancestor. General Pinkard didn't die at home after the war. He died on the battlefield."

"Who told you that?"

She pointed. "Pinkard's statue."

"The inscription? But it only gives his name."

"I don't mean the inscription." She smiled again. "I mean his horse."

"His horse?"

Angela raised her chin as if preparing to address the multitudes. “Traditionally,” she said, “statues of mounted soldiers reveal the way they died. If the horse’s front hooves are both off the ground its rider died in battle, if one’s off the ground he died later of wounds suffered, and if the horse stands on all fours the rider died of natural causes. If Kelbrick’s account were true—”

“The horse would not be rearing,” the sheriff said.

“Correct.”

“Actually, I’ve heard that,” he said. “But I’ve also heard it isn’t always true.”

He could see she didn’t like that a bit. “It isn’t?” she asked.

“Not always.”

She was frowning now. “Well, even if it isn’t . . .”

“Yes?”

“. . . it sure worked this time.”

Hold the Phone

Sheriff Chunky Jones was hauling a one-pound bass out of Harrell's pond when he looked up to see his former schoolteacher Angela Potts standing beside him.

"I figured you'd be here," she said. "Your office has been trying to reach you. Where's your cell phone?"

He dug it out of his tackle box. "Guess it's not turned on. What's up?"

"The crime rate, that's what." She turned to leave. "Come on, we'll take my car."

"What about my fish?"

"Throw it back," she said.

***

Angela updated him on the way into town. Jessica Biggs, a local hairdresser, had this morning reported the theft of an expensive crystal vase from her home during the night.

They arrived to find Jessica sitting on her porch. "My ex-husband stole it," she told them.

"Did you see him?" the sheriff asked.

"Ralph? No. But I saw him earlier last night. He was sneaking around in the trees across the street, watching my house. The jerk."

The sheriff studied her front yard, which was thick with tall bushes. "How'd you see him from here?"

"I wasn't here at the house." She pointed to a small fenced area in the side yard, where a Beagle puppy looked back at them. "I'd gone out to feed my dog."

"But we had a power outage last night. This whole area would've been pitch dark."

"I had a flashlight—and besides, the moon was bright enough that I saw him."

"Okay. So you saw Ralph from outside. What'd you do then?"

"I called the police. That's the good thing about telephones—they work even when the power's out."

"And who responded to that call, Ms. Biggs?"

"Your deputy. The younger one . . ."

"Prewitt?"

"Right. He came out here and checked across the street but told me he saw no one." She added, "Ralph's good at hiding."

"What happened then?"

"Nothing, until I got up this morning and discovered my vase was missing."

"But—again—you didn't actually *see* Ralph take it."

"Come on, Sheriff. He's the only other person who has my door key. And only he knew where I keep my crystal, and how much it's worth."

The sheriff sighed, then had a thought. "Don't you chain-latch your doors?"

"Not the one into the garage. Because the overhead door's usually down."

"And last night?"

"It stayed up because of the power outage. I could've manually lowered it, but I forgot."

Sheriff Jones nodded and pocketed his notepad. "Okay. I'll go question Ralph."

"One more thing," Angela said to Jessica. "Dispatch said you called the police from your home phone—but you just told us you made the call from outside your house."

"I did."

"So you used a cell phone instead?"

"No, I used my cordless. Its range is fifty yards from the base unit in the den."

Angela nodded, then paused for a moment. "I assume you're not fond of your ex-husband."

"Are you kidding? He's dumb *and* worthless," Jessica growled. "The only people he knows are his idiot poker buddies. He *should* be in jail."

"Any idea why he'd want your crystal?" the sheriff asked.

"To sell it, I guess."

"If he's so dumb and doesn't know anybody who's not, who would he sell it to?"

Jessica shrugged. "Beats me."

"Well," Angela said, and rose. "Many thanks. We'll be back later, with the polygraph."

"Polygraph?"

"Lie detector." Angela ignored the sheriff's surprised look. "It's standard procedure."

Jessica's face went pale, her eyes widened. Sweat broke out on her forehead.

"Is something wrong?" Angela asked.

"Actually," Jessica said, "maybe I took that vase over to my mother's."

"Your mother's?"

"I bet I did." Jessica swallowed. "Gosh. I'm sorry . . . I guess this was a false alarm."

***

Ten minutes later, while Angela was driving him back to his car, the sheriff said to her, "Polygraph?"

She grinned. "Just the mention of it can detect a lie."

"But *you*," he said, "detected *this* lie. How'd you know she wasn't telling the truth?"

"Simple," she said. "You have a cordless phone, at home?"

"Sure. Why?"

"Did you use it last night, when the power was off?"

"I don't know."

"Well, I know: you didn't use it. You know why? If you'd tried, it would've been dead."

He turned to look at her. "That's crazy, Ms. Potts. Like Jessica said, telephones work during power outages."

"Telephones do, but cordless phones don't. The base unit that they communicate through has to be plugged in to electricity."

He blinked. "No foolin'?"

"No foolin'."

By now they had reached the little country pond where she'd found him, earlier. "You know," he said, as she pulled up and stopped beside his cruiser, "I never did turn my cell phone on."

"So?"

"So I got an extra fishing rod in the trunk," he said, grinning. He pointed to the pond. "How about it?"

Thursday's Child

Tom Fetterman was late again.

He had eaten lunch at a McDonald's on Powell, four blocks from the bank where he worked, and was sitting on a sunlit bench in Union Square when he realized it was one-thirty. He jumped to his feet, gulped the last of the cookies his mother had tucked into his pocket this morning, and headed north.

Mr. Lindamood would be furious. The third time in two weeks, and Tom had already been warned. Why couldn't he remember to look at his watch? For the hundredth time Tom wished he could think, and plan, and recall things the way other people did.

He knew the only reason he had the job at the bank (he ran errands, stocked the supply shelves, etc.) was because his mother was the sister of the CEO.

"And it doesn't matter if they don't respect you yet," she had told Tom a few weeks ago. "You'll convince them. You're a Thursday's child, Thomas—you have far to go."

But Tom wondered about that. Did she mean he would go far in life, or that it would take him a long time to do it?

He thought he knew the answer. After all, he was thirty years old, unmarried, slow-witted, and living with his wealthy mother. How much more pathetic could he be? Because of her and her resources, he even had an electronic "leash"—a monitoring device he kept on his person, that would alert the police to his whereabouts in case he should wander too far afield. It had already been put to use, in fact. Twice. In both cases, his embarrassment at being picked up and escorted home had been erased by the pure love on his mother's face at his safe arrival. And afterward, he had vowed to try even harder to make her proud of him.

But here he was, in trouble again. In his frustration he kicked at a rock on the sidewalk, and realized too late it was a piece of the cement. He hurt his foot and stumbled. Behind him, he heard someone snicker.

Tom felt the beginnings of tears in his eyes.

Finally the bank was in sight, an old-fashioned gray building set back fifty feet from the street. Tom wiped his eyes with a shirtsleeve, quickened his pace—and stopped short.

Something about the bank was different.

So dense about some things, Tom was oddly perceptive about others. He stood there a moment, looking around. A string of cars and a KCY-TV Action News van were parked at the curb, an old lady trudged along near the shops beside the bank, and half a dozen pigeons flapped and pranced around the windswept shrubbery that bordered the sidewalk.

Nothing wrong here, folks. Tom relaxed and kept going.

Then it struck him.

The glass door of the bank lobby was closed and shaded. It should have opened at one o'clock.

At that moment, a short man carrying a briefcase and a gun burst through the bank's door. He backed a few steps toward the street, then fired a shot at another man who came through after him. As Tom watched, stunned, the second man winced and grabbed his chest like an actor in an old Western. He fell heavily to the sidewalk just outside the door.

The gunman turned and bolted for the street—and straight toward Tom Fetterman, who had jumped behind a tall shrub between the building and the curb.

The robber—that assumption seemed a safe one—was twenty feet away, and closing fast. One thought locked itself in Tom's mind: If he stayed hidden, the gunman would pass right by without seeing him.

But he suddenly knew he couldn't do that. All his life he'd wanted to prove his worth, to rise above his handicap, to earn the respect of others.

Here was his chance.

Quickly, before he could think about it, he stuck out his right foot. The gunman tripped over it, went airborne, gasped a common but descriptive four-letter word during his flight, and crashed headfirst into the cold steel post of a parking meter beside the curb. The gun clattered to the ground.

With a trembling hand Tom grabbed the pistol and aimed it at the robber. He appeared to be out cold. The brief-case, Tom saw, was belted to the man's wrist. Four feet above his sprawled form, inside the glass face of the parking meter, a tiny red flag said VIOLATION.

As if from a great distance, Tom heard the alarm go off inside the bank. About time, he thought. He felt good, cocky almost, but still he couldn't stop shaking.

Where *was* everybody? Then he understood: the gun-man must've warned those inside not to look out the door. The bank had no front windows.

"Somebody call the police," Tom shouted. Just in case they weren't coming already, because of the alarm.

Not that he really needed them . . .

Tom blinked. For the first time his mind grasped the full significance of what had happened.

He was a hero. A *hero*. Soon the bank employees would realize the danger was past and rush outside to investigate. Tom could see it now: Afternoon, Mr. Lindamood. No, everything's under control—here's your thief and there's your money. All in a day's work.

His head was spinning. He could picture himself in the newspapers, and on TV. A promotion, probably.

Then he frowned. Something about that bothered him.

TV. That was it—the TV van. What was *it* doing here?

Tom saw movement from the corner of his eye. As if triggered by his question, someone was running toward him from the Action News van, waving his arms like a man possessed.

"What the hell are you doing?" the guy yelled. He was big and red-faced, with some kind of video equipment on a strap over his shoulder.

Tom just looked at him and continued to point the gun at the robber, who was now holding his head and moaning.

"Who're you?" Tom asked. Something was definitely wrong here.

The big man stopped and put his hands on his knees, gasping for air.

"Frank Morris, from KCY. Do you realize what you've done?" He focused on Tom for the first time. "You really *don't*," he said in amazement.

Tom stared at him.

"We're doing a crime segment here," Morris said. "It's been running a month now, don't you watch the news?" He paused to catch his breath. "You know what a dramatization is? There are two cameras on you right now from that building across the street." He turned and signaled to someone, watched for a moment, then set his equipment down and faced Tom again. "Come on, help me with this man."

Together, they eased the robber to his feet. He had a blue goose-egg above his right eye.

"Easy, Danny," Morris said. He glanced at Tom. "We should get him to a hospital."

"But the guy who was shot . . ."

Morris gave Tom a tired look. "The guy with the ketchup on his shirt? That's Jack Cunningham. He's been told to lie there until we wrap the scene. He doesn't even know you've blown everything. Give me a hand here."

In a daze, Tom helped load the injured man into a green Ford parked near the news van. Frank Morris went around and opened the driver's door, then turned to Tom.

"See if you can do something right," he said. "Go tell Cunningham and the inside camera crew what happened." With a final shake of his head, Morris got in, started the Ford's motor, and pulled out into traffic.

Tom Fetterman looked around. A crowd was gathering now on the sidewalk, and familiar faces were poking through the shaded door of the bank.

Tom just sighed. A hero, indeed.

***

"You okay, Wilburn?" the driver said. He crossed Market, downshifted, hung a left. The gray warehouses of Mission Street flashed by outside.

The man in the passenger seat groaned. "I guess. Least I still have the money." He touched his forehead. "What happened back there?"

The driver blew out a lungful of air and checked the

mirror. They'd stopped only once, minutes ago, to switch cars. "I was watching when you came out," he said. "I saw the guy trip you. The window of the TV van sitting next to us was open, so I grabbed some camera stuff and came running. Lucky break."

"You did good." Wilburn grimaced, squeezed his eyes shut, leaned back against the headrest. "Tell me something: Who's Frank Morris?"

The driver accelerated through a yellow light. The traffic was thinning a bit now. He looked at his passenger and grinned.

"Ever see *Escape from Alcatraz*? Clint Eastwood?"

"No."

"Well, Frank Lee Morris led the only group ever to make it off the island."

Wilburn opened one eye. "Where'd they catch him?"

The driver looped onto the Bayshore Freeway and pointed the car south.

"They didn't," he said.

***

Tom Fetterman hadn't known the city had so many police cars. As he watched, another one screeched up to the curb, its lights strobing. Ever since Morris had driven away, Tom's bottom had been warming the fender of a Toyota parked near the TV van. He was keeping a good distance from the bank, and from Randall Lindamood. Tom wasn't eager for those inside to find out how stupid he'd been. But how was *he* to know it was a staged robbery?

He saw a policeman bending over the man lying outside the bank door. The guy still hadn't moved. Tom figured he must've hit his head the way Danny had when he fell. The ketchup on his shirt had leaked onto the sidewalk.

A TV reporter came jogging up to join the commotion. Tom heard him say KCY had been down the street covering a campaign luncheon. A different crew, Tom figured.

The pistol was still in his hand. He looked down at it.

Blanks. Unbelievable.

The crowd was bigger now. Tom saw a waitress from the coffeeshop next door point him out to a police officer, saw the policeman turn and march toward him.

Tom stood up straight.

"I'll take the gun," the officer said. Tom handed it over, watched it go into a plastic bag. "Your name, sir?"

Tom told him.

"You work here at the bank?"

Tom nodded, and reached for his wallet. It wouldn't be the first time he'd had to show his bank ID to prove it to someone. But then, a second after his fingers entered his back pocket, Tom understood everything.

It happened that way sometimes. He would be standing there totally lost, and all of a sudden the clouds in his head would clear, and his thoughts would snap together like puzzle pieces. The blood, the gun, the briefcase, the TV van, the escape—it all made sense now.

He saw a scowling Mr. Lindamood hurrying toward him, and realized the policeman was asking him something else.

"—said she saw you help the suspect into a car?"

Tom nodded.

"Why'd you do that?"

"His partner told me to." Tom saw Mr. Lindamood roll his eyes.

"His partner?" the officer said.

"I think so, now."

"What'd he look like?"

Tom hesitated. "I can't remember."

"What kind of car was it?"

"Don't know that either."

"He's an idiot," Mr. Lindamood said, to the policeman. "He doesn't know anything."

"Yes, I do," Tom said.

Something in his voice must have had an effect. The policeman's eyes narrowed. "What is it you know?" he asked.

Tom stared off down the street, in the direction the getaway car had taken. *I'm a Thursday's child*, he said to himself. *I have far to go*. He found himself thinking about his mother.

"I'm supposed to wear it around my neck," he murmured. "But I don't like to."

Mr. Lindamood laughed aloud. "Forget him, Officer. I told you, he's a fool."

But the policeman was still watching Tom. "What is it you know, son?" he asked again.

Tom's eyes cleared, his hand still touching his empty pocket.

"I know how to catch them," he said.

***

"You ain't the only one who did good," Wilburn said, with a weak grin. They could see the airport up ahead now, on the left.

"What?"

Wilburn held up a wallet. "I lifted this from the guy who tripped me. While he was helping you get me into your car."

"A lousy billfold? Are you crazy?"

"Maybe not." Wilburn took something from one of the wallet's pockets and studied it. "This looks expensive."

The driver turned to look, saw the black credit-card-sized device with the red blinking lights. "What the hell is—"

And then he noticed the rearview mirror.

Behind them, the first sirens started to wail.

A Matter of Honor

Morgan Hobbs lowered his newspaper. Twenty feet from his rocking chair on the hotel's porch, a young man was standing alone in the street.

"I'm calling you out, Mister."

Hobbs and the old man sitting beside him exchanged a glance.

"What's your name, son?" Hobbs said.

"I ain't your son. Name's Jim Parker."

"And?"

"And I intend to kill you."

"Why is that?"

Parker raised his chin. "I'm told you insulted my wife."

"I don't even know your wife."

"Then you shouldn't've insulted her."

"Insulted her how?"

Parker cleared his throat. "Her . . . honor."

Hobbs removed a cigar from his pocket. "Who told you

this?"

"Didn't give his name. He's at the saloon, got one ear missing."

Hobbs took a match from the old man and lit the cigar. "And you believe him?"

"You're denying you insulted her?"

"Yep."

"Why should I believe you over him? You're not from here."

"Neither's he, if you don't know his name." Puffing, Hobbs fanned out his match. "I'm here on business."

"What kind?"

"Looking for somebody. Man named Woodrow Temple. Heard of him?"

"No."

"Killed a friend of mine."

"You the Law?"

"Temple'll wish I was," Hobbs said, "when I find him."

Parker snorted. "I don't care why you're here. We fighting or not?"

Hobbs squinted at him through a cloud of smoke, then turned again to the old man. "You gonna say anything?"

"Your affair, Dingo. Not mine."

Parker blinked. The words hung there in the dusty air. "You're Dingo Hobbs?"

"I prefer Morgan," Hobbs said.

But Parker's face had already changed. His gun hand drifted over to fiddle with his shirt buttons.

"If you're Dingo Hobbs, and I draw on you," he said, "you'll kill me deader'n a pine knot."

"No need for that. Go on home, let me finish reading the news."

The young man swallowed. Sweating. "It's not that

simple."

Hobbs looked past him at the gathering crowd. "Now's not the time, son, to worry about pride."

A sad but determined look flickered in Jim Parker's eyes, and Hobbs realized this wasn't going to work.

"What's she look like, your wife?" he asked.

Parker frowned. "What?"

"You heard me. Tall? Short?"

"Short, and redheaded. What does that—"

"And she's not home right now, is she?"

"What? Course she's home."

"You sure?" Hobbs studied Parker's mud-caked pantslegs. "You come straight here from home?"

Parker hesitated. "I been settin' fenceposts. Why?"

"Well, when me and my friend here rode in awhile ago, a one-eared man was hugging a gal like you described, in yonder alley."

"What?!"

"Maybe someone wants you dead, Parker. Maybe he's lying, to try to get him both a lady and a ranch."

Parker seemed to consider that. And the more he considered the darker his face became.

"I'll excuse you," Hobbs said, "if you're needed elsewhere."

Parker nodded. "Much obliged. I believe I am."

Hobbs watched him march to the saloon. He paused outside the batwing doors, jaw set, then pushed inside.

"Hope you know what you're doing," the old man said.

Hobbs snapped open his newspaper. "What do you mean?"

"I mean my eyes ain't bad, and I don't recall seeing nobody hugging no woman in an alley."

"Me neither," Hobbs said, around his cigar. "But

Temple musta seen *us*. The fact he made up that story shows he's desperate."

"Like I said, hope you did right."

"What I did was save that kid's life. Or maybe my own."

"Yours?"

Hobbs shrugged. "He looked like he'd be fast."

"Faster'n you?"

"Don't know," Hobbs said, glancing at the saloon. "But I know one thing."

"What's that?"

Hobbs smiled. "He'll be faster'n Woodrow Temple."

John M. Floyd

The Home Front

Sunday, May 23

Dear Margaret,

Arrived at Elmendorf on Friday. The barracks are okay, but it's sure not as good as home. Miss you already.

Really enjoying the scenery. When the weather's clear you can see Mt. McKinley (Denali), and it's 150 miles away. Drove around some yesterday, saw a real moose. Will send pictures.

Say hello to your mom for me and make sure Steve Crawford stays out of trouble. See you at Christmas.

Love,

Charlie

May 29

Dearest Charles:

Everything's fine here. It was so good to hear from you. Air Force life sounds exciting. My mom says thanks for asking about her, she's doing great as usual. She's keeping busy at the church and so forth. I'm fine too, except Uncle Ned works me pretty hard at the store (Ha). I saw Steve Crawford the other day, I think he misses you almost as much as I do. By the way, he says he's trying to clean up his apartment a little so he can start looking for a new roommate. He figures whoever he finds will want the place kept neater than you did (Ha).

I do love you, Charles. Please be careful up there.

All my love,

Margaret

June 1

Hi Charlie —

How are things in the Far North? Better than here I bet. I bumped into Margaret last week and she gave me your address—I guess you've forgotten your old buddy Steve-o, right? Seriously, all is well here in Corn Country. I hired on yesterday with the railroad, hot work but good pay. My parents are still on me about college (what's new?) but I just don't know yet. Maybe next year.

I've been doing some housecleaning around here, and found some of your stuff. I'd pack it all up and send it to you, but I doubt you'd need it there. It's just a few books and a pocketknife and a couple of video cassettes—one's that old porn movie you bought in Chicago, the other's *The Sound of Music*, how's that for variety? Anyhow, I stuffed it all back into the closet, it'll be there if you want it.

Gotta go, I'm taking Betty Goodman to the show tonight.

Your old bud,

Steve

Tuesday, June 22

Dear Steve,

Thanks for writing. Regarding my things, just hang onto them. I won't be up here forever, you know. And keep checking on Margaret for me. I haven't heard from her in a while now, figure she must be busy with the store and such.

See if you can find a box of tomatoes to send me. I know that sounds funny, but they can't grow them very well up here. Something to do with the short growing season. Plenty of sunshine but not enough heat. Or so they tell me. Pretty country, but I miss Illinois.

Take care of yourself.

Your friend,

Charlie

July 3

Dearest Charles:

I'm sorry it's been so long since my last letter. I guess I just couldn't really think of much to say.

My uncle hired a new boy at the general store, his name's Jason Dallman. He says he remembers you. He's a good guy, reminds me a lot of you at times.

I'm glad to hear you're happy there. Take a lot of pictures, Charlie, you're the only one from here ever to become a world traveler (Ha).

Love,

Margaret

July 17

Hello Charlie —

I don't exactly know how to tell you this, so I guess I'll just come right out with it. I think Margaret is falling for that new guy at the general store, his name's Jason Dallman. He seems okay enough, I guess, even looks a little like you from a distance.

The truth is, Charlie, you're a nice guy and all that, but this Jason's a nice guy too, and he's here and you're not. Worst of all, her mother seems to like him, too.

Let me know what you want me to do, old buddy. I know how much Margaret means to you.

Steve

Saturday, July 24

Dear Steve,

Have been in a stew ever since your letter. I've thought about this long and hard, and I don't suppose there's anything you can do, or me either. Just tell her, when you see her, that I truly do love her—that's what I keep telling her in my letters to her, though I haven't heard back from her in a long time now. I knew something was wrong. And you're right about her mother—Mrs. McCarthy is a stern woman, and Margaret does pretty much whatever she says. I can't help liking the old gal, though, even if she does favor this Jason guy. She probably thinks he'd make a good son-in-law, a better catch than me, and I'm sure she thinks she has Margaret's best interests in mind.

It occurred to me after reading your letter that her mom's birthday is the end of next month (August 28th), and it probably wouldn't hurt for me to send her something, I always have. I've known the whole family since I was a little kid.

Do this for me, Steve: Pick out a pretty birthday card, and bundle together some nice chocolates and an arrangement of dried flowers or something. Put that *Sound of Music* tape in too—I know they have a VCR, and she once told Margaret that's her favorite movie. Don't mail the package yet, just keep everything boxed up and ready.

I've enclosed a check for twenty dollars (though I already owe you more than that for the tomatoes).

Thanks for being there, Steve-o. Don't know what I'd do without you.

Your old pal,

Charlie

August 5

Dear Charles:

I haven't written in so long because something has come up in my life. I don't really know how to say this.

Jason Dallman and I have been dating for some time. I don't know how it happened, it just did. I mean, we work together at the store all the time, you know? Anyhow, we have become pretty close, and I haven't seen you in so long I just don't know my own mind anymore. I do like him, and Mom does too. I know you think I rely too much on her opinion sometimes, but since Daddy died she has also become a friend to me too, and if she feels Jason is the right person for me, I have to consider that. I hope you understand.

Please don't be too upset. Whatever happens, you'll always be very special to me.

Sincerely,

Margaret

August 13

Hi Charlie —

No good news. Margaret goes out with Jason almost every night now. Things are getting pretty serious.

One question. Her mother's birthday is only two weeks away. Do you still want me to send your package of presents? I say forget it.

Let me know.

Steve

Wednesday, August 18

Dear Steve,

I understand what you're saying, and I value your opinion. What I have to remember, though, is that if I really love Margaret I want whatever's best for her, even if it's not what's best for me. Her mother has apparently given her good advice in the past, and who knows, if she believes Jason Dallman is Mr. Right, then maybe he is. For once I must put personal feelings aside.

Go ahead and mail the package to Mrs. McCarthy. Even if Margaret and I are finished, my feelings toward her and her mother will always be good ones. There is one thing, though, that I'd like you to change: Put Jason's name on the package rather than mine. I've decided to be unselfish in this.

I repeat, make sure it's a pretty card, print Jason Dallman's name on it, and mail the package of gifts as if it were from him instead of me. Remember, her birthday's the 28th, be sure to send it in plenty of time.

I really believe, in my heart, that this is for the best.

Thanks for everything.

Your friend,

Charlie

P.S. Switch the tapes.

Debbie and Bernie and Belle

Bernie Langford sat alone on the bench at the edge of the park, staring at the red brick building on the far side of Western Avenue. Steam rose in wispy clouds from the pavement; rainwater pooled on the sidewalks. The sun had come out again, warm on his shoulders.

The rain had been light but steady, and his umbrella hadn't done much good: his shoes and socks and trouser legs were soaked. So was the seat of his pants, from its contact with the bench. But none of that mattered a whit to Bernie Langford. The only thing on his mind right now was inside the building across the road.

He had arrived in the taxi around ten, after a two-mile chase through the drizzle and the midmorning traffic. Just after climbing out of the cab, he saw her going up the steps of the brick building. He almost shouted to her, but hesitated, and then it was too late. The front door opened and she disappeared inside. He stood there awhile in the rain, staring helplessly at the front of the building, and after a dozen passersby had given him odd looks he opened his umbrella and trudged over to the park bench to wait.

She was still there, and so was he.

Bernie rubbed his eyes, ran a hand through his wet hair, and looked at his watch. Half past noon. Three hours since her phone call to his apartment. He'd been in class at the time, and when he returned he'd found her message on his machine—a message that left no room for misunderstanding. It was over, she said. She was leaving town today. She'd also said she didn't want to see him or talk to him any more before she left. What she hadn't told him, among other things, was where she was going, when she was leaving, or how she was getting there.

Some of that he had figured out already. The where and how were easy—she was probably headed to her friend Lucy's apartment in New York (she had talked of little else for the past few weeks) and would almost certainly fly. The when was another matter. After receiving her message he frantically checked all the airline schedules, and found eight possible flights. By now, three of them had already flown, and another two were too close to make. The next possibility was at three o'clock.

But he'd had one stroke of luck. After checking the airline schedules he hailed a cab and went straight to her place—he was afraid to take the time to walk to his parking garage to get his own car. When his cab arrived at her apartment, she was climbing into a taxi of her own, and Bernie pointed and thrust a wad of bills into his cabbie's hand and gave chase. Five minutes later he glimpsed her going into the building across the street—and here he sat.

And here he would sit, watching that door, until she—like the sun—came out again.

Suddenly he heard a BANG, and whirled around in

his seat.

Standing in the middle of the footpath six feet away was not a mugger or a terrorist but a little blond girl in jeans and a T-shirt. She was chewing something and watching him solemnly. A brown cloth purse was slung over one shoulder. Something was clutched in her right hand, but he couldn't tell what it was. After a moment of dead silence she stuck out her tongue, inflated her cheeks, and blew a wobbly pink bubble. It grew to the size of a grapefruit, then gave a wet POP and shriveled up. That was the sound he'd heard. Immediately she started chewing again. She looked about ten years old.

"Whatcha doin', Mister?" the little girl asked, around the wad of gum.

"I'm waiting for somebody."

"I got a new yo-yo." She opened her right hand, by way of proof.

He gave her a tired nod. He wished she'd go away.

"I can make it walk the dog," she said. "Want to see?"

"Not right now. I'm kinda busy."

She studied him with an expression that clearly said he didn't look very busy. After a while she looked past him at the building he'd been watching. "Who you waitin' for?"

Bernie sighed. "A girl."

She popped her bubble gum again.

"Your girlfriend?"

"Yeah. My girlfriend."

The little girl lapsed into silence for a minute or so, letting the yo-yo wind and unwind on its string. Bernie tried to ignore her. What was she doing out here anyway? She wasn't even wet.

Somewhere down the street, he heard the multiple horns of a traffic jam. The sun sparkled like diamonds on the damp pavement. Rainwater dripped from the oaks lining the sidewalk.

"Why?" the little girl asked.

Bernie looked at her again. "Why what?"

"Why're you waitin' for your girlfriend? Why don't you just go get her?"

He started to say something, changed his mind, then decided what the hell. "I don't think she wants me to." He pointed to the building. "Besides, that's the YWCA over there. Know what that is?"

"No."

"It's like a girls' club. No men allowed."

She seemed to think that over. "Not even at the front door?"

He blinked. She was right, of course. There would be nothing wrong with his strolling over to the front office and asking to have her paged, or whatever they did there. But in this case that wasn't an option. "There's more to it than that," he said.

She watched him, chewing her gum. The popping had stopped.

"What are you doing out here by yourself anyway?" he asked.

"My uncle works down the street. When it stopped raining I came out to practice my yo-yo."

And antagonize heartbroken fools, he thought. He went back to his vigil.

"What's your name?" she asked, out of the blue.

"Bernie. Bernie Langford."

Another silence.

"Why doesn't she want to see you?" the kid asked.

He shifted on the bench. His shoes made a squishing sound.

"We had a fight. A big one. She said she's leaving town today, to think things out." He paused and felt a lump in his throat. "I'm scared she won't come back."

Now the yo-yo had stopped too. The ten-year-old stood as still as a portrait, staring back at him.

"And you want to catch her when she comes out. You want to talk her out of leaving."

Bernie swallowed, thinking. Was that what he wanted? One part of his mind said Of course it was, that's why he was here. He didn't want her to leave, and this was the only way he could think of to stop her.

But his better judgment told him something different. A confrontation now wasn't the answer. She'd told him she didn't want to see him, for any reason, before she left. If he showed up here now, she'd just get mad and run, and that wasn't a good way to part. What he really needed to do—

He sat up straight. The answer was standing right here beside him.

"I should send her a message," he said, under his breath.

"What?"

He turned to the little girl. "Listen, kid—" He paused. "What's your name?"

"Belle. Why?"

"Listen, Belle." He leaned closer, and lowered his voice. "What if I gave you a note? A note from me to my girlfriend. Would you take it to her, give it to her for me?"

"A note," she repeated.

"That's right. I could write a message right here, on a sheet of paper—" He fished a dry notebook out of the coat draped across his lap (thank God for the umbrella after all, he thought) and ripped out a sheet. "—and you could find her for me, and deliver it. What do you think?"

The little girl frowned. "I dunno."

"I could pay you. How about ten dollars?"

She looked up at the brick building across the street.

"How would I find her?"

"Just ask at the front desk." Surely there had to be a front desk. "Or look around for her, when you get inside. I'll describe her."

She chewed her lip a moment. "Ten dollars . . . ?"

"Make it twenty. How about it?"

That seemed to make up her mind. She nodded, untied her yo-yo, and stuffed it into her purse. "Deal."

Wasting no time, Bernie dug a pen from his jacket and wrote a short message on the sheet of paper. It said, in neatly printed letters:

DEAREST DEBBIE,

I LOVE YOU. I ALWAYS HAVE. PLEASE DON'T LEAVE ME.

BERNIE

He read it through once, started to add more, then decided not to. Maybe simple was best. At least it was the truth.

"Here." He folded it once, pressed it into her palm, and followed it with two wrinkled ten-dollar bills. When she had the money tucked away in her purse and the note held ready, he hunched forward again, his eyes on a level with hers.

"Her name's Debbie Wilson," he said. "She's tall and slim, with light green eyes. Her hair's cut to about right here, kind of reddish brown. She's wearing"—he thought a moment—"a green flowered dress, and white earrings. They look like seashells. Okay?"

Belle nodded again, holding the note in a deathgrip. "You can count on me, boss," she said, and grinned. With that, she dashed down the footpath to the curb, stopped to look both ways, and took off for the steps of the building across the street. She hesitated at the door, as if wondering whether to knock. Finally she just turned the knob and walked in.

Bernie waited in silence, watching the front door so hard his eyes began to water.

Four minutes later the little girl appeared in the doorway, pulled the big door shut behind her, and ran down the steps and across to the park.

For a moment she just stood there and looked at him, panting a bit.

"Well?" he blurted.

She looked a little embarrassed. "She was easy to find. But you were right, Mister. She doesn't want anything to do with you."

Bernie's heart sank, even though he had expected that. "What'd she do when you gave her the note?" He dreaded the answer—but maybe the kid was mistaken.

"She threw it away. And she said to tell you to go to—well—to go to a bad place." Belle frowned, then seemed struck by a thought. She leaned closer to Bernie and said, "She looked *rich*."

Bernie nodded miserably. "She is. That was one of our problems." He glanced again at the building. It was just like Debbie, he thought, to decide to spend her last hours in town at a place like the YWCA, when she could just as easily be sipping drinks at the Yacht Club or the Delta Crown Room. She always chose to try to conceal the fact that she'd been born wealthy. Most of her friends didn't even know it. But in her relationship with Bernie she brought the subject up constantly—she'd always been afraid (with the wholehearted agreement of her mother) that Bernie was only interested in her money. Actually, nothing could have been farther from the truth. "I wish she didn't have a penny to her name," he added.

The little girl seemed deep in thought. Finally she looked up at him. "Let me try again." And before Bernie could reply, she turned and streaked away toward the Y, her yellow hair gleaming in the sun.

This time she was gone ten minutes, which he took to be encouraging. When she came back again, though, he knew as soon as he saw her face that things had not gone well.

"At least she listened," Belle said. Her bubble gum had disappeared: another bad sign.

Bernie waited, but she didn't seem inclined to file a report. "What happened?" he said finally. "This is my life we're talking about here."

The ten-year-old shrugged. "I told her what you told me. That you care about *her*, not her money." She narrowed her eyes. "She said if that's true, why'd you let her pay for your last year's tu . . . tu . . ."

"Tuition."

"Right. And she said you still owe her three hundred dollars for getting your car fixed. Is that true?"

It was true. But the money for school had been a loan. So had the car repair bill. Debbie had told him he could take as long as he wanted to repay her. Now she apparently didn't think he cared at all about honoring the debt. She was wrong, but what mattered was what she thought.

"Look," he said, snatching his wallet out again. He counted out two twenties and two more fives. "Fifty bucks. It's all I have. She'll get the rest soon as I finish classes next month and sign on with Drew Hopkins." Bernie was in his last semester of accounting, and already had a job offer with the CPA firm of Polk and Hopkins, in a building right here in this area. Not fancy, but not bad either. "And I'll never ask her for another cent. Tell her that."

The little girl looked uneasy. "I don't think she wants—"

"Take it. Maybe it'll make her see I'm sincere. All I'm after is another chance. Okay?"

"I guess so." She took the money and crossed the street again. The door to the Y opened and closed and she was gone.

When she reappeared this time she looked angry. Her face was flushed a deep pink. Without a word she plunked down beside him on the wet bench, gazing straight ahead at the sparse traffic. At last Bernie could stand it no longer.

"Why are you looking that way? What'd she say?"

Belle turned and stared him in the eye.

"You should let her go, Mister."

He held his breath. "Why?"

She reached up and scratched her forehead, then adjusted the little purse-strap on her shoulder. The first gesture seemed so childlike, the second so grown-up.

Bernie watched her, waiting.

"I think the money made her even madder. She took it all right, but she said what was fifty dollars when she'd supported and waited on you hand and foot for the past two years." The little girl looked down at her sneakers and shook her head. "Let her go. You'd be better off."

Bernie couldn't believe what he was hearing. There was no doubt the kid had her facts straight. But he'd had no idea Debbie felt quite this way. He'd always tried to do his share, or thought he had. What he really had was a knack for bringing out the worst in people, he decided.

"She say anything else?"

The little girl swallowed, looking uncomfortable. "She said she'd spoiled you. She said she'd paid for everything and never questioned anything. The apartment rent, your education, your gold watch—"

That touched a nerve. "She didn't buy this watch. I did."

"She said she paid for it, though. Her money bought

everything, and now she's tired of it." Belle shook her head again. "I think you're wastin' your time, Mister."

Bernie sat very still, staring down at the muddy ground between his shoes. He felt numb and weak and sick, as if all his muscles had turned to jelly and leaked out his pant legs.

Finally he took in some air. "Okay. I guess it really is over."

He removed his wallet again and looked through it to give her something else for her trouble. Then he remembered he had nothing left. "I'm sorry," he said.

"It's okay." She stood up and gave him a sad look. "Want your twenty dollars back?"

"No, you keep it. But there's one more thing I need you to do." He unstrapped his wristwatch and handed it to her. It was a gold Pulsar, and expensive.

"Take this to her," he said. "Tell her she's mistaken about me. Tell her, material things just aren't that important to me, and she can keep this to remind her I'm being honest with her."

He paused, his heart aching. What he'd said was true: if she was indeed gone, he didn't want the watch. He'd only bought it because of something she had teased him about weeks ago. "Have you *ever* been punctual, Bernard Langford?" she'd said. He remembered trying to look offended. "Certainly not," he'd replied. "I never even had the chicken pox."

Both of them got a laugh out of that. Several days later, when he showed up with the new watch, she kissed him and commented on his thoughtfulness. The memory saddened him. Both the laughing and the kissing were done now, for good.

He focused again on the ten-year-old.

"All I need is her love," he said. "Sounds corny, like a song, doesn't it? But it's true. It's all I've ever needed." He suddenly felt tired. "Tell her that."

When he handed the little girl the watch, he saw tears in her eyes, and felt miserable all over again. She stared at him a long time, and it occurred to him that her face looked a bit more mature than it had half an hour ago.

Don't ever break anyone's heart, little Belle, he thought. Not the way she's broken mine.

"Good luck, Mister," she said, blinking a little. Without warning, she darted forward and kissed him on the cheek.

Then she turned away, clutching the peace offering and heading for the Y.

Bernie watched her go, then rose to his feet. There was scarcely a cloud in the sky now, and though it was humid it wasn't terribly hot. He sighed one last time, looked around at the sun-dappled park, slung his coat over his shoulder, and trudged to the curb to look for a taxi.

The traffic was still thin. No cabs in sight, or buses either. He was about to start the long hike back to the campus when he saw Debbie Wilson open the front door of the YWCA.

Halfway down the steps she spotted him, and they stood frozen a moment, staring at each other across the narrow street. Her face had gone cold and hard, and in it he saw everything he needed to know.

But he couldn't just walk away. He might've been able to a minute ago, but not now—not after actually *seeing* her. He had to tell her, and tell her himself, that she was wrong about him.

He jogged across the road and stood facing her. They stared at each other in dead silence.

"Hello, Bernie," she said.

He swallowed hard, but stayed quiet. He didn't trust his voice enough to speak.

"If you'll excuse me, I have a plane to catch." She shouldered past him and stood stiffly at the curb a few feet away. After a moment a taxi appeared, but she made no attempt to signal it. When it had passed she turned and looked at him, and he saw the glimmer of tears in her eyes. She raised a hand and swiped them away, almost angrily, and when she did Bernie saw she wasn't wearing her engagement ring.

She noticed that he noticed, and glanced down at her finger. There was a suntan line there, where the ring had been.

"Guess that makes it final, doesn't it," she said. The coldness had gone from her voice now. It just sounded sad.

Bernie didn't know how to respond to that.

"It can be sized, you know, if it doesn't fit," she added. "The money should cover it."

Finally he found his voice. "What did you say? The money . . . ?"

She seemed not to hear him. "I hope you'll be happy, Bernie. I really do."

"Wait a minute, Deb." He felt on the edge of panic. Here he stood, with his true love about to march out of his life, and he didn't even know what she was talking about. "What money? What do you mean?"

Though her anger seemed gone now, she gave him a look you might give a child who's done something disappointing.

"I mean the eight hundred dollars, Bernie. That's what I mean. And the ring." She swallowed. "You have a right to it, I realize that. I just didn't think things had gone that far." Tears welled in her eyes again, and her face turned red.

He took a step closer. "Eight hundred *dollars* . . . ?"

Suddenly she flared. "The money you asked me to loan you, ten minutes ago. Have you forgotten?" Her expression hardened. "You couldn't even ask me yourself, you had to get a little girl to do it for you."

Bernie was stunned. A terrible thought leaped into his mind.

"The ring," he murmured. "She told you I wanted it *back*?"

Debbie only stared at him, her cheeks wet and shining. Then she swung around to face the street again, and this time she did raise her hand for a taxi. Fifty yards away, one put on its blinker and headed for the curb.

Bernie paid it no attention. A lightbulb went off in his mind. "Good God," he said.

Debbie Wilson, who had opened the door of the waiting cab, hesitated. She watched him as he pondered this new information.

"I can't believe it," he thought aloud. He blinked at her. "You never said a word to her about my watch, did you. Or about the fifty dollars I gave her, either."

"Fifty dollars? What are you talking about? And what watch?"

Bernie's head was spinning. The answers were falling into place.

He asked Debbie, "What did she say to you? What'd she say the first time you saw her?"

"The little girl?" Debbie frowned. "She said you were waiting for me, outside."

"That's all?"

"Yes."

"She didn't give you a note?"

"A note? No. What kind of note?"

Bernie felt numb. "What about the second time? What did she tell you?"

"She said . . . she said you wanted to borrow some money. A lot of money."

He nodded, thinking hard. "She'd found out you were wealthy. What'd you say?"

"I told her you already owed me three hundred dollars.

I was, well, getting a little mad at you. Then she said you needed it badly. That you'd lost your job—"

"I don't have a job. You know that."

"You comin' or not?" the cabbie shouted.

"Hold on," she shouted back. To Bernie she said, "I thought she meant the Hopkins people had withdrawn their offer. Bernie, what is all this? What's happened?"

"Just go on. She told you I needed a loan . . ."

"Yes. Eight hundred. She said you felt you deserved it, this one last time. And"—she paused—"she told me you wanted the ring back."

Bernie said nothing.

Debbie cleared her throat. "She said you had another girl. She said . . . we weren't engaged any more."

He blew out a long sigh. He felt himself staring into the distance, adrift in his thoughts.

She looked at him hard. The truth was beginning to sink in.

"You didn't say any of that, did you," she asked, her face pale.

He shook his head.

"She made it all up," Debbie murmured. Her green eyes, dry now, were as wide as quarters. She had turned to look up at the brick front of the YWCA building.

"Yes," Bernie said.

She focused on him again. "I gave her eight hundred *dollars*, Bernie. And my *ring*."

"I gave her fifty—no, seventy, all told. And my watch." He held up his bare wrist so she could see it.

Their eyes met and held. Somewhere down the street, they heard what sounded like radio music.

Bernie spread his hands. "Well, I know her name, at least. It's Belle, and that's pretty unusual. She should be easy enough for the cops to find—"

He broke off when he saw the look on Debbie's face. She was staring at his chest. "I don't think so," she said.

"What?"

"Were you wearing your coat when she told you her name?"

"No. Why?"

She kept looking at his chest, and this time he looked too. On the top corner of his shirt pocket were his initials, embroidered in blue thread. The initials BEL.

"She's pretty quick, this girl," Debbie said.

Bernie felt as if he'd been punched in the gut. Too much was happening too fast. He'd never been in a situation like this before, ever.

He had been conned—both of them had been conned—by a fourth-grader with a yo-yo and a mouthful of bubble gum.

All of a sudden Debbie giggled. It was spontaneous, like air escaping from a half-filled balloon. She clapped her hand over her mouth—and then giggled again.

"I can't believe it," she said. "I gave her eight hundred bucks, Bernie."

He felt it building up in him, too. Suddenly, after all the anger and tension and confusion, he opened his mouth and brayed laughter. "I gave her my new Pulsar Chronograph!" The shouted words echoed off the sides of the buildings.

They couldn't seem to stop laughing. People on the sidewalks stopped and looked with varying degrees of disapproval. The taxi had long since given up and gone, but some of the cars on Western Avenue slowed down as they passed, both drivers and passengers gaping at them through the windows.

This made Bernie laugh that much harder. Finally they regained control. A few chuckles and giggles sputtered out, but the reckless hilarity had passed.

Still grinning, they looked at each other in the bright

sunlight.

Then Bernie's face went dead serious.

"I love you," he said. "I always have. Please don't leave me."

Her smile lit up her face. Her eyes were teary again, but this time not sad. She took two steps forward and he folded her into his arms. His coat hung down behind her like a cape.

When they pulled apart, she leaned her head back a little to look at him. Her arms stayed clamped around his waist.

"One question," he said, his voice low. "Does this mean you're engaged to whoever she sells your ring to, instead of me?"

"Oh, I think we're still engaged." She brushed her fingers over his bare left wrist. "But I'm afraid your punctual days are over."

"I would hope so," he said. "I've been taking vitamins."

She giggled again, her green eyes dancing. Still smiling, she dried her tears on his sleeve, and they strolled arm-in-arm down the rain-puddled sidewalk toward the campus.

The Willisburg Stage

"Oh, you know how your grandma is," the old man said. He was sitting in a weathered green rocker on the front porch of his farmhouse, whittling on a piece of wood. A pile of pine shavings littered the floor between his boots. "She's probably worried about tomorrow, with your boyfriend coming and all."

Katherine brushed a strand of honey-blond hair from her eyes and squinted into the distance. "No, that's not it," she said. "Something's happened, since yesterday." She turned to look at him. "I think something's scared her."

Ethan Watkins, eighty-one years old that spring, stopped whittling and peered at his granddaughter over the top of his glasses. It was one of those *You don't miss anything, do you, young lady?* looks.

He sighed, long and deep. "Your grandma heard noises. During the night."

"What kind of noises?"

Ethan hesitated, and for an instant Katherine saw something in his eyes. “It’s a long story,” he said.

She forced a playful grin. “That never stopped you before.”

He stayed quiet awhile, toying with his knife and the stick of pine in his hand. His wispy gray hair stirred in the breeze.

Katherine waited. Her mind was on what she’d noticed in his expression a moment ago. It was unexpected, yet familiar: she’d seen the same thing on her grandmother’s face all morning long.

He’s scared too, she thought.

Suddenly Katherine was worried. She recalled how thrilled both of them had sounded when she’d called them from college last week. She’d been here on their farm outside Mesa View for two days now, and when she left, the day after tomorrow, she’d be going away to a graduation and a wedding and a life of her own, and there was no telling when they’d be together again. She wanted—she needed—to know what was going on here.

Slowly the old man folded his knife and tucked it into his pocket, and something about the finality of that gesture told her he’d made up his mind.

“It all started better’n a hundred years ago, almost a hundred and fifty,” he began. “A stagecoach line ran between here and Willisburg, twice a week. The stage office was down on Main Street, next to what used to be Lawson’s Dry Goods.” He heaved a sigh. “The line was owned and operated by two businessmen who moved here from back east—one was Big Walt Beauregard, I forget the other one’s name. Anyhow, Mesa View was good to them. They both became rich, and fast.” He chuckled. “Two reasons for their success. One was, they had no competition, since railroads hadn’t reached these parts yet. The other was, they were crooks. Their prices were too high, the coaches too flimsy, and it was rumored they spent half their time running guns and liquor to the Comanches."

The old man paused, studying the piece of wood in his hand, then tossed it into the dusty yard. Behind them, somewhere in the house, a door slammed.

"The accident happened in the summer of 1867," he continued. "There'd been heavy rains that spring, and a rockslide took out part of the east rim of Palo Remo Canyon. It also took out the road. The stagecoach route had to be diverted around the west end of the canyon, making the trip to Willisburg twenty miles longer. Walt Beauregard and his partner decided that wouldn't do, and hired a crew to shore up the east road, make it passable again." He stopped and scratched his whiskers. "Well, they did it, sure enough, and in record time. Trouble was, they did it wrong. When the stage drivers saw the new road, right on the cliff's edge, they declared it unsafe, and stomped off the job. You can guess what happened next: other drivers were hired, mostly fools who either didn't know the danger or didn't care."

His granddaughter stared at him, absorbed. "And one of them went off the road?"

He nodded. "First trip through. Stage was full at the time, six passengers inside plus the two men up top. The roadway collapsed, simple as that, and all eight dropped over the cliff into the canyon. When word reached town, Beauregard and his partner claimed the driver'd taken the new route against orders, which was a lie, and they refused to aid the families of those who'd died. What's worse, it was discovered later that the two of them had taken out huge insurance policies on their stagecoaches and horses—and only a few days before the route had reopened. No one suggested the owners had planned an accident, but almost everyone agreed that they'd expected one." The old man shrugged. "Whatever the truth was, the sheriff back then and his deputy, my great-granddaddy, ran the partners out of town, and they never came back."

Katherine, watching in puzzlement, suddenly understood.

"The Willisburg Stage," she said.

"What?"

"I've heard of it. I knew I had. It was a story I read in high school, by someone named Greenwood, or Greenleaf—"

"Greentree," he said, nodding. "Edna Earle Greentree. She lived here a spell, back in the fifties." He studied his granddaughter a moment. "Good memory."

"The setting made me think of it, I guess. I mean, how many stories do you read about Mesa View, Texas?"

"Not many. What exactly do you remember?"

"Well . . . the stagecoach, like you said. The accident in the canyon, the controversy, all that. But then it got crazy."

"How do you mean, crazy?"

"Haven't you read it?" she asked.

He shrugged. "I want to hear your version."

"Well," she said again, concentrating, "in her story, the victims weren't actually dead. I mean, their souls were in limbo, sort of, and just rode the plains, searching for the two men—the partners—who'd caused their deaths. I remember that now. And sometimes at night, the folks who lived near there would hear sounds as the stage went by, sounds of horses and harnesses and old broken wheels—"

She stopped.

"Grandpa," she said, her voice low, "you aren't saying you believe any of that, are you? You're not saying that's what Grandma heard last night?"

They sat and looked at each other.

She turned her palms up. "Grandpa, that was *fiction*. It was an entry in a book of ghost stories."

The old man drew a deep breath. He seemed tired.

Before he replied, he fished an old briar pipe out of the pocket of his overalls, followed by a scarred lighter and a pouch of Borkum Riff. While he opened the pouch he clamped the stem of the pipe between his teeth and spoke around it.

"The characters' names," he agreed, "were fictional. The background—her tale of the accident and its aftermath—was true. The facts are on record, in the *Herald* office in town. I've read them." He took the pipe from his mouth and packed its bowl with tobacco. "The rest of her story was taken from the legend that came later—a legend everybody between here and Willisburg had heard long before Edna Earle Greentree was able to tie her shoes or stay inside the lines in her coloring book. You understand what I'm saying?"

Katherine was still staring at him, hypnotized by him. *He does*, she said to herself. *He actually believes it.*

She cleared her throat.

"The stagecoach," she murmured. "Have *you* ever heard it?"

"Better'n that."

She blinked at him. "What?"

"I've seen it," he said.

***

Somewhere far away, a dog barked. Chickens pecked and clucked in the side yard, a horsefly buzzed past, the May wind whispered in the trees beside the house. For a moment Katherine thought she heard the honk of a car in town, three miles away.

"You've . . . seen it," she repeated.

The old man took his time getting his pipe started, then snapped the lighter shut and put it away. "You've heard the background," he said, "and you've read her story. Now I'll tell you mine."

She watched him exhale a plume of smoke and settle back in his rocking chair. The eyes behind his glasses were dreamy and unfocused.

"I was twelve at the time," he said. "I know that because it was the summer after the Hindenburg blew up in New Jersey in May of '37. Funny the way you remember certain things." He took his pipe from between his teeth and examined it for a minute. "Anyway, my bedroom was in the back corner of the house, where you're staying, and I was on the way to breakfast one morning when I heard my folks talking in the kitchen. Well, something made me stop and peek in through the door, and when I did I saw my mother standing beside the stove, stirring eggs in a skillet. 'It sounded like horses,' she says, over her shoulder. 'I'm surprised they didn't wake you too. Sounded like a team of horses, pulling something big—like a wagon.' My dad, sitting at the table behind her, seemed to puzzle on that awhile. Finally he says, 'You sure it was a wagon?' And something about the way he said it, and the way Mama turned and they stared at each other, made little shivers go up and down my spine."

Ethan had stopped rocking now, and sat still in his chair, gazing off into space. At that moment, as he re-lived that day long ago, Katherine thought she caught a glimpse, beneath the beard and the spectacles and the wrinkles, of that little boy.

"It was while I was standing there watching them look at each other," he said, "that my kid sister—that's your great-aunt Clara, rest her soul—pushed past me into the kitchen." A flicker of a smile touched his lips. "When they saw her, and me too, they quick changed the subject, but I'd already seen the look on Mama's face. She was scared, and Pa too, and I'd already heard enough about the legend to know what he'd meant when he asked her if it was a wagon."

Katherine waited for him to continue. When he didn't,

she asked, in a small voice, “What happened then?”

He glanced at her, then slipped back into his trance. “Nothing, until that night. Just after midnight it was, when I first heard the screams.”

His granddaughter leaned forward in her chair. “Screams?”

“My sister’s,” he said. “Clara’s. And not just crying, mind you—she was hollering bloody murder. Pa got to her first, Mama and me close behind, and when they got her quieted down she told them she’d had a nightmare, the worst nightmare of her life, she said. What was it about, Pa asked her, and when she told him I thought Mama was going to pass out cold.”

“It was about the stagecoach,” Katherine whispered, surprising herself. “Wasn’t it?”

The old man nodded. “It had pulled up in the front yard, Clara said, not far from the porch. Two men were sitting on top, one of them with a shotgun across his lap and the other holding the reins for a team of four black horses that snorted and pawed the ground. Half a dozen more people were inside the coach, she said, and all of them—she started crying again when she told us this part—all of them were looking at her, all those inside and on top too were just looking at her with their cold dead eyes, and empty faces. And just before she woke up, right at the point where she had realized it was a nightmare, one of them spoke to her. One word, she said, that was all, but it was clear as could be. One of them opened his mouth and looked straight at her and said: ‘Beauregard.’”

Katherine gaped at him. “Beauregard?”

He nodded again.

“One of the partners,” she murmured. “So Clara thought . . . she thought they were looking for him?”

“She didn’t think anything,” he said. “She was just a ten-year-old kid, scared silly, telling us about her dream.”

“But you think they were,” she said.

“Yep. I think they were.”

She hesitated, feeling lightheaded, listening to the dry rustle of the wind in the oak branches beside the porch. She couldn’t hear it so well anymore, she realized. Her heart was beating too loud.

“What about the other one?”

“The other partner? Beats me. They just called the one name.”

“What happened next?” she asked.

Ethan Watkins blew out a sigh.

“What happened next was enough to make us forget all about the Willisburg Stage, at least for a while. And enough to make me, for the first and last time in my life, want to kill a man with my bare hands.”

Katherine, sitting wide-eyed on the edge of her chair, heard the bitterness in his voice.

“He came the next afternoon,” Ethan said. “The day after Clara’s dream. An East Texas cattleman, he told us. And a real character he was, with a big hat and a cigar and a diamond pinky-ring and a fancy car that he drove up and parked right behind Pa’s old buckboard we used to ride to town in.” He paused for a beat, remembering. “He was small, really, not even tall as you are, and kinda slimy-looking. I mean, he was well-dressed and all, but . . . slimy. He looked like if you shook his hand his fingers would slip right out, you know? Not that I did, mind you. He paid no attention to me. He was only interested in my dad. ‘I want to buy your farm,’ he says, just like that. ‘I’ll pay top dollar.’

“Pa just stared at him. ‘Not for sale,’ Pa tells him, and the stranger did something odd then. He just looked down at his boots and chuckled, like he’d heard a fine joke. ‘Everything’s for sale, Mr. Watkins,’ he says.”

Ethan fell silent a minute, his eyes unfocused again. His granddaughter watched him, trying to figure what all this was leading to.

"Pa told me to go inside," Ethan said then. "And I did. But I went straight to that window there, and watched them. And listened. It was so quiet I could hear Clara singing to herself, way out in the back yard.

"'This is my home, Mister,' I heard Pa say. 'I grew up here, like my neighbors down the road. You're wasting your breath.'

"This time the stranger didn't laugh. He just stood there on the porch steps and chewed on his cigar. 'I've already talked to your neighbors,' he says. 'You see, it's not just *your* place I want, Mr. Watkins. I need all the land around here, between here and the Palo Remo. And I need it *now*.'"

Katherine leaned closer, her elbows on her knees. "But why?" shc asked.

Her grandfather turned to look at her. "What?"

"That's hundreds of acres, right? Thousands, maybe. Why'd he want it?"

"Good question. My pa asked him the same thing. His answer was, he wanted to build a park. A resort. Hunting, fishing, golf, the works." The old man smiled. "But it was a lie. Margie Simpson told Pa a couple days later she'd seen a team of surveyors out behind Albert O'Brien's farm the week before, when Al was off visiting."

"Surveyors?"

"Not for the land," he said. "For what was under it. Margie described their equipment."

Katherine frowned, then understood. "Oil," she said.

He nodded. "God knows there was never any found on our place, or on Al's either, as it turned out—but Lew Pritchard had a big well come in a few years later, and Willie Beale too."

He was quiet a moment. "Oil was what our stranger was after, all right, only nobody knew it then."

Ethan Watkins shifted in his chair and started rocking again. "Anyhow," he continued, "the stranger said he'd talked to our neighbors, so Pa asked him what they said. 'Well, Mr. Watkins,' the stranger says, 'turns out you and I are a lot alike. You see, my colleagues said they'd leave this deal up to me to decide. And your friends down the road said the same thing about *you*.' When Pa asked him what he meant by that, he said the neighbors were tempted by his offers, but they'd decided they wouldn't sell unless Pa did. Simple as that. 'So it all boils down to you and me,' the stranger says.

"Pa stood up then, straight and tall. 'I already gave you my answer,' Pa says.

"For a minute or so the guy just got a funny look on his face. 'That's your final word?' he says. Pa told him it was. 'Then I think it's time we talked to your wife,' he says to Pa.

"It got real quiet then," Ethan said. "I was still standing in that window there, watching them through the curtains, and when I turned around I saw my mama was right behind me, looking over my shoulder. She had her hair tied up in a bun like your grandma does, and was drying her hands on her apron. We glanced at each other just long enough for me to see she was as confused as I was, then we both looked out the window again.

"'What do you mean, talk to my wife?' Pa asked him. 'Well,' the stranger says, kinda smug, 'I'd like to ask her about a man named McAllyster. Edward McAllyster.'

"Behind me, I heard Mama suck in her breath, and when I looked at her she was pale as a bedsheet. Out on the porch, Pa took a step back, and groped behind him for the arm of his chair. He sat down slow and easy, like a man twice his age. And even though I didn't catch on right away to what was happening, I was plenty spooked, I'll tell you that. I'd never seen either of them act that way before."

Katherine asked, in a hushed voice, "What *was* happening, Grandpa?"

The old man brushed some stray pine-shavings off the legs of his overalls. "It's something I've never told anyone else, Katie Girl. Something better forgotten, probably. Mama had told us, though, Clara and me, soon's we were old enough to understand. I think now that she and Pa had always suspected something like this might happen someday." Ethan hesitated, then looked his granddaughter in the eye. "Ever heard of the Ouachita Kid?"

Katherine almost grinned, then realized he was serious. "The what? Wichita Kid?"

"Ouachita, like the river," he said.

She shook her head.

"Well, long story short, he was kind of a second-rate outlaw. Made the history books by killing a bunch of folks up in the plains. A bad one, he was." The old man paused as if collecting his thoughts. "Anyway, one night in the winter of 1922, the Kid was eating supper in an Oklahoma cafe. He picked a fight, for some reason, with the guy sitting at the next table. The Kid pulled a gun and said he was gonna plug him, right there—and he would've, too, except a little waitress named Lizzie Smith bashed the Kid over the head with an iron skillet. Killed him dead as a doorknob." Ethan sighed. "Turned out the local sheriff was the Kid's cousin, and the waitress was arrested for murder. Two days later she told a deputy she'd seen a mouse in her cell, snuck out when he came in to look, got clean away, and was never found. End of story."

Katherine watched him, saying nothing.

"The Ouachita Kid's real name was Edward McAllyster," he said. "And Lizzie Smith, when she got married a year later, became Elizabeth Watkins."

Katherine blinked. "Your *mother*?"

He nodded.

"And this stranger . . . he knew all this?"

"He'd found out. Somehow."

Katherine thought that over. "But—she was innocent, right? She saved a man's life. Besides, how much time had passed? Fifteen years?"

He shrugged. "She had run away. And there's no statute of limitations on murder. Like I said, I think she and Pa'd always figured someone would eventually find her." Ethan sighed again. "Anyhow, back to what I saw—I stood there and watched her walk through the front door to the porch. When she got to Pa's chair she laid a hand on his shoulder and he put an arm around her waist.

"Then she looked up at the stranger. 'Why're you doing this?' she asked him. His expression never changed. 'I want this land,' he says to her. 'And if I buy yours, the others'll sell me theirs.'

"'Or you'll turn me in?' she asked. He just shrugged and smirked a little. 'No need for that, Miz Watkins. Besides you and your husband, I'm the only one who knows. And I can forget things pretty dern quick, when I want to.'"

"But . . . that was blackmail," Katherine said.

Ethan nodded. "That it was. But they had no choice." He puffed on his pipe a moment, deep in thought. "I watched as my pa went to find the papers, watched Mama cry into her hands when he signed the deed over. The stranger handed him a check, but I don't think Pa even looked at it. Then he told Pa he wanted us out of the house by such-and-such a day, and smiled at us." Ethan exhaled a perfect smoke-ring and watched the wind unravel it. "I think I could have killed him then, Katie Girl. I really do. If I'd owned a gun, or if I'd known where one was right that second, I think I could've killed him as he stood there grinning on the edge of our porch."

A long silence passed. "Anyhow, that's what I *wanted* to do," Ethan said finally. "What I *did* was go out the door and stand beside my pa while the little man put the deed in his pocket and strutted to his big car and drove away. None of us ever saw him again."

Katherine sat motionless for a full minute, watching her grandfather look off into the blue distance. The story was turning out to be more complicated than she'd thought.

Three things, specifically, were bothering her. One was this business of ghosts and goblins riding around the countryside in the middle of the night. That was just too weird. The second was that she knew her great-grandfather couldn't have sold this place in the late 1930's. Her father had grown up here, after all, and she and her folks had come here to visit every year for as long as she could remember. And the third thing—well, it was a combination of the first two.

"Grandpa," she said, "all this about the stranger and the land and the blackmail—what's the connection? What does that have to do with the stagecoach accident, seventy years earlier?"

Ethan took the pipe from between his teeth and studied it. "The connection," he said, "was his name."

"The stranger?" She frowned. "You didn't tell me his name."

"You're right. He didn't tell us, either, until just before he left." Ethan turned then, and looked her in the eye. "His name was Walter Beauregard."

The two words hung there in the air.

"You're joking," she murmured.

"Nope. He was Big Walt's grandson, we found out later."

"Beauregard," she said, thinking over the implications.

"It was a coincidence. Had to be."

"Was it? Remember, this was the day after Clara's dream. And the second day after my mother heard the noises in the yard."

The silence stretched out. Katherine felt a tiny shiver ripple down her back. The wind now seemed chilly.

"In any case, we all stood there gawking at him while he drove away, out of our lives. All except Mama—she was off to one side, looking out over the land, tears rolling down her cheeks."

Ethan Watkins put his pipe down, took off his glasses, and polished them on his shirtsleeve. "It was almost dark, I remember that, and the thick cloud of dust his car raised as it headed up the road. There was a storm brewing off to the west, I recall that too. A big one, judging from the lightning." He shook his head and replaced his glasses. "I don't know how long we stayed out there in the yard. I do know it was full dark, though, when Pa called to Clara and took Mama's hand and we went back inside."

He paused then, lost in his thoughts.

"Next thing we did was have a family meeting. Pa was big on family meetings. He told us, Clara and me, exactly what had just happened—even though I'd heard most of it myself—and that started Clara crying as well as Mama."

Ethan seemed to remember something then, and smiled. "I suggested going after him, and forcing him at gunpoint to give us back our deed. Pa just shook his head. 'We been well paid,' he says to me. 'We'll go someplace else, start fresh.' The idea, of course, was to make us all feel better, and it might've worked if we hadn't seen the tears in his eyes." Ethan pondered that a moment. "It was the worst night of my life, Katie. Mama fixed a meal but nobody ate, we sat together in the living room but nobody said anything, we went to bed but nobody slept.

And then—it was around midnight again, I think—we heard it."

Heard what? she started to ask—and caught herself. Maybe she didn't really want to know. Maybe she should just get up now and go in and help Grandma with supper . . .

"Horses," he said, answering the unspoken question. "A whole team, it sounded like, pulling something big and rickety." He narrowed his eyes, remembering. "It was storming outside, but we could hear 'em anyway, above the rain and thunder. We all ran to the front door, 'cause the noise was coming from that direction, and Pa threw it open and all four of us charged out and stood together on the porch with the wind and rain in our faces, right here where you and I are sitting now—"

He stopped then, and Katherine saw a tremor go through his body. For several seconds he stared straight ahead, his eyes somewhere far away.

But not in miles, she said to herself. In years.

"It was there," he said.

She felt her arms break out in gooseflesh.

"The stagecoach was there in the yard, no more'n twenty feet away. Big and old and dirty, and lit up by the lightning—" He stopped and swallowed again. "At least seven feet tall it was, and twelve long. One of the doors was missing, I remember that, and whole panels had been caved in or torn off. And both right wheels were bent and broken, half the spokes gone. I recall thinking, *There's no way this thing could roll. No way.*"

Another pause. When he continued, his voice was quiet.

"In front of the coach were four horses," he said, "tall and black and shining in the rain, tossing their heads, snorting and stomping, making the stage shake . . ."

He fell silent then, his eyes staring into the past.

His granddaughter watched him a moment, stunned. Finally she gathered her courage. "What about . . . what about the—"

He turned to look at her.

"The passengers?" he said.

She nodded.

"They were there, just the way Clara told us in her dream. A stage full of dead people." Ethan shook his head. "They were dried up and dead. And yet they weren't. They were sitting there looking at us through the downpour, watching us watch *them*. I'll never forget that feeling, long as I live." Another shudder went through him. "And then one of them—it was the driver, up on top—" Ethan paused and said, "He spoke to us."

The old man's eyes had glazed over again, and Katherine realized she was hardly breathing. She thought she could hear his watch ticking.

"His voice was deep, and . . . it echoed, almost. But like Clara'd said, it was clear." Another pause. "He looked at us—he looked at Pa, actually, he looked right at Pa—and he said four words. He said: 'We have him now.'"

They both sat very still.

Off to the west, a white cloud of dust followed a tractor home from the fields. A new breeze stirred the pine shavings under their chairs. The sun, lower now, painted the floor with the patterned shadows of the porch railing.

Katherine's heart sounded, to her, like a drum in her chest.

"We have *who* now?" she whispered.

Ethan Watkins's eyes came into focus. "Who do you think?"

"But . . . it was the wrong man. You said so yourself. This was the grandson of the one they really wanted."

Ethan shook his head. "Didn't matter. He was a direct descendant. Blood kin. They wanted a Beauregard—and they got one."

Katherine's mouth felt as dry as paste. "Got him how? You just said you never saw him again."

"Nobody did. The sheriff found his car the next morning, parked by the side of the road with the driver's door open. They never found Walter Beauregard III."

For a while, neither of them spoke. Finally Katherine turned to him again, hugging her elbows.

"What if," she said weakly, "what if someone just kidnapped him? Or killed him, and buried the body? You said yourself he looked rich. And maybe . . . Grandpa, maybe the stage *was* a dream. A dream, like Great-Aunt Clara's was, the night before."

Her grandfather looked at her lovingly then.

"It was no dream, Katie Girl. All four of us saw it, not just me. Besides, there's proof, if you want it, right here in this house, in the hall closet behind the boxes of old shoes and seed catalogues."

She blinked. "What kind of proof?"

He leaned back in his chair, more at ease now. He thought a moment, then said, "Just after they—the driver—spoke to us, and just before they left, the second man, the one riding shotgun, reached behind him and brought out a mailbag. An old leather pouch it was, with a belted flap and slickered to keep the rain out. Without a word, he swung it back and forth a time or two and tossed it across the yard and onto the porch. It landed right here at our feet, between Mama and me." Ethan stroked his beard, deep in thought. "Then the driver flicked the reins, cracked his whip . . . and they were gone."

Katherine swallowed. "A mail pouch? What was inside it? Mail?"

"No. It was empty—except for one thing."

"What? A letter? A message?"

The old man started to shake his head, then stopped.

"Yes," he said thoughtfully. "It *was* a message, in a way."

She frowned, working it over in her mind. What was he getting at? What could possibly—

Understanding hit her like a slap in the face. She felt her stomach twist.

"The deed," she said.

He nodded. "Safe and snug. The deed Pa had signed over to Beauregard six hours earlier."

There was a moment of total silence.

Finally Katherine rose, her legs unsteady beneath her, and stumbled to the edge of the porch. She held fast to the whitewashed railing and gazed out at the yard and the trees and the road and the rolling pastures beyond.

"I don't know how long we stood out here after they left," Ethan said behind her. His voice was low, and with the corner of her mind that was still listening she knew he was again immersed in his memories. "When we went back inside, even after some of the shock wore off, Pa couldn't seem to take his eyes off the deed. Finally he got up and put it back in his desk, and hid the mailbag in the hall closet. Then he tore Beauregard's check into a hundred pieces."

He was quiet then, and Katherine turned to look at him. Despite the warm sun on her back, she still felt cold.

"Nobody slept that night," he said. "Nobody except Clara, that is. She'd been calm through the whole thing, as if she knew now that they'd never really meant us any harm—this time." Ethan stirred and seemed to wake from his reverie. "We agreed later, the four of us, never to discuss what had happened. Not with each other or with anyone else. And we didn't."

Softly Katherine said, "You never told *any*one?"

"Only your grandma, years later." He smiled a little. "Not that it surprised her. Oh, it scared her, that's for sure, but it didn't surprise her. She grew up near here, and knew the legend. She'd heard the stories all her life, like me."

Katherine had a thought. For a moment her fear was forgotten, replaced by curiosity. "Grandpa," she said, "over the years, all those who heard the stage, who talked about it, who spread the stories—didn't anyone else ever *see* it, like you?"

"Not that I know of," he said.

"But they heard it."

"Yes."

Katherine turned this over in her mind. "And did you ever hear it? Again?"

He frowned. "I thought I did, a couple times. Once out back, feeding the chickens, another time in the south pasture at sundown, stringing fencewire."

"But nothing happened, except that once," she said. "Not to you, or to any of the others who heard it. Right?"

"Right. Far as I know."

She paused a moment. "But you think, this time, it—they—are coming back. You think they're coming back here again. Don't you."

Very slowly, he nodded. "Yes. I do."

"Because of what Grandma heard last night?"

"It's just a feeling, Katie. I can't explain it."

"But . . . what would they want, Grandpa? What would they be after?"

A silence passed.

"I don't know," he said.

***

It was three hours later. Supper had been tense, with little conversation. Katherine Watkins was standing alone now behind the farmhouse, leaning against the fence beside the barn. High clouds drifted past, tinted orange by the last rays of the sun. Within seconds they faded from view. Night came fast out here, and with the night came the cool, even in late spring.

Katherine flipped down her sleeves and buttoned the cuffs.

She turned to look at the house. The sound of the television floated by on the wind, and soft light spilled from the windows, painting fuzzy yellow squares on the dooryard grass. All of a sudden, along with the voices and music from the TV, she caught the scent of her grandfather's pipe, and a moment later saw his shadow pass an open window.

She couldn't help smiling. This afternoon, on the porch, her mind had been occupied with other things, but now the tangy smell of Ethan Watkins's pipe reminded her of her childhood, of her summer visits to this house, of sitting on his knee while he and her grandma played Rook on the checkered kitchen tablecloth. It reminded her of how much she loved them both.

Katherine turned again, her forearms resting now on the top rail of the fence, and looked out at the shadowy back pasture. Stars were beginning to wink overhead.

What is happening here?

This afternoon's story had shaken her more deeply than she'd realized. She'd barely been able to eat her supper at all, and now, after thinking the whole thing through, her stomach still felt queasy. At one point during the meal tonight, while her grandmother had gone to get their dessert from the kitchen, Katherine had excused herself for the bathroom and had instead spent several long minutes standing outside the door to the hall closet, wondering whether to open it and look inside.

She had decided not to, and had returned to the table convinced there was no leather mail pouch, and even if there were, it certainly hadn't come from the ghosts of a wrecked stagecoach. *Good grief.* It had taken her awhile, she admitted, but she had finally come to her senses.

The sad truth was, her grandfather was old. God knows she loved him and always would, but he was an old man now and these spooky legends he'd heard all his life were beginning to work on his mind.

Off to the south, a train whistle hooted mournfully, and she turned to study the dim glow of lights on the horizon. Mesa View, she said to herself, and smiled. It was an interesting town, a town full of good people and, for her, good memories. But how could you take it too seriously? There wasn't a single mesa to be viewed, in any direction.

Her thoughts returned to her grandpa, and she wondered whether the town had a practicing psychiatrist. She doubted it.

Her head was beginning to hurt. She sighed and rubbed her eyes with her knuckles like a little girl.

The one thing that still worried her, now that she'd sorted the whole business out, was something Ethan had said to her just before her grandma had called them to wash up for supper. Two things, actually. Two sentences: *It's just a feeling, Katie,* he'd said. *I can't explain it.*

Just a feeling. Still, that bothered her. Ethan Watkins's "feelings" were not to be taken lightly—whether he could explain them or not. Her grandfather had always, as long as she could remember, been able to sense things no one else knew. Even tonight, at the supper table. He had taken a long swallow of iced tea, set down his glass, and asked when the wedding would be. Not as a joke or anything; he was just making conversation.

She felt a tremor of unease along the back of her neck. She and Scotty hadn't told anyone about their decision to marry, not even their closest school pals. And yet Ethan knew.

Oh well, she thought. At least they would like him. Everyone liked Scotty Treppendahl.

The thought of Scotty, as always, made her feel better. He'd be driving in tomorrow, would stay here tomorrow night, and the following morning they'd travel the five hours to his folks's home to spend the weekend before heading back to college for graduation. The wedding was set for July, a tiny ceremony with only a few friends. Forty-seven days from now.

Katherine Treppendahl, she whispered to herself, trying the name on for size. It had a nice ring to it.

The wind picked up a little, rippling her hair and the fabric of her shirt. Absently she turned up her collar. On the eastern horizon, a full yellow moon began to climb the sky—

She gasped.

Behind her, she'd heard a noise. The sad, creaking sound of old wood straining against old nails, and the rusty rattle of chains and harnesses and traces . . .

She found she couldn't move. Her heart was in her throat, her muscles locked tight. Panic scratched at the door of her mind, trying to get in. With a tremendous effort, she clenched her fists and whirled around—

Nothing there. Thirty feet away, the old gate to the back pasture bumped and creaked in the gusty wind, dragging its chain sluggishly to and fro along the metal latch that held it shut.

She stood there looking at it, dizzy with relief, waiting for her heart to slow down.

"You're a fool, Katie Watkins," she said aloud. There are no ghosts, there are no dead men riding the plains, there is no Willisburg Stage. Not any more.

Another snatch of music glided past. It was vaguely familiar, a rock-beat intro to one of the new CSI series. Still trembling a bit, Katherine glanced at the house; she saw her grandfather's silhouette rise from its chair and move away, probably in search of the TV remote. Seconds later the theme was cut off, replaced by the champagne music of Lawrence Welk. She grinned in spite of herself. Some things would never change.

She drew a long breath and let it out in a whoosh.

Everything's going to be all right, she decided.

She gave the pasture gate one last, triumphant look, pushed her hands deep into her pockets, and trudged back to the house.

***

At exactly ten minutes past midnight, Katherine Watkins sat bolt upright in her bed. Her nightgown was soaked in sweat, her hands shaking.

She looked around her at the moonlit room: ancient dresser, handmade rug on the floor, lace curtains in the window . . .

She stared at these things, yet saw none of them. All she could see were the remnants of the dream. Fighting it, she squeezed her eyes shut. Warm tears rolled down her cheeks and dropped into her lap.

The images remained, vivid and real, etched into her mind.

In the dream, she was standing behind the house at night, beside the wooden fence that bordered the dooryard. The stagecoach was parked on the grass between her and the barn.

The whole scene was bright as day, floodlit by the full moon. She could see every detail: the bare, rotten wood of the coach's side panels, the torn curtains in the windows, the warped brake-lever, the twisted bars of the luggage rack. As she watched, a small piece of the undercarriage broke loose, fell to the ground, and disappeared.

Ahead of the stage, four giant black horses shifted restlessly in their traces, their breaths smoking in the chilly air. Above it, two men sat in the driver's box, looking at her. One held a rusted shotgun across his lap, the other held the reins. Their clothes were filthy and tattered, faces shadowy beneath wide hats. A shaft of moonlight glinted off the driver's cartridge belt. Inside the coach, six dark figures huddled around the windows. All of them were staring at her.

The Katherine in the dream held onto the fence and looked back at them, her mind spinning, her legs rubbery with terror. And just as she realized that it was really a nightmare, just as she was about to wake up, one of the passengers leaned forward over the others and spoke to her. One word only, as clear and sharp and resonant as the last note of a bugle at taps.

"Treppendahl," he said.

Vacationland

The young lady in the black dress stood beside the hotel's admissions desk, reading a Gray Line brochure she had taken from a rack on the countertop. She had the sophisticated, self-assured look of a businesswoman between appointments. Her outfit was smart and tasteful, her hair short, her eyes gray. She was tall and tan and lovely, and she was a thief.

The dark-haired man sipping coffee in the lobby restaurant watched her closely as she replaced the brochure and walked around the handful of pale tourists waiting to check in. Her expression was one of extreme boredom, though her eyes darted about constantly, missing nothing. When she strolled past the elevators and headed for the entrance the man in the coffeeshop put down his cup, rose to his feet, dropped a couple of bills onto the table, and followed her out through the front door.

Bellboys crisscrossed the area just outside the doors, unloading luggage and guests. The dark-haired man stopped there a moment, taking in the view.

It was a fine day. April was always a good month in central Florida—budding trees, reasonable temperatures, and not nearly so many tourists or afternoon rainshowers as would come later, in the blazing heat of summer. And what tourists were here were usually older and less troublesome. The kids were still in school.

He caught up with her on the sidewalk in front of the hotel. "Pardon me," he called, from ten feet away.

She turned and regarded him coolly as he approached. She was even more striking up close, he saw. The gray eyes and the blond hair and the jet-black dress against the backdrop of swaying palms and blue sky made him think of a magazine ad, or a sexy perfume commercial. As he stared at her, the sun and the light breeze turned her hair into a halo.

"What do you want?" she said.

He cleared his throat. "I want to ask you a couple of questions, if you don't mi—"

"Actually I do mind. I'm in a bit of a hurry." She started to turn away.

"I'm sure you are," he said. Something in his voice made her pause, and she turned to face him again. Their eyes met and held. Just for an instant, her gaze flicked past him to the front doors of the hotel, then returned to his face. For the first time, she looked uneasy.

"Who are you?" she asked.

He smiled. "My name is Lawrence Hammett. A pleasure to meet you, Ms. . . ."

"Jones," she said.

"Right." If her name was Jones, he thought, he was the King of the Gypsies. "I assure you, I'll only take a moment of your time."

She looked him up and down. He cut an elegant figure, and he knew it—tailored pinstripe suit, hundred-dollar tie, brilliantly polished shoes, hanky arranged just so. She seemed unimpressed.

Just as she opened her mouth to reply, one of the bell-boys approached them. The girl froze. "Excuse me, Mr. Hammett—" he began.

Lawrence Hammett cut him off with one upraised hand, without ever taking his eyes off Ms. Jones's face. The bellboy said no more, and Hammett knew without looking that he had gone.

"Let's sit over there, where we can talk," Hammett said, as if there had been no interruption. Before she could reply he had steered her away down the sidewalk to the northeast corner of the hotel, where two wooden benches faced each other in the shadow of a tall hedgerow. "Now," he said, as they were seated, "isn't there something you'd like to tell me?"

She sat and stared at him, her fists opening and closing. Her efforts to appear nonchalant were failing fast. After a moment she seemed to try to lean backward to check out the hotel entrance, but that failed also. The hedge was too thick to see through. She turned to face him again, raising her chin in defiance.

"I demand to know," she said, "what this is all about."

Hammett held up a hand then, and silenced her as effectively as he had silenced the bellboy. He was no longer smiling. "What this is about," he said, "is an incident that took place in the lobby a moment ago. One of the hotel guests seems to have had a small . . . problem."

The young woman stiffened, her face pale. "I beg your pardon?"

"An older gentleman," Hammett explained. "He's misplaced something, he says. I thought . . . well, I wondered if you might be able to shed some light on it for me."

She managed to swallow, and sat up a little straighter in her seat. "Are you . . . accusing me of something?" she asked, in a shaky voice.

"Not directly. I just thought we should, well, talk."

A car horn honked somewhere beyond the hedge, and she jumped. She raised a small hand to her throat and rubbed it slowly.

"Who are you?" she asked again.

"I told you."

"Not your name," she said. "Who *are* you?"

He was quiet a moment, studying her face.

"Are you a cop?" she asked.

That amused him. "If I were a cop," he assured her, "we wouldn't be having this discussion."

"Who then? Security?"

"No."

Some of her color had returned. He could read her thoughts: *If he isn't the police and he isn't a house detective . . .*

Then her face sagged, and again he knew what she was thinking. She'd remembered the bellboy.

She cleared her throat. "But . . . you work for the hotel?"

"Not exactly," he said.

"What do you mean?"

"I own the hotel."

She blinked. For a long moment neither of them spoke. High overhead, the cool wind rattled in the palms.

"You own it," she said, looking dazed.

Lawrence Hammett drew a deep breath, let it out slowly, and leaned forward to face her, his forearms propped on his knees.

"Listen to me, young lady," he said. "I was serious a minute ago when I said we needed to talk. I know you took the old man's wallet; I saw you. But I don't want to have to report it."

She sat and gaped at him.

"Why not? you might ask," he said.

She swallowed. "Why not?" she asked, in a tiny voice.

He clasped his hands and gazed straight into her eyes.

"Let me bore you with some statistics," he said. "It may surprise you, but fully one third of all the cars rented in the United States are rented in Florida. Hard to believe? It gets harder. One half of all the cars rented in Florida are rented here in Dalton County. And of all the car rentals in the nation . . ."

He leaned closer. "The point is, we're a tourist paradise. The theme parks, the studios, the resorts—we're probably the number one vacation choice in the world. Are you starting to get the message?"

She just stared at him, waiting. She seemed to be holding her breath.

"Now, consider this," he continued. "According to the paper this morning—this very morning—tourists are saying they're afraid to come here any more. Afraid to *come here*. You know why?"

"No . . ."

"Tourist crime, Ms. Jones. Crimes against tourists, against visitors to our city. It's logical, if you think about it. They're unfamiliar with the area, they're wealthy, and they're naive. Easy pickings. If it's allowed to continue, if even the *perception* is allowed to continue, businessmen like me could be in real trouble, Ms. Jones. No one wants to come to a place that isn't safe, where he thinks he'll be a target. He'd rather stay home. Stay home or go someplace that *is* safe, like the Grand Canyon or Yellowstone or Niagara Falls. Get my drift?"

He fell silent a moment, watching her face.

"My final point," he went on, "is that I don't relish the idea of telling that man back there in the lobby that he had his pocket picked in my hotel. What I had much rather do is go back in there and tell him one of my staff found it on the floor of a hallway. No problem, no robbery, no bad press. Everybody's happy." He paused. "You follow me so far?"

The girl in the classy black dress was no Alberta

Einstein, he decided, but she was no dummy either. She followed him loud and clear.

"What do you want, exactly?" she asked, as a formality. Whatever he wanted, she would do; both of them knew that. She'd scrub the hotel restrooms for a year if he told her to, as long as she didn't have to go to jail.

"What I want," he said, "is to keep this quiet, which I imagine is fine with you. What I also want—what I demand—is that you never, ever, come back to this hotel again, for any reason. In fact, I want you to stay away from all the big hotels, period. If you're foolish enough to continue this line of work, that's up to you, but it'll have to be done elsewhere, and preferably in another city. Understand?"

She was nodding vigorously. The cool, self-confident businesswoman was long gone. All she wanted now was for this to be finished. Here she was, caught with the cookies by the owner of the cookie-jar himself, and she was being offered a second chance.

"Speak, then," he said.

"Agreed." She took a shaky breath. "Agreed. You got a deal."

Silently he held out a hand, palm upward. Without hesitation she took the fat wallet from her purse and gave it to him. He rose, holding the evidence, and she followed suit. For a moment they stood there looking at each other in the cool shade.

"I don't ever want to see you again," he said. "I hope that's clear."

"You won't," she assured him, "and it is."

With that, she snapped her purse shut, hitched its strap over her shoulder, and left. She almost ran down the sidewalk to the landscaped parking lot, her high heels clicking musically on the concrete.

***

Lawrence Hammett watched her until she vanished from sight, then he turned and strolled past the hedge to the front of the hotel. Once again he found himself enjoying the brilliance of the sun, the soft caress of the wind, the elegant beauty of his surroundings. A jet droned overhead, and birds played and sang in the hedgerow. Two hundred yards from the hotel was the entrance to one of three area marine parks; even now he could hear the distant barking of seals and the murmur of crowd noise. This was an exciting city, he thought, for the hundredth time. A good place to live and work.

Just outside the hotel's front doors he saw the bellboy who had approached him earlier, and as they passed he pressed a twenty-dollar bill into the young man's palm. He had the same arrangement with bellboys all over the city, and it was worth every penny. What could be better, when using a false identity, than being addressed by that name in public, by someone credible? And what did it matter that all these boys thought they were being paid to help a lonely snob impress an occasional young lady?

The man calling himself Lawrence Hammett—an alias that combined the names of his two favorite mystery writers—walked through the doors and into the lobby, where he found a newspaper and eased into an armchair. The blonde's victim had left, which wasn't surprising; it usually took these old geezers several hours to realize their losses, whether they were wallets or diamond brooches or Rolex Oysters. All he had to do was watch for the people who lifted them.

He decided he would spend another hour or so here, then move on to the other hotels on his route. It was early yet.

He sat quietly in the leather chair in the center of the lobby, the newspaper open but unread in his hand, his eyes on the crowd, the first wallet of the day satisfyingly heavy in his pocket, and waited . . .

John M. Floyd

Remembering Tally

"Try to look impressed, sir," Fenton whispered.

J. Talmadge Byrd snorted as they stood in the office doorway. It was his first visit to what his campaign staff called their "blue-collar location"—a large, seedy-looking room on the second floor of a West Side office building. Two of the walls were lined with huge windows, open not only to the gloomy day but to the rather appropriate odor of the nearby stockyards. "I'm a candidate for governor, Freddie," Byrd replied, pasting a wooden smile on his face for the assembled crowd. "Not an actor."

"Begging your pardon, sir, it's the same thing."

Which was about as close as Fenton ever came to opposing a statement made by his boss. As Tally Byrd's personal secretary and PR advisor, he made it a point to agree with Byrd's every opinion—or at least appear to. It was rumored that Freddie Fenton, probably the most shameless yes-man in American politics, had never entered the office of any superior who was seated at a desk; he always waited until the occupant was standing, since that made it easier for Fenton to stick his nose in the proper place.

"Members of the media," Fenton called, pushing past Byrd and waving a sheaf of papers, "gather round, please. Ground rules. Over here, please."

The half-dozen TV and newspaper reporters exchanged glances and rolled their eyes, but they obeyed. They knew that Byrd would probably soon be the next governor of their state, despite a number of recent lapses in judgment, both professional and personal. Due mainly to the skills of both his campaign manager and Freddie Fenton, Byrd had escaped disaster when the press got wind of his alleged ties to Organized Crime, not to mention a number of recent affairs with subordinates and staffers.

Thankfully for people like Byrd, politics—like the stock market—is an inexact science, and the most corrupt and least qualified candidate sometimes manages to emerge as the front-runner in the polls. Members of the news media merely sighed and shook their heads and mumbled the same words into their drinks each night: *Only in America.*

This group of reporters would have been amazed to know—and of course so would Fenton and his boss—that within the next half-hour, here in this room, Talmadge Byrd's gubernatorial campaign would come to an abrupt end.

***

While Fenton stood in the circle of journalists and reporters and read through a list of what was acceptable and what wasn't, retired oil baron Tally Byrd—slim and silver-haired and five-foot-four on tiptoe—strutted about the long room with an outthrust chin, slapping backs and braying jokes and pumping the hands of the more notable attendees. Several minutes had passed before he made his way to the old metal desk set farther back in the room. The nameplate on the desk said NANCY WESTBROOK, and the lady standing at attention beside it introduced herself in a tiny voice as the head of this particular campaign office.

The dapper little candidate studied her a moment as she rattled on about the certainty of his upcoming victory. She was a large woman with thick makeup, a shapeless dress, carrot-red hair, and a blue-and-white BYRD FOR GUV button pinned to her collar. As if he cared, she pointed out to him two of the other volunteers—a bald man with a bowtie and a very pregnant young lady—who were seated at desks between him and the far end of the office. Both were speaking on the telephone, and neither looked up. Work at a well-run campaign site never ceases, Ms. Westbrook explained proudly—even during the final minutes before a press conference.

As she rambled on, Byrd tuned her out and began rehearsing his speech in his head. He was halfway through it when he noticed something strange near the back corner of the room, past the volunteers' desks.

"Your safe's open," he said.

Ms. Westbrook stopped in mid-sentence. She followed his gaze, then smiled. "Oh, that. It's not a safe, I'm afraid. I mean, it is a safe—but there's nothing in it. We keep no money or confidential papers. No one here even has a key."

Byrd was not impressed. He had run a successful oil company for many years, and rules were rules. "Shouldn't its door at least be kept closed? For appearance's sake?"

"Well, that's a long story," she said. "You see, this isn't the best part of town, and we've had a few bomb threats, bricks through the window and so forth, and everybody's a bit jumpy. Anyhow, little Sherry Jackson—she's the pregnant lady back there, my best worker—almost quit a few weeks ago. She'd convinced herself that sooner or later we'd all be either burned up or blown up. Then one day somebody suggested that if there's a dire emergency she should just jump into the safe and pull the door shut. It'll lock if it's closed, it's probably bullet-proof and fireproof, and she's the only one around here tiny enough, even when pregnant, to fit inside." Ms. Westbrook smiled. "She's been satisfied ever since."

Byrd smiled also. From the corner of his eye he saw Freddie Fenton standing nearby with several others, some of them reporters, who also appeared to be listening to Westbrook's story.

"That's fine in theory," Byrd said, amused, "but how would she breathe in there, if things ever actually went that far?"

"See how big her purse is? I'm told she keeps a canister of oxygen in it, like a little scuba tank. Enough to last until a rescue, anyway." Nancy Westbrook's face suddenly darkened, and she included Fenton and the others when she spoke next. "Don't any of you say anything to her about it, though. That's her business, not ours."

"I agree completely," Byrd said. "Whatever makes my people happy makes me happy." What would really make him happy, he thought, would be for his "people" to shrink a few inches; this woman towered over him. With a glance at his watch he turned to look for Fenton, who—apparently reading his boss's mind—silently mouthed: "Three minutes."

The TV cameras were rolling now, and several were aimed in the candidate's direction. Having noticed this, Talmadge Byrd turned back to Ms. Westbrook, took her hand, and dipped his head in an elegant bow. "Keep up the good work, my dear," he said warmly.

At that moment the phone rang on Nancy Westbrook's desk.

She picked it up, listened a moment, and handed it to Byrd. "For you, sir. Whoever it is says it's urgent."

With a sigh he came around the desk and plopped down in Westbrook's chair. It was too high for him, which irritated him all the more; his feet barely touched the floor.

"Tally Byrd here," he barked into the receiver. "But I warn you, I don't have much time."

"You have a lot less than you think," the voice on the phone said.

Something in the tone of that statement made Byrd pause. "Who is this?"

"Listen to me carefully, Mr. Byrd. There is a bomb in the bottom right drawer of the desk where you're sitting—it's locked, by the way—and you have exactly two minutes and twenty-eight seconds before it explodes. Do you follow me so far?"

Talmadge Byrd's mouth dropped open. He suddenly found it hard to breathe.

"But I warn *you*—don't try to run. I'm watching you right now from a window across the street, through the scope of a .303 Lee-Enfield sniper rifle. You make any move toward the door, I put a bullet through your head. Nod if you understand."

For a second Byrd stayed frozen, then slowly nodded. His eyes darted to the long wall of eight-foot-high windows, and through them to the office buildings on the other side of the street.

The voice continued. "Why, you might ask, am I taking the trouble to tell you you're about to be vaporized? Well, that's complicated. You see, I am experiencing a rare bout with my conscience. It was my original intention to blow all of you away at once—the explosive charge is certainly big enough—but then I realized that would be a waste. It's mostly you I want, so I've decided to let you make the decision."

Byrd was holding his breath. A corner of his mind registered the fact that the cameras were still on him as Fenton and the media crews made final preparations. For all the good that did him now, he thought. "What decision?" he murmured.

"Whether to let them live," the voice said. "At this point, you see, you have just under two minutes until detonation. If you choose, I will allow you to sound the alarm so the others can escape. There's plenty of time—just shout 'Bomb!' or 'Fire!' or whatever suits your fancy, and we'll watch, you and I, while they stampede out of the room. That's one option. The other, of course, is to do nothing, in which case you'll still die, but everyone else'll die along with you." A short pause. "Zero hour is three o'clock exactly. One minute and thirty-five seconds from now."

Byrd licked his lips. He was sitting rock-still, moving only his eyes. The crowd at the front of the room was paying him little attention. Fenton seemed to be arguing with someone about how to position the microphones and the podium. Now and then someone glanced his way, but no one seemed to want to interrupt what was apparently an important call. The cameras were still rolling, probably to get filler footage before the main event.

He swallowed. "Why are you doing this?" he whispered.

A short laugh. "If you mean why the bomb, it's because I think you have to be stopped, Tally. Pure and simple. If you mean why the choice . . . I suppose it's a test. For months now you've been preaching to the whole state that the only thing you care about's the people and their welfare. 'Whatever I do, it's for the good of my fellow man,' you said. Well, here's your opportunity. At least a hundred of your fellow men are right there in that room with you, and you've got just over a minute left. They can still make it out if you tell 'em now." He paused. "Not many of us get a chance to control the way others will think of us after we're gone, you know. If you do this, you'll be remembered as a hero."

Byrd hesitated, sweating. His eyes swept the office. The guy was right, the crowd had grown—reporters, lawyers, the mayor, assorted friends and enemies. Dozens of faces he didn't even know. But as he scanned their ranks he wasn't thinking of whether to warn them or not. It wasn't *their* lives he was worried about.

There had to be a way . . .

"Fifty seconds," the voice announced.

The candidate's mind was racing. This part of the room was too exposed, the door too far away. Maybe if some people walked past, he could use them for cover—but that was no good either: not a soul was anywhere near him, probably so he could have some privacy. The irony of that was maddening.

"Half a minute left," the voice said.

Frantically Byrd tried to focus his thoughts. Maybe it was a hoax. Hadn't the Westbrook woman said there'd already been several false bomb threats? On an impulse Byrd reached down and tugged on the bottom right-hand drawer. Sure enough, it was locked.

But it wasn't empty. He could hear something . . .

Something ticking.

His heart lurched in his chest.

"Fifteen seconds, Mr. Byrd. Too late now. You really are spineless after all, aren't you?"

Suddenly Byrd had the answer. He knew what to do, and with that knowledge came a surge of hope. He whipped his head around for a look, then forced himself to wait a moment, until the voice spoke again:

"Well, Tally, any last reques—"

NOW. While the guy was talking . . .

Without warning Byrd launched himself from the chair, running as fast as he could—but not toward the door. He ran toward the back of the room.

The young volunteer, Sherry Jackson, looked up as she heard the gasp of the crowd, then froze as she saw Byrd charging straight for her. Before she could react he shoved her aside, sending her sprawling, and snatched her purse-strap from the back of her chair as he passed. The room watched as if hypnotized.

Purse in hand, Byrd sprinted for the safe. When he reached it he tossed the purse inside, wedged his small frame in after it, and pulled the door shut behind him. The heavy, metallic THUD shook the room.

In the ten seconds that followed, no one moved. The office was dead quiet except for the painful moans of the pregnant woman lying on the floor.

It was three o'clock sharp.

***

"I suppose the cameras caught the whole thing?" Freddie Fenton asked.

The time was 3:25, and most of the crowd had been cleared out. Those remaining were Fenton, the mayor, the TV crews and newsmen, a few of Byrd's staff, and several cops from the station down the street. The paramedics had arrived moments ago, and had transported the injured young lady to the hospital. Two firemen hovered over the safe while a welder worked with his torch on the locking mechanism. Muffled thumps and shouts came from inside.

"You bet they did," a reporter answered. He looked so smug Fenton wanted to punch him in the teeth.

"Mr. Fenton?" a voice called. "Step over here a minute?"

It was one of the policemen. Fenton gave the media people a parting glare, then crossed the room to where the cops were talking to a new arrival—a security guard with the letters W. KELLY on his nametag. "What is it, Officer?" Fenton asked.

God, he felt tired.

"Thought you might want to hear this." The cop placed an audio cassette recorder on a desktop and pressed PLAY. "It explains a few things," he added.

For the next two and a half minutes Freddie Fenton listened to a crystal-clear recording of a phone conversation between J. Talmadge Byrd and a man who claimed to be about to blow up the building.

When it was finished Fenton's face was pale as the gray desktops. "Is this for real?" he asked.

"The conversation's for real. The bomb threat wasn't, obviously. We've already sprung the bottom right drawer of the desk—all we found was a regular wind-up alarm clock."

"But—the tape. Where'd it *come* from . . . ?"

"That's the craziest part," the officer said. "Whoever called knew his stuff. That particular phone—the one on the head lady's desk—had been patched into the building's security console, and got recorded automatically." The cop nodded in the direction of the uniformed guard. "Kelly here got a call just after three, asking him to check the tape."

"A building like this has a security console?" Fenton asked.

"It's old, but it works. Unfortunately, for your candidate."

Fenton nodded. His head was aching. "So the guy who called . . . could he really see through the window? I guess he could, if he knew what was happening—"

"Not necessarily. He could've called from right here in the office, with a throwaway cell phone."

Freddie Fenton tried hard to gather his thoughts. It occurred to him that reporters were still swarming all over the room. He looked at the recorder. "Is this the only copy?" he asked, lowering his voice.

"I know what you're thinking," the cop said, "but it

really doesn't matter."

"What do you mean?"

The policeman ejected the cassette and handed it back to the guard. "Whoever it was, was quite a technician. The call wasn't just routed into the security tape, it was sent to the main speakers. Everybody in the building, except those on this floor, heard the whole thing, as it was happening. Over the PA system."

Fenton exhaled and closed his eyes. In his mind he replayed the part of the conversation where Byrd had been given the choice of saving the others in the room. "Sweet Mother Mary," he whispered.

People from downstairs had trickled in now, he noticed. The story was circulating; faces registered shock and disgust. Eager cameras filmed every reaction, recorded every comment. The representatives of the news media, Fenton thought, were grinning like a bunch of Boy Scouts who had just discovered their summer camp was being held by mistake at a nudist colony.

The mayor, who had strolled over, said to Fenton: "Damage assessment?"

Fenton shook his head. "He's finished. It doesn't matter that there was no bomb. What matters is that Tally thought there was, and decided to save his own skin rather than his supporters'. And now everybody knows it."

The mayor nodded sadly. "Hard to believe," he said.

"What's hard to believe," Fenton replied, "is the timing. If that redheaded woman—the location manager—hadn't mentioned the pregnant lady and her plans for the safe . . ." Fenton sighed and ran a hand through his hair. "She must've gone home, I haven't even seen her since she took the call. What was her name? Westwood?"

"Westbrook," the security guard interrupted. "She's

over there, talking to Channel 4. But she only got here a few minutes ago, she rode up with me on the elevator. Said she was told her sister had had an accident, but when she got to the hospital nobody knew anything about it. Crank call, I guess."

A lightbulb came on in Fenton's head. Even as his eyes followed the guard's pointing finger, he knew what he would see. Sure enough, the Nancy Westbrook now being interviewed looked nothing like the woman Byrd had spoken to earlier. This woman was short and blond. There was no sign of the imposter. Once again Fenton huffed out a sigh.

The mayor had come to the same conclusion. "One of the other candidate's people?"

"Who knows?" Fenton said. "Hired by them, maybe. I should've been suspicious—she was almost whispering when she told us her name, and I'm sure nobody questioned the fact that she was at Westbrook's desk. New volunteers are all over the place, here."

They watched together as the real Ms. Westbrook sagged into a chair. Like everyone else associated with Byrd's campaign at the moment, she looked shellshocked. "I think the Opposition must've known Tally pretty well," Fenton added. "Well enough to know how he'd react, anyway."

"I'm glad I know too, now," the mayor said. He tipped his head toward the safe and those working on it. "Would you bet on a man like that to run your state?"

Fenton gave him a glum look. "I might bet on him to run the hundred. He's pretty spry for his age."

Neither of them spoke for a while. Political suicide, never pretty, was always fascinating, and every eye was watching the commotion around the safe, the stoppered bottle that held the evil genie. Freddie tried to imagine the coming storm: national outrage and ridicule, assault charges, probably even demands for repayment of mob funds. A public hanging was not out of the question.

Finally he added, as if to himself: "I wonder if the Other Side needs a good PR advisor."

The mayor pulled his overcoat on. "You might do well there, Freddie," he agreed, his face solemn. "Their candidate's a real workaholic. I've heard he almost never sits down."

Fenton saw him grin before turning away.

At the back corner of the room, the welder was almost done. Fenton heard someone mention that there was no real hurry, since the safe had tiny airholes in the bottom. Talmadge Byrd, of course, hadn't known that, and Fenton wondered idly whether Byrd had filled his shorts after opening Sherry Jackson's purse in the pitch darkness and finding no oxygen canister. He hoped so.

Closer at hand, the new and improved Nancy Westbrook was dazedly taking down campaign banners and posters. Fenton wondered if they were recyclable. After a pause he got up and trudged over to help her, and she gave him a tentative smile. Her eyes, he noticed, were a brilliant blue. He began to feel a little better.

Forty feet away, there were anguished shouts from inside the safe as the torch cut through the last of the door.

A Stranger in Town

The folks of Pauline were content and serene
In the springtime of 1902;
The West had been tamed, their young town had been named,
And the railroad was soon to come through.

There were churches, a school, a town drunk and a fool,
Almost seventy God-fearing souls,
And a mayor and a doc and a jail with no lock,
Overseen by its sheriff, Nate Sprowles.

The fact that old Nate was almost eighty-eight
Was really no cause for concern;
The days when the Law must be quick on the draw
Were gone and would never return.

At least that's what they thought, for their children were taught
To be peaceful and honest and true;
And the streets of Pauline remained calm and serene
Through the summer of 1902.

A STRANGER IN TOWN

There was only one thing that disturbed Ruthie King
And her neighbors who gossiped and spied;
Their concern was the man who had purchased the land
Where the old widow Simpson had died.

He's alone, they were told—not too young or too old,
With a hard little glint in his eyes;
And they only knew that because Myrtle Anne Pratt
Had once seen him come in for supplies.

"He walked easy and slow, kind of watchful, you know?"
Myrtle told her friends later that day;
"And the look in his eyes said it might be unwise
Not to try to stay out of his way.

"He was tall, dressed in black, with a brown haversack
And a hat pulled low over his face;
When he went in the store I observed from the door,
And stayed ready to run, just in case.

"He just gathered his gear and then paid the cashier,"
She recalled as she sipped at her tea,
"And when silly Jane Brett said: 'I don't think we've met,'
He replied: 'The name's Simon McGee.'

"He said nothing more while I watched from the door,
He just solemnly took his receipt;
But something seemed strange as he counted his change
And strode past me and into the street.

"He rode off nice and slow, and as far as I know,
He has never been seen here again;
He just works on his land and he sends in a hand
To buy feed for his stock now and then.

"But what bothers me still," Myrtle said with a chill,
"Was that feeling, when he was around;
It's apparent to me that this Simon McGee
Might be more than just Good Farmer Brown."

"Well, who is he then?" inquired Margaret Fenn—
"He's an outlaw, is that what you think?"
But none of them knew, and so what could they do
Except fidget and prattle and blink?

They also didn't know about Panama Joe
And his band of men, ugly and mean;
For on that autumn day they were making their way
Down the hill toward the town of Pauline.

The first place that they found when they rode into town
Was the schoolhouse behind Reverend Dunn's,
And according to plan, they dismounted and ran
Up the steps, where all five drew their guns.

With a frightening roar the men burst through the door,
And within fifteen seconds or so,
A teacher named Prudence and twenty-one students
Were captives of Panama Joe.

One young hostage was freed so that news of the deed
Could be spread to the folks in the town;
And the rest, left inside, were all hobbled and tied
And then told to stay quiet and stay down.

"We want money," Joe shouted as the schoolyard grew crowded
With parents who quivered with dread;
"Five thousand's the sum, and if it doesn't come
Before sundown your kids'll be dead."

A STRANGER IN TOWN

At the window Joe waited, and anticipated
What the stunned crowd's reaction might be;
So he suddenly shouted: "In case you should doubt it,
There's something I want you to see."

The teacher, still tied, was escorted outside—
As she stood there, eyes teary and red,
She was shot in the back, to give weight to the fact
That the kidnappers meant what they said.

Her poor mother fainted, and those unacquainted
With violence fainted also;
And the rest stood and trembled, and somehow resembled
Young rabbits, in traps in the snow.

Sheriff Sprowles had passed out when first told of the rout,
And the mayor was a coward at best;
But the rest couldn't hide, for their kids were inside,
And no heroes were left in the West.

"What to do?" the men wailed, for their courage had failed,
And the women all started to cry;
And the town of Pauline was no longer serene
As the sun inched its way down the sky.

"If we don't raise the cash," said the blacksmith, Will Nash,
"Then they'll kill 'em, and here's how I know:
That man in the window is Joseph LaPinto—
The one they call Panama Joe."

The name drew a hush, and a sudden cold rush
Of distress as their faces turned grim;
They knew Joe and his cousins had killed by the dozens;
Twenty kids would mean nothing to him.

With a sick, heavy heart the crowd drifted apart
To go gather what funds they could find;
Selflessly the town gave every dollar they'd saved—
But five thousand? That boggled the mind.

At about six o'clock Preacher Dunn and the doc
Counted twelve hundred dollars, all told;
That included all Will's old Confederate bills
And some seventeen pieces of gold.

"Will this much be enough?" someone asked, as they stuffed
Everything in an old leather case;
Doc replied: "I hope so," in a voice tired and low,
And a world-weary look on his face.

As if reading his mind, Joe yelled out: "You will find
You have only a few minutes left—
And if it's not five thousand I'll walk through this house and
Shoot every last young-un myself!"

As this message sank in, the crowd understood then
That they'd not see their children again;
And the friends of LaPinto's twirled guns by the windows,
Stopping only to spit now and then.

Ruthie moaned: "Why'd they *do* this? For surely they knew this—
We're not rich like Hays or Fort Hall."
"That's not it," a voice said, from behind them. "Instead,
It's the killing he loves, most of all."

Too surprised to be scared, the crowd swiveled and stared
To see who the new speaker could be;
Very few were aware that the man standing there
Was the mystical Simon McGee.

Not a sound could be heard, not a one of them stirred
As he stepped forward, cautious and shy;
His dark gaze scanned each face, lingered on the brown case,
And then stopped on the schoolhouse nearby.

As the folks of Pauline watched him study the scene,
The man's name was no longer in doubt;
For by now they had guessed, from the way he was dressed:
He's the farmer we've all heard about.

He knelt in the sand with his hat in his hand,
His shirt and pants faded and black;
And again that odd feeling—ice-cold, yet appealing—
Sent shivers up Myrtle Pratt's back.

For she knew right away what had seemed strange that day
When his trip into town had been done:
The McGee she had seen at the store in Pauline
Hadn't been wearing a gun.

He was wearing one now, and it seemed that somehow
The picture at last was set right;
There were times when a gun seemed a part of someone,
As a sword was a part of a knight.

While she figured this out, the whole crowd heard a shout
That resounded across the schoolyard:
"One more minute!" Joe cried, and the stranger's blue eyes
Became focused and narrow and hard.

His assessment complete, McGee rose to his feet
And said calmly to Dr. Malloy:
"If I've figured this right, I believe you folks might
Need to find a delivery boy."

In the silence to follow, Will sobbed, his voice hollow:
"Won't matter, one way or another."
But the doc had divined what McGee had in mind,
And the two stood and studied each other.

"There are five," the doc said, his sad eyes filled with dread,
But the stranger's stayed steady and cool;
With a resolute face he picked up the brown case
And walked slowly away toward the school.

In the building Joe's band dozed and dawdled and fanned,
But a glance at the yard cured their boredom;
With a signal LaPinto sent men to each window,
And all five watched the stranger stroll toward 'em.

McGee passed by the spot where the teacher was shot
And then stopped thirty feet from the door;
At the top of the steps stood LaPinto himself—
In the wide-open windows, four more.

The sun sat like a pearl on the edge of the world,
The men poised like the shadows of death;
The only sounds were the cries of the children inside,
And the small, waiting crowd held its breath.

"Bring it closer," Joe said, with a nod of his head
Toward the case McGee held in his hand;
"Come and get it," he cried, and then tossed it aside
In a looping arc over the sand.

For a second their eyes watched the case—an unwise
Thing to do then, McGee would have guessed;
For in that second or so, he killed Panama Joe
And then, lightning-fast, all the rest.

So quick had it been, said a student, John Quinn,
Who had watched from the doorway, tied down,
That all five men were dead with a bullet in the head
'Fore the brown case had even touched ground.

When the echoes abated, those there stood and waited,
Stunned, frozen like statues, eyes wide;
Then the crowd, though still shaken, all seemed to awaken
And surged past McGee like the tide.

When the kids were collected, untied and inspected,
They were found to be fine as could be;
After all that was done, the group turned, one by one,
To find their friend Simon McGee.

But he'd gone, so they stayed and watched pale sunlight fade
From a day that, like them, had grown old;
And while sad for young Prudence, they thanked God their students
Were safe—not to mention their gold.

The next morning the preacher said words for the teacher
And put the five men in the ground;
Then, as they had agreed, the group rode to McGee's
To thank him for saving their town.

When they got to the farm a cook said, with alarm:
"All you men just mount up and be gone."
And when several persisted she sternly insisted:
"He just wants to be left alone."

So the men rode away, saying: "If not today,
He'll be thanked when he comes in to town."
But he didn't come in—he sent helpers again
When the need for supplies rolled around.

They continued to wait as snow covered the state
And as Christmas drew friends old and new;
And the town of Pauline was again quite serene
In the winter of 1902.

Then one day there appeared, with a badge and a beard,
A man who began to inquire:
"I'm in search of a killer, his name's Simon Miller—
Word is, he came north to retire.

"Miller's tall, with gray hair, and wears black everywhere,
And he moves kind of slow, like a cat."
But the townsfolk replied, their eyes honest and wide:
"There is no one around here like that."

Since it soon became plain that his quest was in vain,
The man left the next day on his horse;
And the looks folks exchanged when he rode out of range
Showed neither regret nor remorse.

No one else ever came, or repeated that name,
And life in the town of Pauline
Floated smoothly along, like a softly-played song
That was soothing and quiet and routine.

But fools they were not, and nobody forgot,
And as Myrtle Anne Pratt liked to say,
No one had to tell *her* McGee was a killer—
Only a killer could've saved them that day.

When he died of the flu in 1922,
Mourners numbered two hundred or so;
And there among many were gathered the twenty
He'd rescued from Panama Joe.

"Though few of us met him, we'll never forget him,"
Said John Quinn, the mayor-to-be;
For the plaque they'd installed in the new school's front hall
Said: IN MEMORY OF SIMON McGEE.

Last Chance

"They're here," Sam said.

I looked up from my newspaper. Across the table from me, Sam Hudson was working on a stack of pancakes three inches thick. Nothing unusual, there. Every day since our retirement, Sam and I had met at this corner booth in the Last Chance Cafe. And every day he consumed sausages and eggs and blueberry pancakes while I consumed the morning paper. What was unusual was that today Sam's face was dead serious.

"Who's here?" I asked him.

He stopped chewing, swallowed, and said, "The aliens."

For a minute I didn't think I'd heard correctly. But before I could say anything, I saw him look past me and blink. I turned to see Suzie Neiderman, the owner's twentysomething daughter, approaching. She plunked another orange juice down in front of Sam, smiled and fluttered her eyelashes at me, and left. She knew I didn't need anything. I never ate here; breakfast was Raisin Bran and milk at home. We both watched her leave—Suzie had that effect on males of all ages—and then Sam focused again on me.

"I had a dream," he said. "Aliens landed here, sometime yesterday."

I folded my paper and regarded him a moment. Sam was always kidding about something, it was just his nature, but right now he was sober as a Baptist at a tent revival.

"What do you mean, here? In town?"

"West of here, out in the flats. But they've reached town now, and they're about to take over." His point made, he took another huge bite of sausage. If we were being invaded, he apparently wanted it to happen on a full stomach.

"I didn't see anything about it in the news," I said, tapping the paper. "Or out there either." I nodded toward the window, where Highway 42 disappeared into the desert. The Last Chance, located here at the edge of town, had been well named: there was nothing west of this point. No food, no water, no people. Just sand and cactus.

"Joke all you want. The fact is, goofy as it sounds, E.T.'s evil cousins have arrived."

"And you really believe this."

"I believe it because it's true," he said. "They're here."

"And what are they here to do?" Might as well play along with him. I figured Doc Brown had changed his medication again. Sam was one of those people who got tipsy after one beer—a new brand of allergy pills could probably make him see dancing elephants wearing Easter bonnets.

"They're here for two purposes," he answered, still solemn. "To recruit helpers, and to drain our brains."

"To drain our brains."

"That's right."

I barely kept from grinning. "To absorb our knowledge, you mean?"

He sat back and stared at me as if I had grown a third eye. "They don't need our knowledge, Joe. I mean, very simply, they—and the locals they've already taken into their ranks—are going to destroy our minds. Drive us insane." He shook his head, probably at my ignorance, and went back to his intake of cholesterol. "When that's been done," he added, "they'll be able to control us. To take over with no resistance."

"Drain our brains," I said again.

"Right."

"And this'll happen to everybody?"

"That's the plan."

"Well, it hasn't happened to me yet," I told him.

"I'll have to take your word for that," he said, chewing. "Doubt I'd be able to see much of a change."

"Very funny." I looked out the other window at my neighbor Carl Huggins, who was being hauled down the side-walk by a dog on a leash. He was brown and longhaired, with droopy ears and an oversized tail. The dog, not Huggins. But neither of them looked braindrained.

"So who have they infected so far?" I asked Sam. "The whole town, or just those with weak minds? Lawyers, maybe?"

"Sure, laugh about it. But it's happening, I tell you. People are becoming . . ." He leaned forward, darting cautious looks right and left. "Forgetful."

"Forgetful?"

"That's how it starts. I saw it in my dream. And once it starts it happens fast."

"Let's see if I have this straight," I said. "At first we start to forget things—"

"Little things."

"—and eventually—"

"Within an hour or so."

"—we go totally zonkers."

"Totally." He finished his eggs and began mopping up his syrup with the last forkful of pancake.

"How are they accomplishing this? Did you see that too?"

"Not specifically."

"What's that supposed to mean?"

"It means I don't know for sure. But unlike you, I at least have an analytical mind."

"And?"

He narrowed his eyes. "I think it's the water."

"The water?"

"Other ways, too, probably. Food, air conditioning, who knows? But especially the water."

"How exactly do you figure that?"

"Because it'd be so easy," he said. "It all comes from one reservoir. Besides that, you and I don't seem to be affected, right? And neither of us drinks water."

"I drink water."

"I mean normally, around the house. I drink Cokes all the time, and you drink that sorry canned lemonade you like so much. I bet you a dime to a donut we're the only ones in town who haven't taken a single sip of tapwater, or coffee or tea, since yesterday."

A silence passed. I could hear the faraway clatter of dishes in the kitchen.

"You hate it when I'm right," he said. "I know you do."

"You're not right, Sam. What you are, is as crazy as these folks you dreamed about."

He nodded, looked down at his empty plate, and carefully smoothed the checkered tablecloth. "Call me what you like. But I would advise you to believe me. In fact, I would advise you to come with me."

"Come with you where?"

He glanced out the window, and just for a second I

could see the fear in his eyes. "Anywhere, long as it's away from this town. The only reason I came here to the café was to warn you."

"And to have breakfast."

He smiled for the first time today. "Well, that too."

"Besides, you can't leave town—you told me your car's in the shop."

"I'm in the old Mustang. It smokes and rattles, but it might get us far as the county line. I think that'd be enough." He raised his eyebrows the way he always did when an idea struck him. "Unless we take your truck."

"Can't. Tim Rawlins borrowed it, to haul gravel for his driveway. I'm afoot today."

"You walked here?"

"Why not?"

"Well, the hell with this." He threw a few bills on the table and rose from his seat. "We'll go in my junkheap. Come on."

"Now wait a minute, Sam—"

"Humor me, okay?"

I sighed and stood up, tucking my paper under my arm. Crazy or not, I couldn't let him go off alone. Both of us waved goodbye to Suzie and I followed him toward the door.

And then he stopped. I almost walked into his back.

"What is it now?" I asked.

He didn't reply. He was staring through the front window at the parking lot, a blank look on his face.

"Sam?"

"I can't remember where I parked," he said.

"So? How many '72 Mustangs can there be, in the lot?"

He frowned. "Mustangs? Horses, you mean?"

I studied his face a moment, and felt a shiver ripple down my spine. Slowly I turned to look at Suzie. She was watching us, but her smile seemed frozen. Her normally bright eyes had darkened into chips of coal.

What the hell . . . ?

And then I noticed, for the first time, the other customers. Everyone in the place looked as dazed and dreamy-eyed as Sam, some more so. And all of them had breakfast plates in front of them. All of them had eaten, or were eating, food served by the cheerful and gorgeous Suzie Neiderman. All except me.

Oh my God.

My heart pounding, I dropped the newspaper, grabbed Sam's arm, and steered him out the door.

He just looked at me with an increasingly vacant stare. "Where we goin'?" he murmured. Outside, I saw Carl Huggins sitting on the sidewalk. He looked lost. His dog and leash had disappeared.

"Someplace where you can throw up," I said. "And then we're taking a trip."

"What kinda trip?"

"A long one." On my way here I had seen one of the funeral home's black Cadillacs parked in its driveway, and I knew where the director hid the keys. The Caddie would get us a lot farther than Sam's old Mustang.

Halfway across the lot, I looked back. Suzie, her weird smile in place, her gaze hard and glittering, was still watching us. Then I saw her nod to several of the slack-faced diners. They stood and started shuffling in our direction.

I turned to look up the street. The black car was still there, less than a block away. Pulling Sam along, I picked up the pace.

"I do hate it when you're right," I told him.

The Sixth Victim

The five student nurses stood at the security desk, waiting. Outside the glass doors, a landscaped lawn gasped in the August heat.

"No answer," the guard said, one hand over the phone's mouthpiece. "He's not in his office."

One of the students, Nancy Hines, nodded. "We're a little early—"

"May I help you, ladies?" a voice said. They turned to see a blond man in a white lab coat approaching. The lettering stitched to his pocket said DR. G. ROBERTS.

"We're nursing students, visiting from the university," Nancy said. "Our instructor arranged—"

"Of course. Come on, I'll show you around. I'm Gerald Roberts." He nodded to the guard and led them down a corridor. Their footsteps echoed off the bare walls.

"As you probably know," he said as they walked, "we're a state-operated mental health facility. We house approximately eighty patients, here."

A tall student named Ellen Varner asked, "Why the security?"

Dr. Roberts gave her a sad smile. "Not all our patients are stable. One, a man named Ernest Leach, is actually rather dangerous." They turned a corner into another hallway. "But all patients are given free access, within the confines of the building. Even Mr. Leach."

"But if he's dangerous . . ."

"Well, he's no threat to the staff or patients. They're like family to him. He's a potential danger only to visitors." Roberts paused as if to let that sink in. "So the guard's purpose is twofold: to control access in or out, and to protect people like you from people like Ernest Leach." Another smile. "I don't mean to alarm you. Only to caution you."

"What has this Mr. Leach done?" Ellen said.

Roberts looked her in the eye. "He's an axe-murderer."

***

For the next ten minutes Dr. Roberts escorted them through the facility. Nancy Hines took detailed notes. The other four students, to Nancy's annoyance, couldn't seem to take their eyes off the doctor. Not that she could blame them—besides his looks and his title, the man exuded confidence like an aroma.

When they passed a restroom sign, all the ladies except Ellen Varner excused themselves to powder their noses. Ellen remained in the hallway with Dr. Roberts.

When they reconvened, Nancy leaned close to Ellen's ear.

"What's the deal?" Nancy whispered. "In the car your bladder's the size of a golf ball. Here, you don't need to go?"

Ellen grinned. "He isn't wearing a wedding ring."

"So?"

"So I dazzled him with my charm."

Nancy blinked. "Don't tell me you got a date with him."

"No—but he's going to let me meet this Ernest Leach guy."

Nancy stopped in her tracks. "What?"

"Tonight, around six. The doc wants to avoid him while the whole group's here. He says Leach is too unpredictable."

"But—"

"After the rest of you're gone, he and I'll talk to the patient. I'll catch a cab home."

Nancy gaped at her. "But Leach is dangerous, Varner. What did Roberts call him—an axe-murderer?"

Ellen Varner turned to check on the rest of the group, which had gone on ahead. "Take it easy. Gerald will—"

"Gerald?"

"Dr. Roberts," she said, "will be with me the whole time. A controlled interview."

Nancy was still doubtful.

"It's a great case," Ellen said. She leaned forward and lowered her voice. "He told me Leach went berserk and killed five people—"

"Five people?!"

"—with an axe one night. They were all thugs and dope-heads, so it was kept fairly quiet, but he was later convicted. And listen to this: When the verdict was announced, Leach pulled out a hatchet he'd smuggled into the courtroom and chopped off his lawyer's toes."

"He *what*?"

Ellen nodded. "He swung and missed and whacked off three of the lawyer's toes. Then Leach chased him out into the street, bleeding and screaming, until the cops tackled Leach and wrestled the hatchet away. The poor lawyer flipped out, never tried another case." She stopped to take a breath, eyes sparkling. "After an appeal Leach was declared insane. He's responded well here, Roberts said, except he sometimes insists he'd like to claim one more victim. Make it an even half-dozen."

Nancy swallowed. "My God, Ellen—"

"All Leach does now, Roberts told me, is wander around and visit the other patients." Ellen looked down the hall. "Uh-oh."

The blond doctor and students were waiting for them at the end of the corridor. As Nancy and Ellen scurried to catch up, Nancy happened to glance through an open doorway. A dark-haired man in jeans and sneakers was sitting there, at someone's bedside. Nancy paused, then saw the man scowl at her.

She moved away fast as he rose and came to the door. "Young lady?" he said to her back.

Nancy turned again, her cheeks hot with embarrassment.

The dark man's eyes were black and piercing. They made her skin crawl.

"What are you doing here?" he asked. He looked past her at Ellen and the other students, including them in the question. Apparently he hadn't yet noticed the doctor, who was standing beyond the group.

But the doctor noticed *him*. Roberts hurried forward, a look of open concern on his face.

Nancy began to back away from the dark man.

And then he saw Dr. Roberts. "Well, well. What have we here?"

They all froze. Roberts didn't reply.

Without looking away, the dark-haired man reached a hand out to the corridor wall and pressed a button.

Still the doctor said nothing. Nancy, her nerves on edge, blurted, "We're students. We're just visiting."

The dark man shifted his gaze to her. Understanding dawned; his face softened.

"Ah. The student nurses." He checked his watch. "You arrived early, I see." To the doctor he said, "And you—I believe you have something that belongs to me?"

Dr. Roberts slowly took off the white coat and handed it to the dark man. Moments later two orderlies as big as linebackers emerged from a stairway. Each took hold of one of the blond doctor's arms. Glaring, he allowed himself to be led away.

The five students stared after him, stunned. Then all of them turned to look at the dark-haired man, who was pulling the coat on and adjusting his cuffs.

"What's going on?" Nancy asked, in a small voice.

He sighed. "Security lapse. Probably the new guard at the front desk—he hasn't met all the patients yet. And two of my staff are at a conference."

"Your staff? But who—"

Then the answer hit her, and she sucked in some air. Beside her, Ellen's mouth fell open.

"My God," Nancy whispered, nodding at the three retreating figures. "That man's Ernest Leach, isn't he."

The real Dr. Roberts frowned. "Excuse me?"

"Well, isn't he?"

"No. But sometimes he thinks he is." Roberts shook his head sadly. "That's a concern, actually. If he were ever alone with someone, an outsider . . ."

Nancy just stared. "I'm confused. If he isn't Leach—"

"You have to understand," Roberts said, "that Ernest Leach isn't crazy. He's just mean. That's why he's in prison, over in Petersburg."

"But . . ." Nancy looked down the hall again. "Who—"

"That's Morris Baker," Roberts said. "Leach's seven-toed lawyer."

Smoke Test

It was ironic, Larry thought. Susan always liked the fact that he could fix things. *Nice to have a handyman for a husband*, she used to tell her friends. It was probably one of the few things she did like about him.

And now it was going to kill her.

Larry hummed to himself while he knelt in his swimsuit on the bedroom carpet beside the closed bathroom door. On the other side he could hear his wife's singing, and the steady hiss of the shower. An added benefit: the noise covered the sound of his tools.

Forget about that, he told himself. For the moment he had to ignore the singing, and the shower, and the ticking clock, and the roar of the night surf outside the window, and anything else that might distract him. Susan had always said he was absentminded, and maybe it was true. He was always forgetting to take his TV dinner out of the oven or turn off the sprinkler or some such thing. On one memorable occasion, Susan's dog had died when she was out of town because Larry had forgotten to feed him.

The truth was, he usually had other things on his mind.

But tonight he couldn't afford to let his attention wander, not for an instant. There would be no rehearsal, no smoke test. This time the trial run would be the real thing.

Finally he was done. The waist-high light switch on the bedroom wall was wired and ready. Larry stood, put down his tools, turned off his flashlight, and admired his work. In the darkened room the light switch looked just like it always had; there was no way to tell that the plastic on/off toggle was now metal, and wired directly into the juice.

Larry grinned. Ten minutes from now, give or take, Susan would finish her shower and put on her robe and open the bathroom door the way she always did. Then she would step barefoot through the door onto the carpet and turn on the bedroom light, also the way she always did.

But when her finger touched the switch this time, she would get the surprise of her life. The last surprise of her life.

Okay, Larry thought. So far so good. Susan was still singing, the shower still showering. And he had one more thing to do.

Sweating even in his swim trunks, he hurried to the kitchen, filled a bucket with water from the sink, lugged it back to the bedroom, and emptied it onto the carpet outside the bathroom door. The water was a nice touch. The hot switch alone would deliver enough current to kill her, but standing in a pool of water would guarantee it.

Afterward, he would repair the wiring, throw away the metal toggle-switch, fill the tub and flood the bathroom as well, and dash back out to the beach for a midnight swim. He had already made sure he was seen an hour ago, strolling to the beach by the usual path, but had then crept back to the house through the shadowy underbrush, and would soon sneak out again by the same route. The next time he left the beach, an hour or so from now, he would once more make sure he was noticed. He might even decide to scream and carry on a little, for the benefit of the neighbors, once he "discovered" his wife's body. He could picture it now: It was terrible, Officer. I came in from my nightly swim and there she was, lying there . . .

He would give a fine performance, of that he was certain. He might be out of work for the moment (a condition of which Susan regularly reminded him), but he *was* an actor—a fairly good actor, in his opinion. With the right money and the right connections, he would someday be a *great* actor.

And tonight was a step in the right direction, at least in the money department. Dear old Susan might not be much to look at anymore, but she was obscenely rich. And Larry had made sure the will was written the right way.

Suddenly he heard the shower cut off. He checked his watch. He had about three minutes left—it always took her that long to towel off, slip on the bathrobe, step through the door. Quickly he took the empty bucket back to the kitchen, refilled it, left it there on standby, and returned to the bedroom.

One last time he padded to the area outside the bathroom door, making sure everything was set, that everything looked and felt right. He stood there a moment in the dark room with his back to the door, the wet carpet cold on his bare feet, imagining what was about to happen and relishing the idea of living with Susan's money but without Susan.

Then he realized, with a lurch of his heart, that he'd left all his tools scattered on the floor. He didn't even remember where he'd put his flashlight. None of that would matter to Susan, of course—she'd never see any of that anyway, in the darkened room—but it might matter if someone heard her scream or saw a flash of sparks and called the police and caught him here. His whole plan depended on his fixing the switch and getting out of the house fast and unnoticed, and he couldn't do it without his pliers and screwdriver and flashlight.

He couldn't believe he'd been so careless. He had to locate and gather his tools now, and do it quick. Good God, he said to himself, I really *am* absentminded.

And with that thought in his head, he switched on the light so he could see . . .

Appearances

He drew a shaky breath and punched in the numbers. His mouth was as dry as sandpaper when he heard her pick up the phone.

"Yvette?" he said. "It's Tommy."

A silence passed. "Who?"

"Tommy Bridges. I sit beside you in chemistry."

He heard slurping sounds, and finally realized she was chewing gum. Somehow, that made him feel better. The image of perfect, golden-haired Yvette McKenna smacking away on a wad of Juicy Fruit made her seem more accessible, more . . . human. To the rest of the high school she was head cheerleader and prom queen. To Tommy Bridges she was a goddess.

"So?" she asked, smacking.

He swallowed. "Well, there's a big concert downtown tonight, and—"

The chewing sounds stopped. "ZZ Top? You got *tickets*?"

"Five rows from the stage." He almost revealed that

he'd bought them at half price from his flu-stricken cousin Edward, but caught himself just in time. "Will you go with me?" he added, holding his breath.

Another long silence. "Maybe."

"Maybe?"

"Call me again at one o'clock."

Tommy exhaled. "One this afternoon?"

"No, one tomorrow morning, Bridges. Of course this afternoon." The smacking had started up again. "I'll tell you then whether I can go."

"Ah . . . okay. I'll call you at one." There was no reply—she'd already hung up the phone.

Tommy replaced the receiver and sat looking at it, dazed. He decided it didn't matter much that she hadn't said yes. What mattered was that she hadn't said no.

He was still staring at the phone when it rang again. He almost jumped off the chair. The caller, it turned out, was his friend Rufus Landers, asking if he wanted to go to the state fair. Tomorrow was the last day.

Tommy hesitated. He wasn't wild about the fair right now, but if he stayed around here waiting for one o'clock he'd go insane. He agreed, pulled a sweater over his head, and checked the two precious concert tickets he'd tucked into his wallet. Remembering Yvette's apparent fancy for chewing gum, he found a stick of Doublemint and put it in too, just in case, beside the tickets. Pleased with himself, he stomped downstairs and out the front door. He still felt a little giddy, as if wandering around in a dream.

Maybe it *was* a dream, he told himself. *Yvette McKenna.*

He felt a twinge of panic. How exactly should one act, on a date with a girl like Yvette? He remembered the old joke about the dog that, after chasing cars all his life, finally caught one and then didn't know what to do with it.

Tommy was so preoccupied he almost didn't notice Lizzie Kelso, who was raking leaves in the front yard of the house next door. The Kelsos' lot was thick with pecan trees, and even though cool weather had barely begun here in the South, pecans always shed their leaves early. The entire yard was a crunchy brown carpet. Right now Lizzie had her back to him, intent on her task. Every few minutes she paused, scooped up a handful of nuts, and tossed them into a washbucket.

Normally Tommy would have called a greeting to her and kept going—after all, he and Lizzie had seen each other almost every day of their seventeen years. Today, though, the sight of her reminded him of something. He jogged toward her, stopping to pick up a couple of pecans from the cleared area behind her. "You missed some," he called.

Lizzie turned to look at him. "You up already? It's only eleven."

"I don't sleep till noon *every* Saturday." The two pecans in his hand cracked as he squeezed them together, rotated them, and squeezed again. "Besides, I have a social engagement."

Lizzie had already resumed her raking. "Let me guess. You're meeting Goofy Rufie at the fair."

Tommy frowned. It annoyed him a little that his two closest friends didn't care much for each other, but what annoyed him more was that Lizzie always seemed able to read his mind.

"What I came over here for," he said, picking out chunks of pecan, "was to ask you something."

"Well, ask me then."

"It's about the concert tonight."

That got her attention. Very slowly, she turned to him. A tiny half-smile was on her lips, and her eyes . . .

Her eyes looked different, somehow.

Tommy watched her a moment, puzzled, then gulped

the last of his pecan and dusted his palms together. "What I was wondering was, I need somebody to watch my little brother tonight while I go. My folks'll be out, and I said I'd stay with him, but now that I'll be gone too, well—"

He stopped in midsentence. Lizzie's face had changed again. Whatever it was that had shone in her eyes for an instant was gone now. Her half-smile was still in place, but now it seemed frozen, and forced.

"Sure, I'll watch Petey for you," she said. "Just send him over when you leave."

She resumed her work. Tommy studied her back, wondering what was wrong. He tried thanking her but she didn't respond, and after a minute of stony silence he turned and left.

***

"Why is it," Tommy said, "that you and Lizzie don't like each other?"

Rufus Landers took a bite of candied apple and wiped his mouth on the sleeve of his sweatshirt. "I like her okay," he said, chewing. "She just thinks she's smarter than me, is all."

"She is smarter than you." The two of them were strolling the midway, just inside the entrance to the fair. Their only stop so far had been at a snack stand, where Rufus had wolfed down two chili dogs and bought his apple. Tommy had declined. He was saving his funds for tonight. "She sure was in a funky mood today," he said.

"Girls are like that," Rufus said wisely, glancing around at the rides. "Wanta try the Scrambler or the Spin-and-Whirl?"

But Tommy wasn't listening. The wild euphoria he'd experienced earlier had fizzled, and he felt a little odd. He couldn't seem to get his mind off Lizzie Kelso.

"She seemed okay at first," he said.

Rufus pried a piece of candy from between his teeth. "At first?"

"Yeah, when I told her I was going to the concert tonight she acted fine, like she was pleased about it, you know? Then, when I asked her to keep an eye on Petey for me—"

"Wait a minute. You told Lizzie you were going to the concert . . . and then asked her to babysit for you?"

"Yeah, I guess. What's wrong with that?"

Rufus snorted. "What's wrong is, Lizzie Kelso's had her eye on you lately. Didn't you know that?"

Tommy stopped walking so suddenly a man behind him almost ran into him. "What?"

"She likes you," Rufus said. "It's beyond me why she does, but she does."

Tommy could only stare. "But Lizzie's just a friend."

"She used to be a friend. She grew up. Which is more'n I can say about *some* people I know." Rufus lobbed his apple core in the general direction of a trashcan twenty feet away. "And in case you haven't noticed, Lizzie's no ugly duckling anymore."

"I didn't say she was. She's just—"

"She's no Yvette McKenna," Rufus finished.

"That's right. She's not." Tommy pondered that a moment. "Yvette *looks* like an Yvette, know what I mean? Lizzie looks . . . well, she looks like a Lizzie."

After a pause, Rufus said, "The problem is, Yvette *acts* like an Yvette."

"What do you mean?"

Rufus shook his head. "Good grief. And you think *I'm* dumb." He turned and focused on the rides. "Come on, dipweed. Let's do what we came here to do."

***

Ten minutes later they climbed out of their ride seats and stumbled through the exit chute into the midway. The ground beneath his feet, Tommy noticed, didn't seem to want to stay still.

"I think that thing goes faster'n it used to," Rufus said. Now, from a safe distance, the Spin-and-Whirl looked like a bunch of oversized teacups sitting on a warped saucer.

"You're just a bigger pansy now." Tommy studied his friend's grayish-white face. "Sure you're okay?"

"I will be in a minute," Rufus murmured, and took off in the direction of the restrooms, holding his stomach with both hands. "Don't wait up for me, honey," he called over his shoulder.

Grinning to himself, Tommy continued down the midway. This *was* fun, he decided. The too-loud music, the hordes of happy people, the autumn chill, the smell of machinery and sawdust and popcorn . . .

Then he thought again of Lizzie, home working in her yard. Little Lizzie Kelso, the girl he'd known all his life, the girl he loved like a sister.

Was it true what he'd just heard? Could she have other feelings—different feelings—for him?

Tommy sighed. This kind of thinking made his head hurt. Of course Lizzie wasn't in love with him, any more than *he* was in love with *her*. They were friends, that's all.

But now and then, he thought . . . *Now and then, when she crinkles her eyes a certain way—*

A piercing scream snapped him back to reality. He spun around, expecting to see a body falling from the Ferris wheel, but the scream had come from a middle-aged woman in a pink jogging suit. Her husband had just won her a stuffed bear.

Feeling glum, Tommy wandered over to one of the other booths, where he watched a smug-looking college kid showing his date how to pitch a softball at milk bottles. The date, tall and tan and blond, reminded Tommy of Yvette McKenna. His spirits lifted.

One o'clock, he thought. Thirty more minutes.

He could hardly wait.

And the great thing was, he knew she was going to say yes. The thought was both scary and thrilling. How could he possibly have been concerned about plain old Lizzie Kelso, when the famous and delectable Yvette McKenna was practically within his grasp?

And, wonder of wonders, it had come about because of two very expensive, very scarce tickets to a rock concert. For the hundredth time today Tommy reached behind him to pat the pocket that held the wallet that held the tickets, and thanked his lucky stars that his cousin Edward had been obliging enough to come down with the creepy crud now rather than last month, or last week—

Tommy froze.

He felt no comforting bulge in his hip pocket.

Where was his wallet?

Tommy searched his other pockets. Nothing there. He turned in a circle, looking around, his mind replaying his latest movements and actions. Whatever had happened, it had happened within the past fifteen minutes or so. He knew that, because he remembered taking out his wallet to pay for admission to the Spin-and-Whirl—

He blinked.

The Spin-and-Whirl. Its wild, jerking motion had thrown both him and Rufus around like ragdolls, their bottoms slipping and sliding on the metal seats as they hung on for dear life.

If his wallet had come out of his pocket—and it had—then it had come out during the ride.

He took off at a dead run, dodging his way back through the crowds.

When he arrived at the Spin-and-Whirl, red-faced and

puffing, he felt a surge of hope. The place was deserted, the machinery silent. No one even stood in line. The big teacup-looking cars sat empty in the noonday sun.

With barely a pause Tommy dashed along the railing to the ticket booth. The ride operator was nowhere to be seen. A hand-lettered sign said BACK IN 10 MINUTES.

Tommy felt sick. He had to find that wallet. Not only did it contain his two sacred tickets, it also held his emergency funds. Thirty-eight hard-earned dollars.

Still no sign of the ride attendant. For a moment Tommy considered climbing over the railing and searching each car, but he knew that wouldn't work. His wallet had surely been found by now, and probably by the grungy-looking operator he'd seen here earlier.

But he had to try. He was about to step over the railing when a voice stopped him. Tommy's head snapped around so fast it made his neck hurt.

The man who'd spoken, the operator Tommy had seen earlier, was leaning against the sign on the Spin-and-Whirl's ticket booth, both hands stuffed into the pockets of baggy, grease-stained jeans. Topping off the outfit were a ragged flannel shirt, a baseball cap, scuffed cowboy boots, and a gray beard. Long hair spilled from beneath his cap, and his eyes were bloodshot. Several teeth were missing. Everything about him, even his clothes, looked tired.

"I said, what do you want? I'm on break."

Tommy's heart sank. This guy was no Good Samaritan. He looked more like an extra from *Deliverance*. And since the chances were about a hundred percent that he was the proud new owner of Tommy's wallet, the chances were about zero that Tommy would ever see it again.

But what did he have to lose?

"I think I lost my wallet, in one of your cars," Tommy

said, his voice trembling. "My name's inside it. Thomas Bridges."

As Tommy watched, the man removed a pack of cigarettes from his pocket, shook one out, and lit it with a battered lighter. He exhaled a plume of blue smoke that hung there like a fog in the still air. Squinting at Tommy through the cloud, he said, around the cigarette, "You asking if I found it?"

This is crazy, Tommy thought. He blew out a sigh. "No. I guess not. I'm sorry to have bothered—"

"Stay there," the man growled. He turned, opened a gate in the railing, and limped to a small metal shed that crouched like a puppy amid the giant motors and pulleys. A minute later he reappeared, stepping over cables as thick as firehoses, and held out his right hand. "Look familiar?"

Tommy almost fainted with relief. He opened the wallet. There it was: money, tickets, even the bent stick of Doublemint.

"It's all there. Count it, if you want to."

Tommy swallowed. "I . . . can't believe it."

The man chuckled. "I couldn't either. When I made my walk-through, it was laying right there on the seat of Number Four—"

"No, that's not what I meant," Tommy said, and immediately wished he hadn't.

The words seemed to echo in the quiet.

"I know what you meant," the attendant said. As Tommy's face reddened the man rested his forearms on top of the railing and stared Tommy in the eye.

"I'm not offended," the man said. "But there's something you need to remember, Thomas Bridges. Appearances can be . . . well . . ."

"Deceiving."

"Exactly." He pointed his cigarette like a finger. "You see that bunch over there?"

A ripple of laughter floated over from the other side of the midway. A group of businessmen with suspenders and silk ties and thousand-dollar loafers were trying to toss plastic rings over little revolving pegs without mussing their styled hairdos.

"Be glad those guys weren't the ones found your wallet."

Tommy stared at the man a moment. They both smiled at the same time.

"You're right," Tommy said, the tension gone. A thought occurred to him. "Is there anything"—he shrugged—"anything I can do for you? In return?"

The ride attendant seemed to think that over. Finally he said, "My girlfriend tells me I smoke too much. Maybe my jaws need some exercise."

Tommy frowned, then understood. Grinning, he opened his wallet, took out the stick of gum, and handed it over.

"Good trade," the man said.

They shook hands, and Tommy left. Only once did he glance back, and when he did the man was still leaning on the railing, holding his lighter to another cigarette.

***

Tommy strolled around awhile, lost in his thoughts. He found Rufus sitting on a bench, staring up at a poster for one of the sideshows. On the sign was a drawing of a scaly long-snouted monster in ladies' clothing and a woolly, hunchbacked giant. FREAKS OF NATURE, the sign said. ALLIGATOR WOMAN AND THE MISSING LINK. Rufus pointed to the sign and said, "Looks like they found your real parents."

"You're lucky, Rufie," Tommy said, plopping down beside him. "I was taught not to hit sick people."

"I've recovered. I look sick to you?"

"Just ugly, mostly." Tommy bent down and relaced his sneakers. "Want to ride something else? Or how about another chili dog?"

"Very funny. I figured you'd still be mulling over your love life."

Tommy thought a moment. "Let's just say I've made some decisions."

"What you better make is a phone call," Rufus said. "It's two minutes till one."

Tommy checked his watch and immediately felt better. "I believe I will." He rose to his feet. "Be a good boy while I'm gone," he added, "and don't talk to any strangers."

Still rubbing his stomach, Rufus watched his friend walk away. "Tell Yvette I'm free next weekend," he called.

***

Tommy found a pay phone on the wall of a hotdog stand. Nearby, a bunch of kids in bumper cars were bashing their brains out to the tune of "The William Tell Overture." It was 1:01.

He lifted the receiver and hesitated. Now that the time had come, his hand was trembling. Tommy dropped his coins into the phone, took out his wallet, and studied the two concert tickets.

Two little pieces of colored cardboard. They now seemed more important than ever.

He drew a shaky breath and punched in the numbers. His mouth was as dry as sandpaper when he heard her pick up the phone.

"Lizzie?" he said. "It's Tommy . . ."

Wheels of Fortune

At first Eddie thought he'd been carjacked.

He was parked at the curb with one elbow propped in the driver's window and Del Shannon in the CD player, waiting for the arrival of his wife and his dimwitted brother-in-law, when he heard the Ford's rear door pop open. He turned to look over the seatback, opened his mouth to say *Well, that was quick*, and then clamped it shut before the words could come out.

Staring back at him from the rear seat was an Oriental man in a business suit, with luggage in tow.

"Take me to airport," the man said.

Eddie blinked. "What?"

"JFK," the man said, glancing at what looked like a solid gold wristwatch. "Very fast, please."

Eddie looked into the rearview mirror a moment, as if to remind himself that he was really here and that this was really happening, then turned again to his new passenger. "Mister," he said, "this ain't a taxicab."

The man frowned. "Is yellow car, yes?"

"It's tan, actually, but even if it was yellow, it ain't a taxi." Eddie pointed through the windshield at the normal workday chaos of the city street. "You need a real taxi."

The man shook his head with quick little jerks. "Not can find."

"Sure you can—" Eddie began, but then realized the guy was right. The citywide cab strike was in its second day. "Look," he said instead, "you can catch a bus, maybe, whatever, but you gotta get outa my car. I'm waiting for some people, and they'll be really mad if—"

"Must get to airport *fast*," the man insisted. "Bus make many stops." He nodded as if the matter had been properly settled. "You take."

"No," Eddie said, beginning to lose patience now. "I *not* take. You get out of this car right now, or I'll—"

"Ten thousand dollar," the man said.

Eddie thought he'd heard wrong. After all, the music was loud: Shannon was currently a-walkin' in the rain, tears were fallin', and he felt the pain. Eddie pushed the STOP button.

"What did you say?" Eddie asked.

"I pay you ten thousand dollar, take me to airport. Yes?"

Eddie shook his head sharply, just in case this was a dream. "No," he said. "I can't just *leave*. I'm on kind of a strict schedule here, and I—"

"Twenty thousand."

Dead silence in the car.

"You'd pay me twenty thousand dollars?! To drive you to the airport?"

"Fast," the man corrected.

Eddie swallowed, then asked, "Why?"

"Merger," the man said. "Deal done, if I convince company in Japan quick. Plane leave in eighty minute."

"What kind of deal?"

"Computer. Many billion dollar."

Eddie wiped his forehead. Leaning down a bit, he squinted through the passenger-side window at the crowds on the sidewalk. No sign of Maria or Carlos. "I don't know, Mister—"

"Fifty thousand," his passenger said, pulling out a wallet as thick as a Tom Clancy novel. "Cash."

Eddie stared at the wallet for a full five seconds.

"Buckle your seatbelt," he said.

***

They made the airport in fifteen minutes flat. Eddie screeched up to the terminal, cut the engine, and accepted the huge wad of bills.

"All is there," the man from Japan said as Eddie began counting them. "Help with luggage."

Eddie's passenger—a Mr. Ogama, he had learned—had already hopped out and was marching toward the terminal.

A reasonable request, Eddie decided. He stuffed the cash into his shirt, pulled his passenger's suitcase and duffel bag out of the back seat, and followed. Within minutes, Ogama had checked the larger case and was on his way down the concourse. Eddie hurried alongside with the duffel.

They arrived at the security checkpoint with time to spare.

"Well done," Ogama said, smiling. He took the duffel bag and nodded toward a snack stand. "Buy you cuppa coffee."

As they stood at the counter he asked, "What will you do with newfound fortune?" He seemed in a fine mood.

"A little vacation upstate," Eddie said. "Alone." Definitely alone, he thought. Both Maria and her hoodlum brother were downright scary, even in the best of circumstances. And after today . . .

Eddie sighed. What was done was done. For a long time now, ever since their trip to Rio to visit her other two brothers (who were even more scary), he had dreamed of leaving her. Now he could. He felt good, he felt rich, and he felt free.

The feeling lasted until he noticed the TV on the wall behind the counter. On the screen was a live shot of a man and a woman, both in handcuffs, standing on a city sidewalk surrounded by bulging bank-bags and about a hundred frowning policemen. The sound was off, but you could tell that neither captive was at all pleased with the situation. As Eddie watched, his coffee forgotten, the woman's face glared directly into the camera.

"She looks bossy," the Japanese businessman observed.

"She is," Eddie said, unable to take his eyes off the TV. The picture had cut to the marble-columned entranceway of a bank, and then to a closeup of a vault door.

"On second thought," Eddie murmured, his mouth dry, "I might take a longer vacation. Maybe a flight to Miami."

"Delightful city, hot as hell," Ogama said. He followed Eddie's gaze. Now the man in handcuffs was staring into the camera.

"He looks mean," Ogama observed.

"He is," Eddie said. Without taking his eyes from the screen he added, "Or maybe farther. Maybe Europe." After all, he still had a passport in the glove compartment.

"Also interesting place," Ogama said brightly. "And cooler."

On the TV, the camera had widened its angle to include both the man and woman now, and both were pointing to an empty parking space beside the curb and giving the cops a long description of something or someone. Their soundless words were accompanied by vigorous gestures and sprays of saliva.

"They look really upset," Ogama observed.

"They do," Eddie agreed. He considered a moment, still watching the newscast, then came to a decision.

"Mr. Ogama?" he said.

"Yes?"

"How's Japan this time of year . . . ?"

John M. Floyd

Run Time

Warden John Blackledge stood at the window with his hands in the pockets of his jogging suit, looking down at what he called the Free World. The building that housed his office was the only one inside the prison walls that could be accessed from outside, and it was that area just beyond the wall that he was watching now. It was a concrete lot marked VISITOR PARKING, and at the moment it was deserted. The view from his other window, though he hadn't bothered to look through it yet this morning, was a scene that was anything but deserted: that window overlooked the prison yard, and workdays started early at Crowfoot State Penitentiary.

As he watched, a white Toyota pulled into the lot and parked. A little early, the warden noted, glancing at his watch. He liked that. He expected he would also like the young blond-haired man he saw getting out of the car. Though they'd never met, Warden Blackledge knew who he was. The fellow walking up the sidewalk from the visitor's lot was, according to his dossier, an Eagle Scout, a top graduate of the L.A. Police Academy, the youngest person ever to make the rank of detective, and the son of Senator Morgan Grant.

He was about to be Blackledge's next Assistant Warden.

John Blackledge watched him until he disappeared from view, noting with approval his conservative attire and military bearing. The face was different from the father's, but the walk seemed familiar. Blackledge had known Morgan Grant for forty years, all the way back to boot camp. Adrift in memories, the warden went back to his desk and sat down to wait. A moment later he heard footsteps on the stairs outside, and when the new assistant warden opened the door Blackledge rose and came around the desk to shake his hand.

"Allan Grant, sir," the young man said, standing tall and straight. "Pleased to meet you."

"Not as pleased as I am, Grant. Good to have you aboard. Merry Christmas, by the way."

"And to you, sir." The young man hesitated, then said, "I had something in the car for you, Warden, but—well, after thinking about it, I thought there might be rules . . ."

The warden nodded agreement. "Quite right, son. No gifts for superiors. You can't go wrong if you go by the book." He started to turn back to his desk, then paused when he caught Grant eyeing his jogging suit. "Speaking of regulations," Blackledge added, "I realize I'm out of uniform. But the doc says I need exercise, and since our meeting's the only one I've scheduled this morning, I plan to get in some run time when we're done."

Allan Grant didn't seem to know how to respond to that. "Fine by me, sir."

Having settled that, Blackledge rounded the desk again and sat down, and Grant followed suit. After several minutes of small talk, the warden took a pipe from a drawer, packed and lit it, and leaned back in his chair. He squinted through the smoke at his visitor.

"I was a little surprised when I heard about your application, Grant. Young officer like you, with all your honors, on his way up in the department . . ."

Allan Grant shrugged. "It's what I've always wanted to do, sir. You may have heard my grandfather was a warden upstate, in the forties. He always said it was one of the most noble positions a person can hold. I believe that." He stayed quiet a moment. "When I heard you needed a new assistant, well . . . here I am."

A silence passed. Finally the warden rose and moved again to the window. He stared out at the wintry countryside a while, puffing on his pipe, then turned to face his visitor.

"I need to warn you, son, that this is no bed of roses here. I know; I ran a prison in New Jersey for almost twenty years before this one. It's my home state, but I made a lot of enemies there—gangsters, most of them, men like Sal Dinardo and Amos Mott and Ben Rosetti, men who mark you and never forget. Not a day goes by I don't think of that. Understand what I'm saying?"

Allan Grant nodded. "I understand, Warden."

"Trouble is, you might not even have to wait to make enemies of your own. Any of these guys who want me would probably want you too, because of your father's record against the mob. The chance to get both of us, under the same roof, so to speak, could be tempting." The warden paused. "You with me so far?"

Grant set his jaw and nodded again.

"And there's more: the work's tough. The hours are long, the responsibility's heavy, and pay's terrible, and the recognition is almost nonexistent."

A smile flickered across the young man's face. "Don't

sugar-coat it for me, sir. Give it to me straight."

Blackledge smiled also. "Sorry. You're right. I can see you've thought it through." He returned to his chair, where he leaned back and chewed on his pipestem for several seconds, studying the younger man's face. "Your quarters," he said, "will be in Building 4, the other side of the parking lot. You passed it on the way in."

Grant hesitated, then stood and walked to the window where the warden had been a moment before. He peered out through the blinds at the view beyond the walls, and at the small building Blackledge had indicated. "I look forward to it, sir," he said, continuing to gaze out the window. Suddenly his eyes narrowed.

"Anything wrong, Grant?"

"No sir," he murmured, his eyes still on the window. "But something just occurred to me. As your assistant, I am also an aide, of sorts. Am I not?"

"What do you mean, an aide?"

"I assume a certain degree of responsibility for your well-being, your safety. Isn't that true?"

The warden frowned. "I suppose so. What are you getting at?"

Allan Grant turned and looked his new boss in the eye. "What if I decided to kill you right now?" he asked. "What if I walked in here off the street with the intention of shooting you dead? Could I get away with it?"

Blackledge took the pipe from between his teeth and thought a moment. "Yes and no. You could do it, I suppose, but you couldn't get away." He pointed his pipestem at the floor. "There are five people just below us, in the admin office, and two next door. One's a guard, and all seven are armed." He paused a second, intrigued. "Why do you ask?"

Grant took another look out the window, then said, "I

think I've imposed long enough, sir. I'll let you get on with your run time now." He seemed to have another thought. "If you would, though, just remain inside here a while longer. Is that all right?"

"Of course," the warden said, puzzled. It was the first time he could remember being dismissed—not to mention being given orders—by a subordinate. He rose from his seat and the two of them shook hands again. Grant murmured a distracted thank-you for the vote of confidence, then left quickly.

John Blackledge stared at his closed office door for a moment after the young man had gone, then stood and moved to the window. *What's out there that's so interesting?*

Sure enough, the situation outside had changed. A second car was parked in the visitor lot now, just on the other side of Grant's Toyota, and a young dark-haired man was sitting behind its wheel, alternately checking his watch and staring up at the warden's window.

Blackledge stepped back a pace, then peeked out through a corner, between the blinds.

As he watched, the back of Grant's blond head moved into view, and the two young men nodded to each other. It was obvious from their manner that they were strangers. Allan Grant stopped and climbed into his Toyota, and then—as the dark-haired man was getting out of his own car—Grant got out also, and walked around to confront him. Blackledge couldn't see everything at that point because they were standing between the two cars, but it looked as if Grant had something in his hand and was showing it to the other man. Whatever it was, though, it wasn't a weapon—the second man's face was clearly visible to the warden, and its expression was one of mild annoyance rather than fear. After a pause the second man nodded, and it was then that Blackledge realized Grant had probably displayed a badge and ID.

Absorbed, the warden continued to watch as the two men had a short discussion. At one point the dark-haired visitor unzipped his jacket and seemed to be turning out his pockets while Grant observed. Then the two young men exchanged a few more words and parted company; Grant got into his Toyota and left, and the dark-haired man—after standing and watching the departing car—turned and started up the sidewalk toward the warden's office.

For the second time that morning John Blackledge sat down at his desk to await a visitor, but this time he made sure the old service revolver in his top righthand drawer was loaded and accessible.

Two minutes later the office door opened and the dark-haired young man stepped inside. "Morning, Warden," he said, approaching the desk. "The name's Wesley."

Blackledge made no move to get up or shake hands. "And how may I help you?" he asked.

The visitor cleared his throat. "Well . . . first I have something to give you, sir. The guy who just left asked me to deliver it."

As Blackledge watched, keeping his right hand near his open desk drawer, the man called Wesley took from his jacket pocket a small square package wrapped in Christmas paper. He leaned forward and placed it on the desk between them.

"He said if you can break regulations, so can he." Wesley looked a little irritated. "He said you'd know what he meant."

The warden's face softened a bit, then went serious again. "He and I will discuss that later. My new men don't usually start out by disobeying orders."

The young man looked confused. "You mean . . . he works here?"

"Yes, he works here. He checked you for weapons,

didn't he?"

"No, sir. He checked me for cigarettes. He said he was out."

The warden frowned. Keeping his eyes on the dark-haired man, Blackledge rose and walked around his desk. He knew he looked ridiculous in his jogging suit, but right now he didn't really care.

"Then what were you two talking about down there?" he asked.

Wesley shrugged. "Nothing, in particular. He gave me your gift, and a little advice. I'd seen him standing in your window when I drove up, so I waited till you were done. I figured he was a relative or something, from back East."

"What do you mean, back East?"

"His car," Wesley said. "It had New Jersey plates."

The warden blinked.

New Jersey . . . ?

Blackledge's face grew stern again. "Who exactly are you, Mr. Wesley? And what are you doing here?"

"Actually, Wesley's my given name, sir. That was your friend's advice: that you prefer a first-name basis with your staff." Looking flustered, he opened his wallet and held out his police ID. "I'm Allan Wesley Grant," he said. "The new assistant warden."

Blackledge could only stare. And then—

All at once he understood. The early arrival, the stalling for time, the staged performance in the lot . . . even the vaguely familiar gait as the young blond man had approached the office. It wasn't the walk of a Grant that Blackledge had recognized; it was the walk of a Rosetti.

Good God . . .

Slowly, his heart in his throat, the warden turned his head to look at the wrapped package on his desk.

"I was wondering, sir," Wesley said. "Is there anything

I should do right away?"

Warden Blackledge, who had picked up the gift box and was holding it gingerly to his ear, suddenly widened his eyes and dropped it as if it were scalding hot. When he turned to look at his visitor he could scarcely breathe.

"Run," he said.

Partners

"New Orleans," the red-haired man said.

His companion, a tall fellow with a friendly face, turned to look at him from his seat a few feet away. "What?"

"You asked what I was thinking about. I told you. New Orleans."

"What about it?" The tall man took a pipe from a pocket of his coat. Unable to sleep, both men were sitting on wooden benches in a stone-paved courtyard outside their rooms. A few oaks and elms stood nearby, casting gaunt shadows in the moonlight, and soft music strummed somewhere in the distance. The air was chilly, but that was to be expected: it was early March.

"We should have gone there," the red-haired man answered. He shifted a little in his seat, wincing in pain as he did so.

His friend glanced up at him, then went back to filling his pipe. "When should we have gone? Tonight?"

"Why not?"

"You wouldn't want to wait until you're feeling better?"

"That would've *made* me feel better."

The tall man regarded him in amused silence for a moment.

"We couldn't leave," he said, "and you know it. We've only been here a little better'n a week. This is business. These folks are more than friends, they're our partners now."

The redheaded man sighed. "I know that. I've just been daydreaming, that's all." He added in a grim voice, "And I think this could be a no-win deal."

His friend nodded. "I think you're right." He lit his pipe with a wooden match, then fanned it out and flipped it away into the darkness. The music in the distance had stopped now, and it was eerily quiet. "But tomorrow there'll be a crowd of people here, hundreds maybe, and we're the stars of the show, you and me. We're the ones everybody'll be watching." He paused a moment, puffing. "If it doesn't work out, it doesn't work out," he said with a shrug. "But we've been in risky deals before. I was a congressman once, remember."

The other man smiled. "I've never done anything quite that dumb," he said.

His companion blew a series of little gray smoke-rings and watched as the wind pulled them apart. "I heard you used to rassle alligators."

"Alligators," the red-haired man agreed. "Not politicians."

"And you once lived in New Orleans," the tall man said. "You call that good judgment?"

"Don't kid yourself, David my friend. It's the greatest town in the world."

"Great to visit, maybe. But to live in?"

The red-haired man just sighed and looked wistful. "We should have gone there," he said, shivering in the cool wind.

Suddenly they heard someone coming, walking toward them in the darkness. Both of them reached for their guns.

"Crockett?" a voice called. "Bowie? Colonel Travis needs you. Meeting at the north wall."

The two friends relaxed, then looked at each other.

"Showtime," the tall man said.

Clockwork

Standing on the streetcorner, sweating, watching for Wilson, Lenny Sims came to a decision: He needed a career change.

For five years he'd been doing the same thing, day in and day out. He had to admit, the job had its perks: flexible hours, travel, great pay. Besides that, he was good at his profession—and not many were. His was what might be called a specialized field.

Lenny Sims was an assassin.

No, he thought—not an assassin. That word implied covert government-sponsored missions, hi-tech surveillance, military precision. Lenny knew nothing of those things. He was just a hired killer.

And the job had long since lost its appeal. His associates were dangerous and so was the work, even more so than it used to be. Or maybe he was just getting old. In any case, the stress was wearing him down. Like now, for instance.

He checked his watch again. 3:37.

Five minutes ago Lenny had driven a red '06 Camry onto the gravel lot of Prudoe's Auto Repair, near the edge of town. He'd parked it in the back, next to the office, then jogged to this corner, half a block east. The rendezvous point.

But his driver wasn't here. And time was running out.

The clock on the bomb inside the Camry's trunk was set for four sharp.

Thirty seconds later a black Continental roared into view, with Vern Wilson at the wheel. The car screeched to the curb; Lenny wrenched the door open and dropped into the passenger seat. He heard the tail end of a traffic update before Wilson switched the radio off and stared at him. "How'd it go?"

Vernon Wilson was typical of the folks Lenny worked with, these days. Bloodshot eyes, pinched face, ratty hair pulled into a ponytail. He looked like Willie Nelson on a three-day drunk.

"Let's move," Lenny said.

The freeway entrance was a half-mile away. Wilson's Lincoln (or at least the one he was driving today—Lenny had no idea who it belonged to) was still accelerating at the top of the onramp; within two minutes it was part of a metal river flowing south toward the suburbs.

"Well?" Wilson asked. His hands were clamped to the wheel, his bleary eyes on the road ahead.

"Package delivered," Lenny said.

"See anybody?"

"Just some doofus, out in the lot." Which didn't matter. The guy he'd seen—a big longhaired dude with a beard and a Braves ball cap—had looked too dull-witted to be a threat to the operation. In fact he looked more spaced-out than Wilson, which was saying a great deal.

"Think we'll be able to see it from here?" Wilson asked.

Lenny turned to check the rear window. “We’ll hear it, too. This is a big one—it has to be, to take out the building beside it.”

Wilson chuckled. “Well, don’t feel sorry for him. Jack Prudoe’s done his share of—” He blinked. “What the hell . . . ?”

Lenny felt the car slowing, and turned to look. Ahead, traffic in all three southbound lanes was gridlocked. Blue lights strobed in the distance.

“Accident,” Wilson said. “We’ll be here a while.”

“Better now than half an hour ago.” Another look through the back window. “A traffic jam then might’ve done me in. I even found myself worrying somebody’d carjack me at a stoplight, bomb and all.”

Wilson grimaced in what passed for a smile. “Killer becomes the victim, huh?”

“Stranger things have happened. Toyota Camrys are way up there, on the most-stolen list.”

“That’s just cause there’s so many of ’em on the road.”

They were stopped dead now, bumper-to-bumper. To their right, in the middle lane, a guy in a business suit sat red-faced and cursing in his BMW. Horns chimed in from cars up and down the line, blaring their occupants’ frustration.

“Just look at them,” Lenny said. “Places to go, things to do.” He realized that he himself had no place to go. He found himself wondering again what it would feel like to live a normal life, with normal problems and normal complaints.

What the hell was he doing in this business?

“Matter of fact, a red ’06 passed us a minute ago,” Wilson said, apparently still talking about Camrys. He gave Lenny another grin. “Popular car.”

Lenny shrugged. “Long as it didn’t have a racing stripe. Wouldn’t that be a kick in the old—” He paused, watching Wilson’s grin disappear. “What’s the matter?” Lenny asked.

"It did have a stripe. Yellow and white."

Lenny felt his mouth go dry.

Could it be? His orders had been to leave the keys in the ignition—

He sat up straight, squinting at the triple line of stopped cars ahead. "You still see it?"

"Not now. It's probably five or six cars up. Why?"

"The driver," Lenny said. "You get a look at the driver?"

Wilson was gaping at him now. "What's going on here, Lenny?"

Lenny made himself take a slow breath. "What did he look like?"

"I don't know . . . heavy guy, beard, scraggly looking—"

"Baseball cap?"

"How'd you know that?" Wilson asked.

"My God." Lenny broke out a sweat. "It's him. It must be. The guy I saw at Prudoe's."

"What!?"

"He must've stolen the car." Lenny knew it was possible. It was even logical, if you stopped to think about it: from Prudoe's garage, the southbound freeway was the quickest route out of town.

A silence passed. Lenny could feel his chest tightening.

"He stole the car, Wilson. After I left it. And you know what that means, don't you? He's a rolling time-bomb."

Wilson took a second to process that, then swallowed. "He may be a bomb," he said, peering through the windshield, "but he ain't rolling. None of us are, anytime soon."

Lenny squeezed his eyes shut. *This can't be happening.* Dimly he remembered his watch, looked down at it. 3:46. They had fourteen minutes.

And the fact they couldn't see the car didn't matter. They were way too close. A bomb that big, if it didn't kill them outright, would set off a chain reaction, probably every car's gas tank within two hundred yards.

"Get us outa here," Lenny said, his heart pounding. "Fast."

Wilson whispered a curse. Both of them looked left, across the median. The northbound lanes were clear.

"We can cut across," Wilson blurted. "Head back the way we came."

"You mean—"

"Hold on."

He jerked the wheel left, gunned the engine. They had one bad moment when it seemed they might get stuck in the soft grass of the median, then they were across and flying north, back toward town. Lenny began to breathe again.

"That was close," Wilson said, his eyes on the rearview mirror. He licked his lips. "I can't believe you left the damn keys in the car."

"I was told to. It's a carshop—who'd have thought somebody'd steal it off the lot?" What Lenny couldn't believe was that they'd actually seen the guy and the car, right out here on the same road with them. The phrase "small world" flickered through his mind, but he knew it was more than that. "Just rotten luck," he added. The only kind he ever had.

Wilson ran a hand over his face. "The timer's set for four o'clock, right?"

"On the dot."

"So what do we do now?"

Lenny let out a sigh. "Now that we'll be guilty of killing a car thief and hundreds of commuters, you mean?" He couldn't keep his eyes off the mirror, and the now-distant lines of stopped cars.

"Can't help that—the cops can't tie it to *us*. I mean what about Jack Prudoe? We might've dodged getting blown up, but when the boss finds out what happened we'll be on the list too."

"You saying we still have to make the hit?"

"If you like living." Wilson nodded toward the glove compartment. "There's a .38 in there, a throwaway. We can still stop at the garage and do Prudoe. We committed to four o'clock—you got ten minutes left."

Lenny thought it over. Wilson's suggestion made sense. It was the only way to salvage what had become a total screwup.

But no more, after this. They could by God find somebody else. Lenny had made up his mind: This would be his last job.

"Might as well do it right," he murmured.

"What?"

"Nothing. We got no other choice, huh?"

Wilson shook his head.

Their exit was coming up. Lenny took the revolver from the glove compartment and checked its load while Wilson hit the offramp and looped back west. When they reached the garage, he took a side entrance to the lot, and rolled the big Lincoln into the shadows beside the building. No one in sight.

Lenny looked at his watch. 3:55.

"How'll I know Prudoe when I see him?" he asked, watching the side door.

"Don't matter. Do everybody you run into. And make it fast."

"What about you?"

"I'll wait right here."

Lenny got out, the gun sweaty in his fist, and eased through the door into the building. Inside, a cheaply paneled hallway led to an empty office. He glanced out the back window. Sure enough, the red Camry was gone.

On the far side of the office was a half-open restroom

door, with a light on inside. Lenny swallowed, drew a long breath, shoved it all the way open. Nobody home. The only other door was glass, and led to the service bays. As he slipped through it, he heard the ring of metal on concrete, as if a tool had been dropped on the floor. Someone was working, moving around in the bays.

It sounded like just one person. Good.

Lenny raised the pistol and crept toward the noise.

When he rounded the hood of the second car, he saw a man with long brown hair squatting beside a wheel rim, a flannel shirt stretched tight across his back. Lenny held his breath, cocked the .38, and said, "Jack Prudoe?"

The man froze. Slowly he rose to his feet and turned, wiping his hands on a grease-rag.

Lenny's stomach lurched.

It was the guy he'd seen before, in the baseball cap.

"I'm Prudoe," the man said, smirking. "Come back for your car?"

Lenny's knees had gone weak; his pulse hammered in his ears. The bomb wasn't out on the interstate. It was still *here.*

His gun hand, usually steady, began to tremble.

"Since you left the keys, I pulled it in for you." Prudoe glanced past Lenny, and from the corner of his eye Lenny saw the red Camry, sitting in the bay next to him.

And then, as he tried to decide what to do next, the grease-rag in Prudoe's hands spat at him. Lenny felt a blow to his chest. The revolver slipped from suddenly limp fingers and clattered to the floor.

A second later Lenny followed it. He lay on his back in his own blood, staring up into the muzzle of Jack Prudoe's silenced automatic. As if in a dream, he looked past it, past Prudoe's bearded face, to a clock on the garage wall. It said 4:02.

Lenny blinked.

4:02?

"I disarmed the bomb," Prudoe said. "Cars ain't the only things I can fix."

Lenny swallowed. He felt cold, for some reason. "Wilson?" he asked.

"I fixed him too. Saw you two drive up, and snuck around front. When you went in the side door I walked up to his window and popped him. If it's any consolation, the car was already moving. He was about to drive off and leave you here."

Lenny didn't reply. His vision was blurring. Something made him think of Prudoe's confident smirk a moment ago, and his too-tight shirt, and suddenly he understood the reason for both: The man was wearing Kevlar underneath.

"Want some advice?" Prudoe said. "You plant a car bomb, don't jog down the street afterward. Looks suspicious."

"I'll remember that."

"Funny thing is, looks like I got me a Camry out of the deal. Always liked the red ones."

Lenny coughed, felt a searing pain. "Too many on the road, if you ask me."

"With a yellow-and-white stripe?"

"You'd be surprised," Lenny said. But then he remembered Vern Wilson, and the way he had cut the radio off in the middle of a traffic report. One by one, the pieces fell together. Wilson hadn't seen another car, or been mistaken—he had lied. There *was* no other car. He had known about the freeway accident beforehand, from the radio report, had even kept the left lane and made sure he had room between him and the car ahead when they stopped, so they could turn and head back. And he'd known already what Prudoe looked like, and the striped red Camry too. Even without the traffic jam, Wilson would've still said he'd seen the car pass them, and would've found a way to get Lenny back to the garage before four o'clock. He—and his boss—would have wanted Lenny to be blown up along with the target. It all made sense now.

"Killer becomes the victim," Lenny murmured.

"What?" Prudoe asked.

"Nothing."

Maybe this was a fitting end, Lenny thought. Maybe he deserved it.

Prudoe studied him a moment, then raised the pistol. "Any last requests?"

Lenny squinted, tried to focus. Then he looked past the gun again, and realized he could no longer read the hands on the wall clock. "I'd like to know the time. Is it 4:05 yet?"

"Almost," Prudoe said. "Why?"

Lenny gave him a sad smile. As it turned out, he didn't have to answer.

The bomb's backup circuit took care of that for him.

***

Out on the distant freeway, the motorists waiting in the southbound lanes turned and stared in the direction of the explosion. But not for long. Soon they were back to the important things in life, like leaning on their horns and shouting at the cars ahead.

After all, they had places to go . . .